Praise for *The Killing Way*

"Hays turns a time-honored historical legend on its head, creating a new mystery series steeped in Arthurian mythology. . . . The popularity of both historical mysteries and new twists on the Arthurian tales will provide a tailor-made audience for this promising new series." —*Booklist*

"Hays shines in the area where Steven Saylor does: with characters and relationships. The mystery is well created, the political maneuvering is plausible, and we can expect future volumes to take us through Arthur's struggles against the Saxons and his rivals among the Britons. . . . A more than respectable entry in the tradition of Arthurian novels." —Orson Scott Card, on his *Rhinotimes* website

"This may be the first historical mystery set in a credible Dark Age Arthurian world. . . . An impressive (and suspenseful) start to a new series." —*Historical Novels Review*

"In creating this vivid and original detective story, Tony Hays makes thorough and intelligent use of modern research. Yes, it might actually have been like that."
—Geoffrey Ashe, leading Arthurian scholar
and author of *The Discovery of King Arthur*

"This historical mystery combines much of the rich heritage of the legend of Arthur and Merlin with the more contemporary fascination with forensic evidence." —*VOYA*

"Well written and crafted; Hays has the talent for passing on historical details and information without clogging the narrative. . . . A compelling and suspenseful book."
—Brenden DuBois, author of *Twilight*

"Earthy, densely plotted, and likely to have readers eagerly awaiting the next installment." —*Kirkus Reviews*

THE KILLING WAY

TONY HAYS

A TOM DOHERTY ASSOCIATES BOOK

NEW YORK

THE KILLING WAY

Book design by Ellen Cipriano

Maps by Jennifer Hanover

A Forge Book
Published by Tom Doherty Associates, LLC
175 Fifth Avenue
New York, NY 10010

www.tor-forge.com

Forge® is a registered trademark of Tom Doherty Associates, LLC.

The Library of Congress has catalogued the hardcover editions as follows:

Hays, Tony.
    The killing way / Tony Hays.—1st ed.
        p. cm.
    "A Tom Doherty Associates book."
    ISBN 978-0-7653-1945-6
    1. Arthur, King—Fiction. 2. Britons—Fiction. I. Title.
PS3558.A877K56   2009
813'.54—dc22

                                                          2008038104

ISBN 978-0-7653-2591-4

First Hardcover Edition: April 2009
First Trade Paperback Edition: March 2010

Printed in the United States of America

This book is dedicated to the memory
of my brother,
Ronald Douglas Hays
(1949–1990),
who would have written a novel himself had
fortune not treated him so cruelly.

$\mathcal{A}$CKNOWLEDGMENTS

here do you start in recognizing those people who have played a part in a project that has taken more than ten years to bring to fruition? The list is almost longer than the book itself. First, of course, I want to thank my agent, Frank Weimann, for taking a chance on me. For their technical advice and friendship, my appreciation goes to Geoffrey and Patricia Ashe and Dr. Christopher Snyder, who have shared generously of their knowledge of the time and the characters. I also must thank John Paine for his outstanding guidance.

For their generous years of advice, support, and kindness, Dr. James A. Grimshaw, his wife, Dee, Dr. Richard Tuerk, and his wife, Roz, top the list. They all kindly read versions of the book and offered their suggestions. Others who have been integral parts of my life as a writer are former classmates and professors Dr. Bryan Dietrich, Robert Sterling Long, Dr. C. Jason Smith, Dr. Bill McCarron, and the late Dr. Joanne Cockelreas. Among the friends and colleagues are fellow authors Gordon Mennenga, Howard Bahr, Charles C. Thompson II, Kevin and Gail Buckley, as well as Owen Thompson, Kelly Linam, Liz Mills, Lesley Daniel, Marty Alexander, Lesa Plunk, and my good friend Brian Holcombe. I would be completely remiss if I overlooked Stephen Fitzpatrick and Bill and Diane Pyron, old friends from my days in Kuwait.

And then there are those who have been there for me all along the way. My brother, John David Hays, Woodson Marshall, Don Cornelius, Greta Crowe, and my dear, dear aunt Mary Dee Welch and her family, Red and Carrie Nell Shelby, Larry and Joan Phelps, John Roberts and Susan Parris, and the entire Bain family. I can't forget to mention Anna Pastore and Dr. Judy Edwards, friend, colleague, and boss.

Last, and absolutely not least, I want to thank my editor, Claire Eddy, her assistant Kristin Sevick, and all the folks at Tor.

TONY HAYS
Savannah, Tennessee

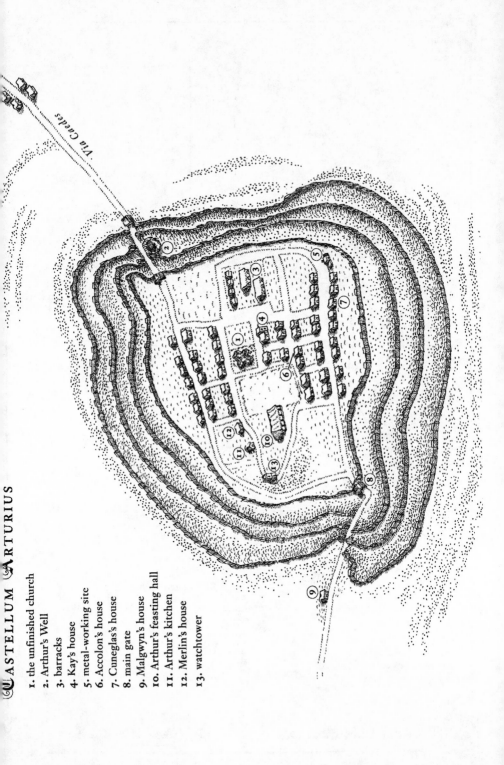

CASTELLUM ARTURIUS

1. the unfinished church
2. Arthur's Well
3. barracks
4. Kay's house
5. metal-working site
6. Accolon's house
7. Cuneglas's house
8. main gate
9. Malgwyn's house
10. Arthur's feasting hall
11. Arthur's kitchen
12. Merlin's house
13. watchtower

Via Caedes

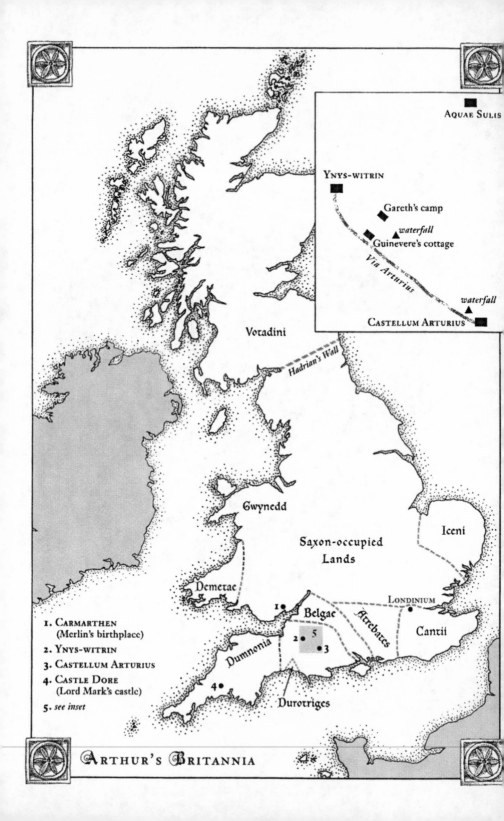

AQUAE SULIS

YNYS-WITRIN

Gareth's camp

waterfall

Guinevere's cottage

Via Arturius

waterfall

CASTELLUM ARTURIUS

Hadrian's Wall

Votadini

Gwynedd

Iceni

Saxon-occupied
Lands

Demetae

LONDINIUM

1 •

Belgae

Atrebates

Cantii

2 • 5
• 3

Dumnonia

1. CARMARTHEN
   (Merlin's birthplace)

2. YNYS-WITRIN

3. CASTELLUM ARTURIUS

4. CASTLE DORE
   (Lord Mark's castle)

5. *see inset*

4 •

Durotriges

ARTHUR'S BRITANNIA

THE KILLING WAY

GLASTONBURY

In the eightieth year from the Adventus Saxonum

I am in my ninetieth winter, the oldest man in the western lands. My eyes and my one hand have not yet deserted me, so I think it meet that I put down in writing some of what I have lived through. And there has been much, from my farming days near the lands of the river Cam to the battles against the Saxons to my days at Arthur's castle. I have witnessed death, devastation, and treachery. But I have also seen goodness in commoner, and king, and in these days that is exceptional and worthy of note.

My days are spent in contemplation and remembrance near the brothers at Glastonbury, that place we used to call Ynys-witrin before the Saxons spread their vile language like a plague across our land. I am not a brother, and I do not live with them, rather in a small house near the abbey. But I take my meals at the abbot's table, and I read the brothers' manuscripts, copy an occasional one if they have need of me and my hand is not too pained. They leave me to myself much of the time, unless the abbot needs advice on treating with the ubiquitous Saxons. He respects my word; no one else in our lands has as much experience dealing with them.

Each person's life brings unexpected events, trials, burdens, each of which tests his soul and his nerve. Such has been my life. As a young man, I thought to be no more than a simple farmer. Now I look back at the different paths I have followed, and I count among them farmer, soldier, scribe, councillor to a king, and now simply a penitent soul looking for reason in all that has passed. Though I could have wished to remain that simple farmer, I cannot count my life as a bad one. I believe that I have done much good with the years God has given me. And I owe that satisfaction to one man.

I never intended to write these words. These memories were saved in the farthest reaches of my mind, back where no one, not the Saxons or anyone, could take them from me. But not a fortnight ago, I argued with Gildas, that fat monk who wrote a tome called De Excidio, *and though it pretends to tell something of the history of this land, Gildas ignores the most important parts. He ignores my Lord Arthur, who gave his life to keep the hateful Saxons at bay, who championed the Christ and ruled these lands accordingly. He ignores the sacrifices of the many for the good of our* patria.

When I pointed out these omissions, he grumbled that they were not important. To him Arthur was just another self-serving tyrant, concerned only with the women he could bed and the food he could steal from poor folk. When I spoke of Gereint, Gawain, and Gaheris, aye, even Guinevere, he laughed at the blood they had spilt on this very land. At that, I could take no more. I tried to strangle him, and though my bones have weathered ninety seasons, it took three of the monks to drag me away from him and back to my house.

No, I cannot leave the field to such as the fat Gildas. He never really knew Arthur, and what he knew of Arthur he did not like. Besides, all Gildas knows how to do is complain. The others who could have written the truth—Bedevere, my old friend Kay, the old abbot Coroticus—are gone.

The tale is not an easy one, filled as it is with betrayal and death, nor does it please me to recall. But though it takes my last breath to finish, it is a task that must be done, for all of them. It is a debt of honor, and one no man can stop me from paying. So, I take a quill in my one hand, misshapen by age, to record what really happened.

CHAPTER ONE

"Pleasure myself with a one-armed man?" the wench had whined. " 'Tisn't likely." But half a chilly night and a full skin of wine later, she chanted a different tune. And I was forgetting that I was half a man.

Until someone grabbed me about the neck and lifted me from between her legs.

Until someone flung me across the hut, and I crumpled against the stone and stick wall.

My attacker first appeared as a fuzzy shape, and anger welled up in me as I shook my head to clear it and the figure became better defined. Then he spoke, and the anger filled my throat and threatened to choke off my breath. "It does not surprise me," the tall, bearded man said with a frown, "to find you wasting yourself with a drunken wench."

Not only had I been savagely torn from a night of drink and pleasure, but the culprit was none other than my Lord Arthur, a man who had saved my life—and the man whom I hated with all my heart.

"I have need of you," Arthur said in his deep, rumbling voice. He tossed a woolen wrap at the girl and motioned sharply at the door. Silly wench was blubbering by then, scared witless of Arthur, and she scampered out of the hut and into the foul night.

"I have no need of you," I answered, groping for the goatskin. But he snatched it from my grasp and poured the wine onto the ground.

"You wound me, my lord."

"You wound me, Malgwyn. Quit sniveling and come with me." His voice changed, perhaps unnoticeable to others, but I had warred with him through too many battles and knew that it portended trouble. "There has been a death," he said, dropping his chin to his chest.

I am called Malgwyn ap Cuneglas. The only thing gentle about my birth was the kiss that my mother laid on my newborn brow. I was born to a farmer near the river Yeo, a man from the west country named Cuneglas. He died when I was but ten years old and my mother when I was seventeen, the year I took to wife Gwyneth, the daughter of my neighbor. She was fifteen and the loveliest lass in our lands. For five years life was as good as I could ask. We farmed and lived and loved. For a while.

Arthur was not king then, but rather the "Dux Bellorum," the general of generals, for Ambrosius Aurelianus and a handful of lesser kings scattered throughout the land. The kings had made an uneasy alliance with the Saxons to fight the Picts, and then the treacherous dogs betrayed us. To Arthur the kings turned; I knew him then only as a whisper on the wind, a story made larger in the telling, of a great warrior who laid a hundred Saxons low with a single sweep of his sword. And, truly, I paid him no mind.

Troop levies had not been made in our region. The Saxons were many leagues away from our lands, and the people found no fear of them; they had once been our allies.

Until.

Until they turned on us, one cool morn while the men of our village were off to market to sell our produce. Until our return brought us death and destruction. As we rounded the road to our village, instead of finding our families eagerly awaiting our return, we discovered our huts destroyed, smoking, burning. We found our women raped and our babies killed. Searching the rubble that had been my home, I found Gwyneth, her legs aspraddle and her throat slit. Our girl, Mariam, still in her first year, had hidden in a storage pit. For a wonder, they had not found the child. I suspected that Gwyneth hid her there when she heard the Saxons come. I took her from the cold pit and cried giant tears, until her wrap was moist with my grief.

The next day I took her to my brother's home in Castellum Arturius—the town was too large for a simple raiding party—and left her with him. With other men of my village, we mounted our horses and rode to find Arthur, to join him.

I did not cry again.

I smiled at each Saxon throat I cut. I smiled at each rotting Saxon body we left on the battlefield. My fellows thought it odd that I smiled so much at death and devastation, and after a while they called me "Smiling Malgwyn." They did not understand that the smile ate at me like a disease.

Arthur saw something in me though. Before one battle, I sat on my horse on a ridge and studied the land before us. Another horse rode up alongside, and I took it for one of my fellows. "If Arthur is smart," I said, "he will place forces in hiding there, there, and there." My finger pointed out low hills. "When the Saxons ride to face our main force, they will be trapped with their backs to the river."

"I agree," a deep voice said. Arthur. "You are Malgwyn ap Cuneglas."

"Yes, my lord," I said, turning quickly and giving the salute, surprised almost as much by his sudden appearance as by the fact that he knew me.

He nodded, smiled faintly, turned his horse and left. Within minutes, the troop dispositions were made as I had suggested. When the Saxons made their charge, the course of battle ran just as I predicted. We crushed a large Saxon force, shoving the last survivors into the river to drown. I was given my own troop of horse to command and a place in the war councils.

Had I known then what that brief encounter portended, I would have killed him there. It would have saved me a great deal of pain and misery.

Arthur's odd pronouncement cleared my eyes, and I began to focus. I yearned to return to the wine and the wench, but the set of his jaw made me want to know more.

"Death is a constant of this life, my lord," I observed. "It is all around us. Why is this one different?"

Arthur lowered himself onto a stool that I had lashed together out of an armload of trimmed branches and scraps of leather. He was dressed as a common man, in a woolen tunic hanging down nearly to his knees and tied at the waist with a leather belt, and *braccae*. His huge feet were covered with leather shoes laced across the top in the Celtic manner. He liked to go abroad in peasant's garb, without the fine linen *camisia* his wealth and station afforded him. A dagger protruded from his belt, and I suspected that one or more of his men lingered in the darkness outside my hovel.

"A servant girl from my hall was found dead an hour ago in the lane. She was lying outside Merlin's home."

"Ravaged?" I gathered my own braccae and slid them on. In front of any other man, I would have been humbled, but we had shared too many campfires to worry about such niceties.

"That is not for me to say, but the poor child was gutted like a deer, slit from throat to belly."

"Odd. But why does the death of a serving girl disturb the great Lord Arthur?"

"There was a knife lying by her body, covered in blood. It belongs to Merlin."

And that explained it all. Merlin, though some called him Myrddin hereabouts, was a harmless old man, a councillor to Ambrosius Aurelianus and Arthur's old teacher at Dinas Emrys, where Arthur was schooled. He came from a town in the far north, Moridunum in Roman days, Carmarthen now. Some said that he was of a long line of prophets, whose deeds gave rise to the town's name, which meant "inspiration" in our tongue.

Once he had given good counsel, but the years had played tricks on his mind, and he thought himself a sorcerer now and sold potions made of valerian root to the gullible. When he was in his right mind, he could cut through the thickets choking a problem and strike at the root of the matter. And, Arthur loved the old cantankerous fool.

The wine's magic was beginning to fade and a pain grew in the back of my head as I, now dressed, rested on my haunches. "So, your much touted devotion to justice is now about to betray you? What of it? You are Lord Arthur. You are as good as crowned as the Rigotamos. Do as you please. No one will argue."

"You know I cannot do that. Vortimer, David, Mordred, and the others are always tormenting me. They snap at my heels like a litter of unruly pups, and they are always looking for some reason to challenge my ascent to the throne." David, a lord of the northern lands, the Votadini, was one of a number of cagey warriors, ambitious and sly. And while Arthur still championed the Christ, Vortimer, and a handful of other lords led a growing movement of those who believed our troubles came because we strayed from the old gods.

The pain in the back of my neck grew even stronger, and I rubbed it with my one hand. "Go away, my lord. I am no help to you, and even if I could be, give me one reason that I should come to your aid."

Arthur rose and crossed the hut, kneeling in front of me and resting his hand on my shoulder. I looked up into his eyes and saw a sadness in their depths. "The murdered girl is Eleonore, your wife's sister."

I considered this for a moment, letting the weight of what he said fall upon me. Eleonore, a warm and wonderful girl. I remembered her as a child, not yet in her teens, helping my Gwyneth with our Mariam, not long, it seemed, before I found Gwyneth bloodied and Mariam hiding.

Damned Saxons! They couldn't have done it; this I knew. But I wanted someone to blame, and if I didn't know who committed the deed, they would serve to fill the role. Or maybe I blamed them for making me less than a man. Arthur and I had done for many of them. But that was before, before the other had happened. And for that, I could blame Arthur.

A man without a limb had no place in our world. 'Twas better to be born with some deformity, for then you might be marked as blessed by the gods, or cursed by them. But one who has lost a limb was given no such choice. The loss of a limb would follow a man into the afterlife and most considered it a punishment for some sin or a cruel nature. Aye, many believed that a man so marked could not ascend to heaven, was doomed to wander the underworld. Such a man could never be a king, for only perfection in a king was acceptable. Losing my arm cost me not only its use but marked me as cursed by the gods both in life and out.

It had happened along the river Tribuit; we battled with an exceedingly large force of Saxons. I remember that it was a pretty morning, but the songs of birds did not grace our ears, rather the clank of metal on metal and that awful, indescribable sound of rent flesh. The enemy had nearly overwhelmed our brave force with their stout spears, lances, and swords, and a handful of us were surrounded on a grassy knoll that sloped into the river.

The more desperate our situation became, the more frenzied the thrust and parry of my sword. I slew twenty of the mongrel Saxons, but with only three of my fellows left, I realized this was the end of my vengeance, the end of my smiles, a reality driven home when a Saxon blade cleaved my right arm at the elbow.

I fell in the blood-dampened grass, my severed member lying with the hand toward me as if imploring me to join it, and waited for peace to come, for my chance to rejoin Gwyneth. But as darkness grew around me, I sensed someone fumbling at the stump of my arm, a leather strap tied taut to stanch the flow of scarlet. As I cried in protest, I was lifted up and placed on a horse; a voice whispered in my ear, "No warrior such as you will waste his life's blood if I can prevent it." It was Arthur.

For days I was delirious with fever and exhaustion, near to death I was told. I awoke two weeks later with the brothers of the small abbey at Ynys-witrin, that place also called Avalon. Arthur had left me in their care. The brothers liked Arthur not and he cared not for them, but they respected each other, and Arthur knew my wound would need careful attention if I were to survive.

Survive, what a hateful word.

When I awoke and realized what I had lost, the last thing I wanted was to survive. Gwyneth gone. The farm gone. Half an arm gone. I cursed Arthur for saving me, cursed him for not letting me die on the battlefield, bathing in Saxon blood. I struggled with learning to write my letters. The brothers had suggested the task as a way to keep my mind active, to strengthen my left hand and arm, and to give me a trade, that of the scribe. But for me it was just something to fill my time, to push out thoughts of Gwyneth and the Saxons and a war that had seen Arthur rise high while others lost everything.

The great man visited me once, without warning. "A good occupation," said a voice from the door.

"Good for something that once was a man," I had answered without turning, already knowing who it was, continuing to scratch the quill across the parchment.

"That is true only if you believe it yourself."

"That is what you and your church say, and the Druids as well."

"Yet, the brothers here have cared for you," Arthur retorted.

"They are kind."

"Perhaps you should learn some of that kindness."

"For what purpose, my lord?" I spat out the words as though they were sour wine.

"In order to turn it upon yourself. You act as a man who has done some great wrong and cannot forgive himself. Be kind to yourself. You deserve it."

"And what should I tell my men, the ones you dragged me from, the ones I should have died with, and betrayed."

"That their time had come and yours had not. That God had more plans for you."

"You are not God, my lord! But you are the archpriest of bastards and the spawn of vermin." In any other time and place that would have earned me a quick death. But Arthur had merely laughed. I think back now and realize that my words were so venomous because Arthur's were so true. And I think he knew that then.

"Learn your lessons well, and keep your mind sharp. I may have need of you again."

He was gone before I could tell him to leave me alone forever.

But though I heeded his words about learning my letters, I kept my mind anything but sharp, except for one irritating puzzle at the monastery that drew me from my melancholy. I learned my letters, and with something of a trade, I returned to Castellum Arturius, intent on making what little money I needed to drink myself into the next life.

I scratched the stubble on my face as I considered Arthur's expression and a burning that was building in my belly.

We had seen each other little from that time to this. Now, Ambrosius was the Rigotamos, and Cadwy and the rest were but memories, old men who bored guests with their tales of battles gone by, for the Saxons' advance had been checked for a time. Ambrosius was readying to step down, and the cloak of leadership seemed poised to fall to Arthur. I watched from afar as he rose high in the esteem of the people, and now he sought election as the acknowledged overlord, the Rigotamos, the high king of the Britons. It was a time of relative peace as the Saxons stayed in the lands of the Cantii and left our western fields and villages alone. And I lived alone in my little hut, drinking, trying to forget I'd ever heard of Arthur.

Eleonore, such a pretty child. Dead, now. I had seen her about the castle in recent days, and she showed a love for life that knew no bounds. I could not imagine her cold and white with death, as I had seen her sister, my beloved. It was as if Arthur had brought death to my family again and had saved me to bear witness to it. With a great effort, I pushed myself to my feet and brushed Arthur's hand from my shoulder, meeting him eye to eye and not yielding an inch. "Listen to me, my lord. Mark you this and mark it well: I will have the truth of it, no matter where it leads. Even if that crazy old fool did the killing. She will atone for another of her family who lies unavenged."

My lord drew himself to his full height, fearsome as it was, his eyes blazing. "Do not forget who rules Arthur's castle."

"Do not forget whom you have sought out," I countered. "I will not spare Merlin if he is the guilty one. And should your hand be seen in my inquiries, it will prove what Vortimer and the others are probably already whispering: that the great Arthur, who champions truth and justice and boasts the Cross on his shield, will conveniently forget such things when an old friend is in jeopardy. And that will force Ambrosius to reconsider his support for you." I chose my words well and knew my target even better.

Arthur's shoulders slumped, and he turned from me. "Of

course, you are right. You are a hard man, Malgwyn. But the world needs such as you. Though if any citizen of this kingdom lies unavenged, Malgwyn, it is not Gwyneth. You repaid her death a hundred times over."

"Her death will never be fully avenged."

"Believe as you wish. Come, I'll show you where it happened."

"Has aught been touched?" I asked him brusquely, struggling into my shirt.

"No. I knew you needed to see her as she was found."

Outside, people were still moving about in the lanes. This was no ordinary night. The entire *consilium*, the entire group of lords from all the tribes of Britannia, had come to Arthur's castle for one purpose and one purpose only—to name a new Rigotamos, a new high king to govern over all.

Oh, the old Rigotamos was not dead. No, he breathed yet.

Most such lords seemed as the one before, one to pay tax to, like all the rest. But Ambrosius was different somehow. He seemed to care about all of the raids by the Saxons, once our allies. "Aye, he has a Roman bearing, that one," my old man would say, leaning on his hoe at the end of the day. "Yep, him and that young one will stand us in good stead." By "that young one" he meant Arthur, a young officer and tax collector for Ambrosius. "A good, stout Roman lad," my father had said.

And when I met him one day, I saw that look in his eye, the one you knew you could trust above all else. His name was well known in our family. Rumors flew that he had been the reason that my cousin Guinevere was cast from the women's community at Ynys-witrin, but few knew the truth of it. A few years later, when we had laid my old father in his grave and the Saxons turned on us, ravaging the land at will, I remembered those eyes, and it was those I sought after the devils butchered Gwyneth when they reduced our village to burning huts and bloodied bodies. That was the beginning; much came after.

Now, Ambrosius was stepping down, and that young officer, the one I had come to trust with my soul yet now hated with all my heart, was said by some to be the next Rigotamos. He had repulsed the Saxon surge, with me at his side most of the time, and his reputation stood high across the land. Ambrosius, fat and rich, had retired to Dinas Emrys, leaving the administration of the various lords to Arthur. But he did not trust his consilium, as well he might not, and worried that some ambitious lord would conspire to kill him and claim the throne for himself. So, by retiring, he removed himself as a target and secured the major voice in choosing his successor.

By that time, I could care less, a one-armed drunk, saved from the grave by Arthur and despising him for it every day. He had made me half a man, and robbed me of my love for killing Saxons, that inner love that kept a smile across my face. No, I was no lover of Arthur.

It was generally assumed that this meeting of the consilium would confirm Arthur's choice. Treachery was a way of life, however. By proposing Arthur as his successor now, and using his power with the consilium to secure the selection, Ambrosius could rest easy. I had to wonder at the conjunction of events— the consilium's meeting and Eleonore's death. Were they somehow connected?

Arthur's castle was an old fort even then. An ancient village from Roman times was located to the northeast, and it was among those once-fine houses that some of the soldiers made their homes. Lord Cadwy established our fort on old Roman ruins near the land called Camel. The young Arthur would not take the bribes offered by the abbots and monks to ignore their levy. It earned him no friends among the priests, but the common man appreciated his fairness, and he rose to Dux Bellorum for our consilium. When Cadwy died, Arthur claimed his fort near Camel, changing its name to Castellum Arturius.

I preferred to be closer to the fort above and lived just beyond the outer gates. Years of use had beaten the main road into more a wide gully than a road, but Arthur had had the route cobbled in recent years. It led past my door and entered through Roman-style double gates, winding sharply up through the four defensive rings surrounding the fort. The massive rings were made of rock walls, dry-stacked in the old fashion, not mortared like Roman builders would have it, sixteen feet thick and reinforced by strong wooden posts every ten feet or so. Each ring of stone was surmounted by a stout wooden rampart. It would take a massive army or base treachery to defeat the castle's defenses.

Guards stood watch at each ring, but they raised a hand and smiled as they saw Arthur with me. Had he worn his warrior's regalia, they would have stood and saluted, but they knew that Arthur did not like ceremony when he dressed as a common man. Arthur could be a fierce and passionate warrior, and for this his men loved and trusted him. Trusted him enough that they accepted that he was a true believer in the Christ and carried symbols of Christianity on his shield, though even some of Arthur's men wished for the return of the Druids. A good man he was, but no special friend of the clergy, and that endeared his men to him as well.

On top of the hill, on the high summit, sat Arthur's great hall. The fletchers' workshops, armorers, the great market, and other shops and timbered houses lay spread gloriously out below. A Roman-style barracks occupied the far end of the plateau from the great hall, at the terminus of the wide lane that ran the length of the fort. All was fresh and clean, the lanes all paved with local stone. When Arthur had taken residence at the fort, he launched an extensive rebuilding campaign, paving the lanes, repairing the buildings, and erecting a new hall for himself.

As we trudged along the lanes, we encountered few people at this hour, two past the midnight, but as we drew closer to Merlin's hut, just east of Arthur's hall, a circle of armed warriors stood guard while a group of young men pushed for a closer look.

The metallic smell of blood hung in the air, like that of a freshly dressed kill in the field. I pushed past the young toughs and through the circle of guards. Eleonore's face was turned away from me, and I was glad for that. Her tender neck looked like Gwyneth's, though, and the sight stole my breath from me. From behind I heard a sudden silence and the rustling of bodies as the crowd parted for Arthur.

I knelt before her and pulled her clothing back from her stomach. She wore an old-fashioned gown, called a *peplos*, with a Roman-type cut, favored by Arthur's circle. A beautiful bronze brooch, shaped like a dolphin, fastened the gown at her shoulder. But when I saw what had been done to her, appreciation for her jewelry fled and I nearly spewed wine over her. Arthur had been absolutely correct. She was cut from between her breasts to her womanly parts and the flesh laid back. Blood lay splattered about her clothing in gobbets. I took her cold face in my hand and pulled it toward me, and the sight of that familiar face sat me back on my haunches as if I were truly drunk. I began to heave again as the bile flooded my throat. This time I couldn't hold it back and my evening's drink splashed all over the cobblestones. She had her sister's face, almost my wife's twin, and seeing her like this was like kneeling in my hut, desolate, so many moons before. For a moment, all around me disappeared, and I felt the rage and revulsion of Gwyneth's death sweep over me again. It was as if I knelt over her still ravaged remains; it was as if she had died once more. My bile heaved and my heart tightened; until, that is, some wag behind me chuckled.

"His lordship not only brought a one-armed drunk to investigate the crime, but one with a weak stomach as well. Perhaps his spine is as yellow as his belly is weak." I didn't recognize the speaker, but I knew that he was a follower of one of the lords of the consilium, a young buck with less common sense than experience and of that not much at all.

I paused to see if Arthur would answer this insolence, but he stood curiously silent, perhaps waiting to see what I would do. I knew too that this was Arthur's way of checking my worth. We had some old warriors about the villages and towns, missing hands, feet, but those who suffered such wounds mostly died from loss of blood or the stinking, choking putrefaction that followed. Those who survived, like me, were left to begging, pleading for a scrap of bread or a jug of wine, losing the last of their pride. A one-armed man served little purpose in any world. Farming required two hands as did most other jobs. Men with one arm had no purpose, no use it seemed. Arthur kept me breathing, gave me a trade to keep me from begging, but he could not return my arm. And now he would see how I had adapted to that loss.

I handled it swiftly, my anger at the child's death venting on the heckler. With a speed that shocked all who saw, I grabbed the feeble throat of the boy and, in one move, lofted him off the ground and pinned him against the wall of Arthur's hall. His eyeballs bulged as I remorselessly cut off his breath.

"As you can see, I need but one arm and one hand to stifle your childish mewlings." I let him drop to the ground, and he clutched his throat. "Another word from you and you'll be as dead as that girl." Coughing and hacking, he scuffled away from me across the cobblestones. "Now, go, before I change my mind and end your miserable life."

I spun around and fixed the crowd of soldiers with a stare. "Would anyone else care to test my spine?"

The young ones took a step back, without knowing it, it seemed. But not Vortimer, who stepped out so that I could see him. He and I had shared a battlefield or two in our time. Bearded with a thick chest, he had not the height of Arthur, or the honesty. The slyness in his eyes worried me, for I could not read him as well as I could read other men.

"Go on now, the rest of you! Get to your homes," ordered the captain of the guard. The handful of others slowly dispersed, leaving me with the guards and Arthur, and, of course, Eleonore.

"Bring those torches in closer," I directed. The glowing, dancing globes of light drew in about me until I could see all too clearly what evil the murderer had wrought on the poor girl.

She looked so different now, so unlike the little girl I had watched grow up. She had been but a child when Gwyneth and I were wed. The youngest of the children, she had been doted upon by her parents. Gwyneth often chided them for spoiling her, but both she and I did our share of the spoiling. Eleonore had bright, inquisitive eyes, and when she visited us, as she was wont to do, she would climb into my lap and beg me to tell her stories. How she would listen to those stories, with those beautiful eyes sparkling. But the sparkle was gone now, fled with the fire of life that had once filled her, replaced with the dull glaze of death. I shivered and steeled myself for the task ahead.

The blood I had first noticed now seemed less marked. There was much, to be sure, but not as much as one would expect from such a wound. No great puddles lay on the cobblestones, and yet the knife had ripped through her body, severing all those great channels that carried her blood. A knife, a single-edged blade, lay beside her, and it was covered with her blood and bits and pieces of her flesh. The great, gaping wound could easily have been made with such a weapon.

Still, something bothered me. I brushed the hair back from her face and neck and saw immediately the knife had not killed her. Bruises showed on her pale neck, in the shape of fingers, and small splotches, where blood had burst to the surface and appeared around her white eyes.

Eleonore had been strangled to death.

No blood had sprayed the lane because her heart had quit pumping before her body had been ripped open. I had seen similar wounds on the battlefield, where a blunt blow to the head had killed, and a later sword thrust produced no great gouts of blood. Why would the killer have mutilated her so when she was already dead?

I motioned for the guards to draw closer with their torches, and, with my initial shock set aside, I studied the gaping wound more closely. A quick survey led me to realize two facts: the blood I had sought on the lane was not pooled in her body cavity, another sign that she had been dead when this butchery had been done, and something more disturbing than the poor girl's identity could ever be.

Her heart was missing.

With all the will I possessed, I strengthened myself and slid my hand into her body, shifting lungs, stomach, but where the heart should have been were those great, severed tunnels and an empty spot. An old monk at Ynys-witrin taught me what I know of a person's insides. It was another of those studies I performed to help forget my missing arm. Preparing the bodies of the brothers for burial had fallen to this old man. He had studied the human body carefully and knew it well. The other brothers were reluctant to touch a dead body, a superstition dating back to Roman days, but one no more necessary then than now. The dead are ever with us, but I had heard tell of priests and ritual purifications, necessities to be performed before a body could be touched. We worried little about that sort of thing in these days. Now, sitting back on my heels, I studied the blood covering my hand, drying into a mortal glove, and tried to think of some reason for this. Rape. Yes, I understood rape. But this was different.

To be certain, I drew her skirts up and examined her womanhood. No tears, no scrapes, no blood, no bruises, nothing. No reason to think she had been raped or even that she had submitted willingly. I had heard enough in the lanes to know that she had her admirers, those who would pay court to her: Kay was one. I had also seen the look of hunger that young Tristan had given her at the feasting that night. He would bear questioning, as would Kay.

"Malgwyn!" a voice hissed, and I looked up to see Kay himself, with an expression of disfavor on his face. "Her honor, Malgwyn. Leave her something!"

"Her honor is gone with her life's breath, old friend. And if studying the most private part of her is the path to her killer, then I must follow that lane wherever it leads." I shook my head, replacing her skirts and smoothing them. "However, that is not the reason this time."

"She was not abused?" Kay asked. He was an exceptionally tall man, and I was forced to stretch my neck to look up at his face, as I was stocky and of medium height.

"No. There is something else awry here. Where is Merlin?"

"I had him taken to the barracks and tied to a post to keep him out of trouble," answered Arthur, more loudly than I thought necessary considering the hour, but I suspected he wanted all to know that he would offer no favor in this matter. In other circumstances, I would have laughed at Arthur's sometimes overwhelming desire to seem fair and just. What man with power in this day and age was either? But this was not a night for jests.

"And your other servants, my lord? The ones that this girl worked with. I'll need to speak to them as well."

"As you wish," Arthur said with a flourish, more for the benefit of his followers, Kay, Bedevere, and the others. He knew that I'd do as I pleased regardless. "You have my full authority in this matter."

"Thank you, my lord."

"I will leave you to your work," Arthur answered. "But, Malgwyn?"

"Yes, my lord."

"Be quick about it." Arthur left abruptly, returning to his hall.

His tone left nothing to the imagination. The longer I took

to divine this matter, the less chance Merlin would have, and Arthur's chances to be Rigotamos would dwindle. The people would demand Merlin's punishment, and for this there could be only one choice.

Arthur loved the old man like a father, and he would hesitate to have him executed, hesitate until the people began to ponder whether he had the strength to rule. As soon as Arthur lost his popular support, the other nobles would pressure Ambrosius to stop championing him as the new Rigotamos, leaving the field open.

"Are you finished with the body?" a new voice asked, one that was as familiar to me as my own. I turned toward the grim face of my younger brother, Cuneglas, named for our father.

He was turned differently, was my brother. He had no liking for the farmer's life and became a thatcher in Arthur's castle. Though I started out as a farmer, fate and the Saxons had robbed me of that life. Despite my missing arm, and by the grace of the monks at Ynys-witrin, I made good money, more than I ever had as a farmer, by writing or copying documents. And so I had spent my days, when the light was good, copying or writing, and my nights drinking to blot out the blackness of my sunny days. My brother and I were not close; we saw each other but seldom. Like our father, he had a gruff bearing, cast by his nature to be sarcastic, and his company was not pleasant. My days were dark enough without allowing him to darken them further with his melancholy moods. A big part of the matter with me had to do with my embarrassment at leaving my child with him and Ygerne, his wife. At first, I was so besotted with revenge that I could think of nothing but seeing her cared for and out of danger so that I might pursue my own mission. Then, when my wound cost me my arm and I turned to drink to blot the thought of my dishonor, I knew she needed a family, not a cripple. So, I stayed away and let my brother see to her raising. Occasionally, I would slip them some money; I spent a little on drink and less on food.

Cuneglas and another man began moving Eleonore. I rarely saw my brother. Indeed I saw his wife, Ygerne, more frequently, and Mariam, my daughter, until recent days—before Mariam stopped speaking to me. But that was my fault, for shirking my responsibility and leaving her to be raised by them.

"It is good to see you, brother," I stuttered somewhat lamely, not meaning it. My hand flew to my empty sleeve, attempting to hide unconsciously what I could not keep from his view.

"Would that another reason had brought us together," he replied.

I had no answer, and I knew that he expected none. A thought struck me, though, now that he had asked about the body. "No. I'd like to look at one more detail." Kneeling beside her again, I held her hands up and saw that a bit of cloth was clenched in one fist. I needed to look at it, but the cloth was held tight in her death grip. "Cuneglas. Please, help me here."

With his two good hands, he pried her fingers apart enough for me to pull the cloth out. It was dark, heavy wool cloth, the type worn by peasants and not uncommon among the Picts. Of itself, it meant nothing. Folk even of Arthur's rank would wear such cloth as an outer garment, covering their precious skin with imported linen beneath. That it was torn and clenched in her fist did offer a clue. She had struggled with her killer.

I checked her fingernails and found some streaked blood on the nails of the hand that clenched the scrap, but I couldn't be sure if it was her own or her assailant's. No flesh clung to them, but that didn't mean she hadn't marked the killer.

With a frown, I addressed the captain of the guard. "Who found her? Was she lying just as she is now?"

"The *vigile* found her," came the answer. Vigiles were another of Arthur's Roman pretensions. Watchmen. Guards. Their function was to patrol the lanes and watch for fires primarily, but for thieves and drunks as well, though there was little stealing within the walls of the fort. Arthur's punishments were harsh when someone erred. "He's back out on his rounds."

The captain's answer tore me from my mind's wanderings.

"Have him brought to me at the barracks. If I am not there, then find me," I ordered. I was turning to face my brother when a thought struck me. "Why are you claiming her body? What of her parents?" This was not our way, and it bothered me greatly.

He shook his head at me. "Dead this month past, Malgwyn. The plague took them. I am surprised you had not heard. She had no one, and since we had Mariam, she came to us. I could not turn her away. Eleonore was Mariam's aunt and your sister-in-law. She was family." As if to punctuate the matter, Kay rose, dusted off his knees, and slipped away from the torchlight, his face as white as that of a dead man. Kay must truly have cared for her. I had seen him walk away from the remnants of a battle, picked at by the ravens and crows, as though he were leaving a banquet.

Nodding at Cuneglas's recitation, I thought I would find myself unmoved at the death of Gwyneth's parents, but they were such simple, goodly folk that my heart sank at the news and I mourned their passing. I suspected that soon, though, a numbness would settle over me, and nothing more could shock me. I looked to the captain of the guards again. "Will your men take her to Cuneglas's house?" He nodded his assent, and I took my brother's arm in my hand and squeezed gently. "Walk with me, brother. The women can prepare her body. I would like to talk with you."

He hesitated, torn, I knew, between his duty to Eleonore's body and his curiosity about why I was involved in the affair. But after a brief pause he started up the broad avenue at my side toward the guards' barracks.

"I knew she worked at Arthur's hall, but I never understood why. Do you know?"

"She needed work. His cook, the old Saxon slave Cerdic, needed another serving girl. There's little else hereabouts for a young girl without parents. I could shelter her, but I needed help to feed my household." It was a common story. Time was yet hard for all in our lands. But his voice a hesitation betrayed, one I didn't welcome.

"What else? The girl is dead. I must know everything if I'm to finish this matter."

He averted his eyes. "Well, Lord Arthur had a hand in her hiring as well."

Sparks flared in my eyes. "How so?"

"Malgwyn, he heard of her plight, of our plight, and came to me one night. He said there was nothing in his kingdom that he would not give to help the family of Smiling Malgwyn."

Damn the man! Did God above appoint him as my eternal tormenter? First, he snatches me from an honorable death at the river Tribuit and puts me in the charge of the brothers at Ynys-witrin, leaving me a one-armed warrior and object of pity. Now, he takes it upon himself to care for my family as if I couldn't. I stopped my silent rampage at that thought.

"Had Eleonore said anything about someone bothering her?" I was anxious to change the direction of this conversation. "Had she mentioned Merlin?"

"She was always mentioning Merlin. He spends half his time at Arthur's table, eating and annoying all who will listen to his tales of dragons and potions. But Eleonore only laughed about him. I saw no fear when she spoke of him."

"Others?"

Cuneglas frowned. "She was a pretty maid, and lacked not for suitors. But she did not seem inclined toward any of them but one."

"Who were they, and who was the one?"

"There was Tristan from the west country, acting in Mark's stead at the consilium. Her chosen swain was Kay, Arthur's lieutenant. Then there was—"

"She was a peasant girl," I interrupted, shaking my head. "You are naming lords and warriors. What use had they for Eleonore, other than pleasure?"

"She was a special one, my brother. Much like your Gwyneth. Beautiful and lively. Quick-witted and saucy. And Arthur had bestowed his blessing on her. All knew that he favored her above the other servants. Though, truly, none knew why."

"But did she fear these men? If she were as protected by Arthur as you say, my head tells me that Kay, at least, would have been protective too. I remember this Tristan as only a foolhardy boy, but the Dumnonii need Arthur. He would do all in his power not to incur Arthur's wrath."

We passed a pair of closed-up stalls and I saw, by our torchlight, shadows lurking to either side of them. Wearing light gray robes and hoods, they huddled closely together. Cuneglas must have seen my look. "Druids. They arrived today, during the procession for the consilium. No one knows why."

"Vortimer?"

Cuneglas shrugged. "I think so, but who can tell? He speaks to the people of the old ways, and the Druids shadow his path, but he keeps himself apart from them, just enough."

Vortimer was Arthur's chief rival for the throne of the Rigotamos. He was the son of Vortigern, that man whose bad decisions brought the Saxons upon us. But Vortimer, through his prowess in battle, had overcome his father's disgrace. Ten years ago, Vortimer's preference for the Druids would have worked against him. But now, a growing wind was sweeping the Druids back across our land, and the people were breathing deeply. Aye, even Mordred, Arthur's cousin, had proclaimed his belief in the Druids. Mordred lusted for Ambrosius's seat too; most thought him too young, but his ambitions were as unfettered as deer in the forest.

I too had watched the procession of the consilium, the council of lords who would choose Ambrosius's successor. I did not remember seeing the Druids during that great parade, but Vortimer was smart enough not to include them in his escort.

I shrugged. Ofttimes I wondered if perhaps Vortimer wasn't right, that we had brought all these wars on our own shoulders by abandoning the old gods. I treasured the friendships that I made at Ynys-witrin among the monks, but I never fully accepted their religious teachings. They tried, though. Oh, how they tried. A part of me wondered if Arthur hadn't taken me there in hopes of converting me to his faith; many were the discussions we'd had around the campfires late at night, and he knew of my doubts about Christianity. Perhaps the Druids followed the right path. Christians. Druids. I knew not which was true. One made gods of things I could see—nature, the growing season, the moon. The other made godlike a man as the son of a single God who wished only that we love one another, and then He was killed, giving himself up for that which He believed. That too was compelling. But my life had taken so many twists and turns that I spent my time wondering why any god would willfully treat a man as I had been. I had done nothing to offend the one god or the many. I had only wanted to love my wife and child, to till the land, to have a simple life.

Our talk flagged until we came to the barracks and training ground. Archery targets sat at one end of the field, wooden shafts still protruding from some. A guard stood at attention at the door of the main structure.

"Do you have Merlin inside; he who is sometimes called Myrddin?"

The guard nodded. "I was told of your coming, master. You are free to enter." He looked at Cuneglas oddly. "But of the thatcher I was told naught."

"He is with me," I assured him, pushing past and into the room. Big, sturdy posts held the roof in place. A pair of tables sat at the far end of the room. Some of the soldiers sat around them, cups and jugs in front of them. The unmistakable smell of *cervesas*, our local beer, pervaded the room. Beyond the tables was yet another massive post.

And there stood a laughable sight if I'd ever seen one. A dried-up, wrinkled old man, dressed in a dark tunic, belted around his nonexistent waist, and wearing of all things a pointed cap, some kind of leather skin stretched over a frame. He was tied to the rear post in the room and seemed to be asleep.

"Merlin, what in the world have you done now?" Not a

proper way to begin an inquiry, but neither was the way I was dragged in.

The old raisin lifted his chin and squinted at me. "Malgwyn, would you please untie me and let me get back to work? I have so much to do. This is nonsense, disturbing an old man's sleep."

We knew each other well, for Merlin had often attended our camps and counseled Arthur before battles. If not for the bloody vision of Eleonore forged into my brain, I would have laughed at the old man.

"Some evil has been done this night, Merlin. And they say you have done it. How came you here? Where were you when they took you?"

"I was in my home, asleep in my bed. Bedevere stormed in with a troop of guards and arrested me. They haven't told me what I've done and haven't heeded my calls for Arthur. But I'm rested now and I must get back to my experiments. What evil have I done? Is this about the hearts? There's nothing wrong with that. I believe in my theory!"

A chill ran through me. "What about hearts, Merlin? What is your theory?"

Even tied to a post, the old fool put on his schoolmaster's face. "Eating hearts is a way to make your own healthy, strong."

"What kind of hearts?"

He looked confused. "Why, animal hearts, Malgwyn. What else could I be speaking of? Arthur and the rest said it was silly to talk of such things, but I know I am right."

I turned to Cuneglas. "Do you know of this?" I had told no one about Eleonore's missing heart. Stories had filtered through the lanes for months of the wandering nature of Merlin's mind. Some said he was possessed by a demon; others claimed that he was anointed by God with special knowledge. I thought he was just an old man, and old men's minds often decline in their last years. Perhaps it was a combination of both, the awful combination of an insane old man's fantasies and reality. And perhaps they had met in the person of young Eleonore.

Cuneglas shrugged. "Just another one of Merlin's latest theories. But some of Arthur's warriors liked it not. Said it sounded too much like human sacrifice and claimed Merlin was advocating bringing back the Druids." He spoke as if Merlin were not there and that bothered me.

"Druids! They are false alchemists, Malgwyn." Merlin spat on the ground. "They should be banned from all Britannia!"

"Not now, Merlin," I cautioned him. "We have other matters to concern us. Are you certain that you do not know why you are here?"

The wizened old face grimaced. "No, I do not. I was dragged out of my bed and brought here. I very nearly had no time to dress."

"But you're wearing a new hat."

"Oh, this," he said, delighted I had noticed it. It's a new idea, a hat that sheds water, designed to let the rain run off it instead of collecting on top. You see—"

"You were brought here because young Eleonore, Arthur's serving girl, has been murdered." I knew I must stop him or he would lecture for hours.

Merlin frowned even more deeply. "Eleonore? But she was a mere child. Who would want her dead?"

"They say your knife killed her."

"My knife?" He cocked his head and confusion spread across his face. "I gave my knife to someone. Someone borrowed it to dress a deer they had killed."

"Who?"

The old man shook his head. "I cannot remember. I have lived too many years to remember that one moment."

So, that was to be his defense. He loaned his knife to someone. But I knew what no one else knew. She did not die by the knife, but by strangulation. Though it would be simple to believe that the old man, in his delusions, had mistaken Eleonore for some animal and killed her for her heart, I heard truth in his voice. Or mayhap I just hoped I did.

The door was flung open behind me and I spun around to see Kay, out of breath, rush into the room. "Malgwyn! Quickly, you must come with us!"

I shot a glance at Cuneglas and jerked my head for him to follow. As we trailed Kay out the door, I could hear Merlin shouting at me:

"I'm not finished with our lesson, Malgwyn! You will return this instant!"

Kay moved at a trot back along the great avenue, and I did my best to keep up, but my training of late had been more in lifting skins and pots of wine than running. Within a few steps I was huffing and puffing for breath.

We stopped finally at Merlin's door, right where Eleonore's body had been found. The body was gone now, delivered, I supposed, to Cuneglas's house where it would be washed and prepared for burial. "I have seen the site of the murder, Kay. What else is there?"

"You haven't seen this, Malgwyn."

He shoved the wooden door open and we both ducked as we entered. A single lamplight brightened the room, and Bedevere stood near a rickety wooden table, a dark lump lying on it.

A sinking feeling filled the pit of my belly, as I looked down on the object on the table. It was wrapped in woolen cloth. I knew what it was when I saw it, but the knowing didn't make the revelation any easier to take. With a deep breath, I pulled an edge of the cloth away. All in the room gasped.

A human heart.

Bloodied, beginning to dry and atrophy, but a human heart nonetheless.

Arthur's hopes for Merlin's salvation suddenly seemed forlorn at best.

CHAPTER TWO

"Malgwyn? Malgwyn?"

It was Kay, pestering me to say something. "What would you wish me to say? That it was a deer's heart? Well, it's not, my friend. It's human, and I'd lay money it's the girl's. Someone took it from her body." There was silence for some moments. Somewhere, outside the door, I heard someone retching, thought it must be Cuneglas.

"Does this mean that it truly was Merlin?" Kay asked. I glanced at him and saw a slow anger building.

"We're meant to think so," I said sharply, more to keep control over him than in truth. Merlin may still have done this deed. The old fool or more likely somebody else was giving me little choice but to tell Arthur what he didn't want to hear. "Who knows of this?"

"Just Bedevere and myself," Kay answered. "Arthur sent us to fetch Merlin some suitable clothes," he stammered. Kay's eyes shot to the object on the table. "So that is Eleonore's heart?"

"Aye," I answered. "Or at least I suppose it to be. I know only that Eleonore's heart is not in her body, and this is a human heart. More, I cannot say. Say nothing of this to anyone.

There is more to this than what it seems." I said it all with more confidence than I felt, but I had no other choice. Something was amiss here, and I felt, rather than knew, that the easiest answer was not the right one.

Kay turned away, his gloved hand to his mouth, and a gagging sound slipped from behind it. I looked away for a moment. Such times deserve privacy.

I pulled the cloth back around the heart and sank heavily into a chair. "Tell me of the girl and the court. I am told that you were fond of her."

It was at that moment, I think, that Kay became a living human being for me. We had known each other for years, befriended each other on the field of battle, watched each other's back when the fighting was fierce. But that breeds a knowledge of a man that has little to do with affairs of the heart. And after my wound, after I dove into a jug, we were not close, a situation more my fault than his. Embarrassment is a strong and bitter disease. So I did not know him, not really. Not until he too sank onto a stool and began to cry.

"I would have had her as my wife, Malgwyn," he said, brushing the tears from his cheeks with weather-roughened hands wrapped in woolen cloth against the chill. His hair was light, lighter than mine. His father wore the purple, I am told, and some say his mother was a Pict. Such pairings were not uncommon. Of this, I understood little. I knew though that he was a good man in battle.

"But she was a peasant, a serving girl only. Surely some girl of higher birth would have been more to your liking."

He looked at me with searing eyes, as if I had taunted his honor. "Never speak of her in that way. She was better than them. Better than all the women of noble family. She had the

fire of the Picts in her eyes, and her spirit was as free as a hawk.
You should know that as well as any man."

It was true that Eleonore shared more with my wife than just
blood. Kay was in love; that much was plain. And love could
make men do horrible, wicked things. But could it make you kill
the one you loved? Maybe, if that love wasn't returned. I had
seen stranger things in my life. But mutilating the corpse? Yes, I
could see a young nobleman, frantic over his actions, doing all in
his power to cast the light of inquiry away from him. No,
though I prayed for a different answer than Kay, I could not ex-
clude him from my list any more than I could Merlin.

"What said my lord Arthur about your match?"

The young man shrugged. "He said naught about it. We all
knew that Eleonore was his favorite, but he had no inclination
of that sort toward her."

"Why say you that?" Lords such as Arthur took women as
freely as they drank wine.

Kay shrugged. "He had Guinevere."

I nodded. Until my farm was raided by the Saxons and my
life torn asunder, my beautiful cousin Guinevere was the first to
bring gossip and shame to our family. Bold and impetuous, she
heeded not the family's commands, and when but fourteen seasons, she joined a religious order at a house near unto the brothers at Ynys-witrin and took the vows of poverty and chastity. I
was married and had my own hovel by then, and I heard the affair had something to do with a young man and an arranged marriage that she fought with all her might. I had battled with her,
begged her not to take such a serious step at so young an age, but
the sisters were so pleased at her zeal that their arguments easily
defeated mine. It was they whom she sought to please, not her
family.

For three years she was a devoted member of the order, but in those three years she grew into a woman, and her nature rebelled against the strictures of the order. She was disciplined for partaking of strong drink, for not performing her daily prayers, for not assisting with the daily chores.

One day a young lord came to call, collecting taxes for Lord Cadwy, and his eyes fell on the beautiful nun. He felt shamed by his lust for her, felt horrible for how the glow of her skin touched him. He vowed never to return to the monastery, to send one of his men to collect the tax. But by the following week the young Lord Arthur had found a different reason to visit the sisters. And the week after, yet another cause arose to bring him within their confines. And Guinevere too watched this intense, devout young man and grew to love him.

For a year they did nothing more than exchange glances, secret smiles. Arthur believed too strongly in the Christ to do something as sinful as to bed a nun. But, as will happen with humans, the temptations became too much and a smuggled note arranged a secret assignation. And the secret assignation ended in a bed of leaves. Two visits, three visits, four visits, and the lovers were caught.

Arthur was shamed. Guinevere was cast from the community and ordered never to return. She had broken her vows. Lord Cadwy kept the affair quiet but forbade them to meet. But Arthur loved her, and though he knew that they could never marry, he provided a cottage for her and visited when he could. As Cadwy and Ambrosius grew older and their power transferred to Arthur, the couple was less careful about their meetings, and rumors began to sweep the land of Arthur's sorceress, rumors that I knew Merlin spread to keep Guinevere's true identity secret. But with the passage of time, so passed the urgency to keep such a confidence. Slowly, Arthur made her welcome at court, though rumors still swirled that she was a witch, and until Arthur would marry her, she kept a cottage in the country, hidden away from view. Even now, when she appeared at feasts as Arthur's companion, people whispered that she was a witch who could cast spells and bring calamity on any who dared question her place at Arthur's side.

I had known the truth all along. Guinevere was, after all, my cousin. Kay and Bedevere, as Arthur's oldest and closest companions, would have known from the first, but I could think of none other.

"I did not see him with other women," Kay continued, "and I would have. Also, he did not tell me to cease my suit, nor did he encourage me. The same cannot be said of that newcomer to the hall, Tristan. He comes from Lord Mark's lands to the west. Aye, he's that distant king's son."

"Why don't you like him? Eleonore?"

Kay's eyes darted away from me. "'Twas more than that, Malgwyn."

"Yes?"

"He brought word from King Mark, word that made Arthur furious."

"Kay!" Bedevere shouted.

"Hush. This is Malgwyn, not some harpy in the streets."

"Mark is not here for the consilium?"

"No. He sent his son in his stead."

"And that word?" I pressed.

Kay glanced around. "This is not for every man's ears. Tristan is charged by his father to bring an offer of a permanent peace with the Saxons to the consilium."

I stood straight up, blood rising into my face. "A permanent peace with those devils? Kay, this cannot be allowed!"

"Calm yourself," he said, rising to meet me and placing a hand on my shoulder. "Arthur is violently opposed to a permanent peace. And the peace they offer is no gift, more a surrender. They demand all the territory of the Cantii and full access through our lands and Mark's lands to the western sea."

"They seek free passage across all of our island," Bedevere said.

"That *is* a surrender." I relaxed. Granting them the land of the Cantii in practice would mean little. They were already well settled there and the right to settle had been lawfully granted to them by Vortigern. But those lands lay close to where the Iceni had lived, and bards sang still of that fearsome woman Boudicca who rebelled against the Romans. As much as we clung to many of our Roman ways, we still had our native heroes. She was one. Arthur would never agree to such an arrangement. He had seen as many burned hovels as had I. And, high lord though he might be—next to Ambrosius—he knew that he would lose his grip at once by agreeing to such a treaty with the Saxons. Their treachery against Vortigern was well known. Vortimer too would oppose such a treaty. Though he championed the pagan Druids, he knew that treating with the Saxons in such a manner would be surrender, not diplomacy. And he did not want to be associated with his father's memory, a father indeed who had tossed Vortimer's mother aside and married a Saxon woman.

"But," I said, bringing the subject back in focus, "Eleonore fed your distrust of this Tristan?"

Kay's face became hard. "He was too free with his hands, and he pressed his suit too hard with Arthur."

"Pressed it how?"

"When Arthur refused his offer for Eleonore, he wanted to buy her. She was a freewoman, of lowly birth though she be, and Arthur was offended, and were Tristan any other than King Mark's son, Arthur would have tossed him from the rampart walls."

I snorted. "I would have done so anyway. But I suppose that's why Arthur's a lord and I'm a one-armed scribe."

Bedevere's head whipped around. "You are far more than that, Malgwyn. You hold a place in our lord's reverence that no one else equals and no one else understands. And your feats at Tribuit are still sung of in Arthur's hall."

Tribuit. Would that I had never heard of that river. I rubbed the stub of my arm at the reminder. Since that day, the smell of fresh blooming flowers left me sick at my stomach. I had lain on a bed of such blooms as my life's blood drained from me, almost, until Arthur pulled me back into this world.

Of the rest that Bedevere claimed, I doubted. But then, how was I to know? I rarely left my hut. Were it not for the women that brought my food to me and the youngster that I had taught to sharpen my quills, I would speak to few. The melancholy which gripped me dug at my throat day and night. I did not feel worthy to speak so I pretended a sourness that was a lie. Before Gwyneth was killed, I had loved to drink and laugh with my neighbors. But those days ended with the beating of her heart.

I turned my attention back to Kay. "Enough of me. Eleonore, Kay? How did Eleonore respond to Tristan's suit?"

"She did not welcome it, nor did she reject it. Eleonore was of a changeable nature."

Once again, it seemed that Kay had as much reason to kill

the poor child as anyone. I sank down and peered at the woolen-covered lump on the table. While he was lost in his own thoughts, I found a piece of leather and bound the now withered, blackened heart in it, wondering at how such a fragile-looking object could be so tough and resilient. "Did you know, Kay, that the human heart is almost indestructible? When we stormed the Saxons in their fort at the river Glen, we threw fire into their huts. Later, as we picked through the ruins for anything worth carrying away, I came upon a Saxon, dead and burned, but in his chest, his heart could still be seen, mighty muscle that it is. I do not pretend to understand it, but when all else is gone, the heart remains."

I paused. How would I know aught of hearts? I had sold mine for the blood of Saxons.

"Who did this, Malgwyn? Who? Merlin?" Kay wasn't interested in my speech on the resilience of the human heart. And he was no more moved by severed limbs and exposed organs than I. But as I had been moved by the butchery of Gwyneth, so was he moved by the butchery of Eleonore. While waiting for my response, he spun around and unfastened the bronze fibula holding his fur cloak around his shoulders. With a flourish, he removed the cloak and laid it across a stool, wincing as he did so. I noticed a woolen wrap around his wrist, the flesh red and swollen.

"How came your injury, Kay?"

He glanced at his wrist and shrugged. "Yesterday morn, I was at sword practice with Bedevere and twisted it. A day, maybe two, and it should be fine."

"Aye," added Bedevere, "and I would have bested him."

Inwardly I chuckled. It did not surprise me that they had been at swords. Such weapons were few in these times, and theirs had been gifts of Arthur's for their loyalty and bravery. They lost no opportunity to display them. I took notice of the fact and began to answer his question. "I do not think so, Kay. He is an old man, and Eleonore was strangled to death. I doubt that a man as old and frail as he could overpower a strong young woman."

"She did not die by the knife?"

"No, 'twas no knife that ended her life. 'Twas human hands that choked the breath from her. The knife was wielded later and removed her heart."

Kay went pale again, raising his fist to his mouth as if to cover a cough. In a second, I heard him clear his throat hoarsely. "But does that not argue for Merlin? He strangled and killed her and then removed her heart for his demonic ritual," Bedevere argued.

"Perhaps. But Merlin is a frail old man. I'm not sure he has the strength to strangle a strong young girl."

"I hadn't thought of that," Kay conceded, turning back to face us. "But sometimes old people have reservoirs of strength that are unapparent."

"And you, Kay? Could you have strangled her with your one good hand?"

His eyes grew large and bright. No fear hid in their depths though. Only anger. And that was a welcome sight.

"I loved her, Malgwyn. I could not harm her."

"Even if she chose Tristan over you?"

"Even then." His eyes held mine, firm and tight. And I was glad to see that too. Men give themselves away with their eyes, as much or more than women do. I needed a colleague in this affair, someone who could lend their ears. Kay and I had fought side by side, saved each other's lives on countless occasions. I could not yet count him out in this affair, but if he was guilty, keeping him close by would give me more chance to watch for a hint of his guilt. If he were not guilty, well, a better companion could not be had.

"I'm sorry, Malgwyn," a voice said from the door. It was Cuneglas, wiping his mouth with his sleeve.

I waved him off. "I understand, my brother. What is sad is that such sights haven't the same impact on me."

"I saw you kneeling beside Eleonore," Kay admonished. "Your heart is not empty."

"No, not completely. But my grief was more about history than the present."

Cuneglas regarded me with something approaching pity in his eyes. "It was all of it that made me vomit. I am a thatcher, not a soldier. My eyes haven't seen many butchered bodies, not as yours have." He paused and passed me a soft look. "She was a young and beautiful woman, one who had become a part of my family. This butchery!" he said with a shiver. "I did not think man capable of such."

"It is not easy to accept, but I have come to believe that there is not much that man is not capable of."

"Your life has not been easy."

"Nor Kay's." I noticed that the tall warrior's eyes were moist and his face strained. "But what is an easy life? We scrape some food from the ground and give a portion to our lord as his due. When he calls, we answer his command and fight and die, often for things that have no meaning for us, but to fulfill some private ambition of his. And, in the end, all is taken from us by the hand of death. Such are our lives, brother, and I see nothing easy in the tale for any of us."

The memory of the bright and beautiful child would not

leave me. And I wondered about the truth of what I had said earlier to Cuneglas. Was it truly history that sparked my revulsion? Or was it the barbarity committed on such a young one? In fact, I had lied to Cuneglas. This butchery was a mystery. I thought of Gwyneth; at least I understood why she died. The Saxons wanted our land, our patria. But Eleonore, carved like a slaughtered deer, made no sense. But sense there had to be, some reason for it!

I stopped and considered my words. "Challenge," I said suddenly. "Challenge is one of the reasons to go forward, the hope of accomplishing something worthwhile, something necessary. It still does not make life easier, but it adds value to the living of it."

Chapter Three

Cuneglas took his leave of us, pleading exhaustion and a full day's work ahead of him, as well as Eleonore's burial to arrange. I watched him disappear into the darkened town and wondered at the different paths our lives had taken. Turning away after a moment, Kay and I crossed the lane back to Arthur's hall. A handful of drunken soldiers lounged about, playing at dice, men I did not know and hence I took them for visitors, here with one of the other lords. I found a servant and gave him the heart, bundled up, and without saying what it was, I told him to stow it away until I should call for it.

Even then, hours after the feasting, the great hall was not yet empty. Ambrosius Aurelianus, Rigotamos of the Britons, lounged beside the table, still snacking. A haze of smoke from the fire hung against the beams overhead, slowly filtering out through the hole in the roof.

With Ambrosius was Nyfain, leaning too close to him for a married woman, I thought. But I often suspected that Nyfain's marriage to Accolon was one of convenience for her and loneliness for him. It gave her enough status to receive invitations to the feastings (due more in her late husband's honor than anything else), and Accolon's pay enabled her to buy pretty things to wear.

"Malgwyn," Ambrosius began, slightly tipsy from the wine. "Arthur told me he was going for you. Have you resolved this affair?"

"No, my Lord Rigotamos. 'Tis too soon for resolution. Did you know the girl?"

"Only that she had a family connection to you. Do you think Merlin did this thing?"

"I do not wish to believe it. But man is an unusual animal. He is as unpredictable as our changeable weather."

"I think he did no such thing," Nyfain interrupted. She wore the plump cheeks of a well-fed woman in her middle years. "Merlin adored the girl. He had no reason to harm her."

"You knew her well?"

"Aye," she said. "She often watched my boy." Nyfain had a young boy, child of her first husband. "'Tis funny that you were the one named by Arthur to see to this."

"Why funny?"

"Eleonore mentioned you last eve. Right after the feasting, she told me she must see you. Something about a conspiracy, murder. I thought she had been sampling the wine too heavily and told her so."

"What say you, my lord? Have you heard aught of such things?" Even as I asked the question, I noticed one of the other soldiers, one casting the die, was listening, it seemed. He looked familiar, but I could not place him.

Ambrosius's face wrinkled into a wry smile. "I am the Rigotamos. Not a moon passes that I do not hear of some plot to murder me. I have seldom found substance to any of them."

I nodded. That much was certain in this violent age. Rumors

of rebellion and assassination floated across our land like ill winds. And a girl was likely to take nothing and make it something.

But if it were true, why kill Ambrosius now? His reign was within days of ending. To kill him now served little purpose, with one exception—Ambrosius's championing of Arthur as the next Rigotamos.

How would a girl like Eleonore know of such a plot, if one existed? Would such a girl eavesdrop on the wrong conversation? No, the answer to her death lay in another direction.

"She was such a pleasant girl," Ambrosius said after another swig from his jug.

"Aye, she was," I agreed.

"You realize that this matter will have serious repercussions for Arthur. If Merlin is truly guilty, then Arthur's patronage will work against him when the consilium votes. If he is not guilty, Arthur will be accused of protecting him. And my support will lose some of its strength."

I nodded. These thoughts had occurred to me. But such conspirators, with the selection of a Rigotamos at stake, would hardly reveal their plans to a serving girl. No, I insisted to myself, Eleonore's death had a simpler answer.

Still, that she wanted to see me lent Nyfain's story a certain credibility. We had spoken on occasion in recent years, but not often and then only in passing.

"Malgwyn, I remember well the way you eyed a battlefield and knew instinctively the best line of attack. I trust you in this, but the consilium is pushing for a vote. I have stalled them for two days. I need you to hurry."

I frowned. "Haste is one thing I cannot promise, Rigotamos. But if there is truth to be found, I shall do my best to find it."

By then I noticed that Ambrosius was drifting off to sleep. Nyfain had deserted us for Mordred and a group of his men, drinking and singing songs in these early morning hours. I watched as Mordred whispered something in her ear, probably negotiating the price of her bed for the night. The pair wandered out the door, arm in arm. Her husband, Accolon, would not see her this night, just as in most, I understood. Nyfain, a woman of noble birth, stripped of her position by her first husband's death at Caerleon, married Accolon to stay close to the court. Though Accolon was no officer, Arthur treated her at court as he would any noblewoman. Of his many faults, pity for others was one.

But though she accepted Accolon for his support and humble house near unto the gate, her heart still lay with the luxuries of the nobles and their vices. In turn, she became one of their vices. For his part, the old soldier hoped she would help him recoup his stature with Arthur, lost long before. The boy, Owain, was abandoned in the middle.

I remembered the day I first encountered the boy. He squatted in front of my hovel, nearly as dirty and grubby as was I. But his eyes were bright and uplifted, holding none of the fear I had seen in other children's eyes when they beheld me.

Just returned from Ynys-witrin with a bundle of manuscripts to copy, I narrowed my eyes at the boy and growled, but he gave not an inch.

"Are you Malgwyn?" he asked without a hint of concern.

"Aye, and who would you be?"

"Owain," he answered spryly. "My mother is Lady Nyfain." And that had explained his appearance. "Father Accolon says you were a great warrior."

"Accolon is kind."

"Would you teach me how to be a warrior?" Something in his voice, a pleading and a forthright manner, softened my heart.

Soon, he was spending more time at my hut than his own. He was an eager lad, and I taught him the manner of mixing inks and sharpening quills. And I told him stories, not of my own exploits, but of warriors long dead. Though I would never admit it, I grew fond of the boy and missed him when he was not around.

I pushed thoughts of Owain from my mind and turned back to the mission. "My lord, do you know where Lord Tristan is?

Ambrosius shook his wobbly head. "No. He took his leave earlier." Leaning toward where Nyfain had been, he spoke as if she were still there. "Did I tell you, my dear, of the day we stormed Caerleon?" But before he could finish the thought, he nodded off again into a drunken slumber.

As we went to leave, Arthur beckoned to us from his chamber. I sighed. I had known this would come, but I'd hoped for further time to study and deliberate. But as Kay and I entered, I saw another man there—Accolon. He looked about at us and seemed confused. "I was told to report to the scribe Malgwyn." I thought then of his wife, just on the other side of the hall, bargaining with Mordred for her favors earlier in the evening. Poor fellow.

He was older than most of Arthur's men, gray in the beard and hair. His cloak was bare in spots where the fur had worn away. I smelled the sickly sweet odor of honey mead about him.

"Have we not served together?"

"Aye, many moons ago we shared a battlefield or two."

"You are the man who found the murdered girl?"

"Aye. In the lane beside the old man's house." His voice was thick and gravelly.

"Was that spot on your regular round?"

"Aye. There are two of us in the lanes at night. We patrol separately the lanes on either side of Lord Arthur's hall and then come up the opposite sides of the town until we meet in the northeast."

"What time did you find her?"

"About two hours past the midnight."

"How long between times that you passed Merlin's door?"

"A half hour, maybe longer."

"Was there any disturbance there earlier? Did you see the maid roundabouts?"

"Not there. Not then." Accolon narrowed his eyes as he concentrated. "Earlier. About the midnight. At the gate on the Via Caedes. She was there with a man."

"Merlin?"

He shook his head. "I could not tell you. He wore a hood and was in the shadows inside the gate."

"Shadows?"

"The moon shadows."

"What caused you to take notice of them?"

He shrugged. "She was laughing and joking."

"And her companion?"

"He said nothing."

"And then?"

"And then nothing. I continued on into the fort to report for watch."

Though it filled in a minor gap, it ended at a stone wall. Almost literally. Also, Accolon's tone of voice bothered me, rubbed me raw. It held an insolence, directed not at me but at the world.

"If there is nothing more, I'm finished with my duties for the night."

"Go then," I said, "but I may speak with you further."

He grunted and left.

"That is not a happy man," I said in the ensuing silence.

Arthur's familiar, deep voice rumbled through the room. "For good reason."

"And what reason is that, my lord?"

"Accolon wanted to marry my sister Morgan. But she cared for him not, and I refused to force her into a marriage not to her liking."

"And, by the looks of him, he had no dowry to sweeten the porridge," I said.

Arthur shook his bearded head. "Once he had, but he is too fond of drink and dice. I would not saddle my sister with such as him."

"And yet you keep him as one of your men."

"Each man needs a job, a purpose. It was the right thing to do. If a man has no purpose in life," he continued, looking straight at me, "then he should look beyond himself and seek a purpose."

"I have a purpose, my lord. To drink and pleasure myself for as long as my body will allow."

"That may take many years. I am about to seek rest, Malgwyn, but I wanted to know if you have discovered anything about this affair."

Impatience had been one of Arthur's faults as a young officer. But since I was young then too, I saw it as boldness, good leadership. In the older Arthur it annoyed me. "I have discovered many things, my lord. And when I am ready to tell you, I shall. But first I have questions for you."

Kay chuckled. "Malgwyn, you take liberties," he said.

Arthur fumed. "Ask your questions."

"What was your relationship with Eleonore?"

"She was a servant here."

"That is all?"

His eyes narrowed and crimson painted his cheeks. "That is all."

"Your interest in her welfare seems out of place, my lord."

"Say what you mean plainly, Malgwyn."

"Were you bedding the maiden?"

"And if I were, it would be my right." Arthur did not believe that, nor did I truly believe that he had a hand in this affair. A custom did exist in those days, called *prima nocte* or "first night." It involved the first night of marriage and a lord's right to take the bride. It was a right Arthur would never claim. But the chance to irritate him was more than I could resist.

I changed subjects abruptly. "Lord Arthur, I shall need to question Guinevere." I was aware that this would enrage Arthur. His cheeks puffed out and turned red. The fire in his eyes matched that of his cheeks.

"Absolutely not!"

"With all the respect due you, my lord, she is my cousin— family—and I have a right and need to speak to her. I'm sorry, Arthur. I must. You charged me to this task, and you must allow me free rein to question whom I please. I have learned enough to know that Eleonore was seeking me out before she was killed. She spoke of it to Nyfain. She may have spoken to Guinevere as well."

"No, I will not have it!" He really had no objection; he was just angered by my disrespect.

"My lord, if you do not allow me the freedom to act as I please, I cannot promise you any results, let alone those you desire. Besides, it's not as if you were married to her."

And at that, Arthur's face, while blushed before, now turned crimson in anger. I stood my ground, giving not an inch to his bluster. His unwillingness, in my mind, to marry Guinevere had been a particular sticking point in our relationship, even in the best of times. For Arthur to marry Guinevere would bring his oft-noted devotion to the Christ into great doubt. It did not matter that many of the people did not share that devotion. In these unsettled times, they looked for consistency, truth, not the mere illusion of it. She was a disgraced sister of the women's community, who had broken her vows and been cast out. Many still lived who remembered how Vortigern had cast aside Sevira, his Briton wife, for Rowena, daughter of the pagan Saxon Hengist. And just as many believed that the calamities that had befallen our lands could be traced to that betrayal.

In both the people's eyes and the church's mind, Guinevere was not fit for marriage to a lord. Indeed, Bedevere once told me that the archbishop of all Britannia, Dubricius, had ordered Arthur not to marry her. It mattered to no one that Arthur had been as much at fault in Guinevere's shame as she had. No one but me. For I could also remember that she had been but a child when she took those vows. Merlin's rumors, intended to protect them both, had created another obstacle. If Arthur were to marry her, the people would think that she had bewitched him, and their faith in him would drop even further.

Kay stepped forward. He could be so silent as to sit in the middle of the room and not be noticed. But given a battle-axe against the enemy, he was like some great animal, fierce and deadly. "Arthur," he said gently. "You know Malgwyn. You know he would not make such a request unless it was necessary. He is Guinevere's cousin. He will treat her with respect." Inserting himself between us, he deftly diverted the argument.

A pause ensued and the crimson drained from Arthur's enraged face. He was protective of Guinevere. He knew people gossiped about her, considered her a lowly consort, not a true wife of a noble. And he knew that his refusal to take her as his bride added to my grudge against him. But knowing these things did nothing to simplify a very complicated matter.

Bedevere, amused by the scene, excused himself to check the posting of the guards.

Arthur laughed grimly. "You haven't changed, Malgwyn. Fiercely independent. One of the shrewdest men that I know. But blinded to any knowledge of yourself. Ask her what questions you will. She'll answer at her own pleasure." He paused, letting that remark sink in. "We are feasting on tomorrow's eve, in honor of the consilium. I would have you attend and observe. Ambrosius has set the vote for the next evening."

"Has this something to do with the murder of Eleonore?"

"No. This has something to do with the future of this kingdom."

"The last time I concerned myself with the future of this kingdom, I came home with this." I tapped my empty sleeve. But I knew what he'd say next, and I knew too that I would be attending the feast.

"The Saxons threaten us once more, Malgwyn. But this time they are using their brains and not their swords. The consilium meets to choose a new Rigotamos. It is a perfect time to create havoc. I have nearly the entire consilium in my castle, under my care. I cannot afford to have aught go amiss. Your battle wound is of no importance; your nimble brain and unclouded mind are. And, I judge, you are not the hard-hearted, uncaring lout you would have us believe. You care, old friend; you just choose to keep it well hidden."

"For half a loaf of hard bread, I would rip your throat out, my lord. You weave words more skillfully than any maker of tunics," I conceded, because he was right. "As you wish. I will attend. Perhaps then I'll have more to tell you about this affair. I must warn you, the evidence does not look good for our friend Merlin."

His head drooped until his beard touched his tunic. "I feared so."

Suddenly, I felt very tired, more weary than I had since my days in battle. The night was gone and the sun would soon be raising its head, and I had had no sleep. I knew that a puzzle such as this one required my strength, my concentration. "I go to take my rest now, my lord. I have seen and done all that I can before daylight."

"Please, Malgwyn, I have a room at my hall for you. Rest there." Arthur was almost pleading.

"Thank you, my lord. But I'll only rest well in my own place."

Arthur frowned. "There are many who would wish that you fail in your inquiry, that Merlin is swiftly dispatched and that his crime can be turned against me, if crime he committed. I fear for your safety. I will set a guard upon your door to watch over you."

I shook my head. "No, that will not do. I'll have no young stripling that I know not standing post." In truth, I needed no such guardian, but Arthur had handed me an opportunity to have my own way without him knowing it.

"Malgwyn, I insist."

This time I frowned and hung my head. "Well, my lord, if Kay would allow me to stay at his house, then I suppose I could agree."

"Is that agreeable with you, Kay?"

My friend nodded.

"Then watch him closely. He is valuable to us."

Headed to Kay's house, we encountered Bedevere, trudging along the muddy, slippery cobblestones.

"You seem lost in thought, old friend," I greeted him. He looked up, his dark eyes framed by heavy eyebrows and a beard that reached high on his cheeks. I did not know who had befriended Arthur first, Kay or Bedevere, but they held equal esteem in Arthur's eyes. Of late, Bedevere had been touring the borders to the south, marking the settlements of the Saxons—new settlements, that is. Kay and Bedevere were as different as night and day. Kay was tall and prone to anger. Bedevere was stocky and taciturn.

"And you seem sober."

I chuckled. "You were never one to throw compliments about freely."

"Forgive me, Malgwyn. I have been in ill humor of late."

"And why is that?"

"My vote has been courted by two other lords." Bedevere's words drew a dark cloud over me, as dark as the moon was on this eve.

Kay and Bedevere both commanded regions of our land, scattered about the countryside, thus giving them seats on the consilium.

"Who?"

Bedevere shook his head regretfully. "I am not at liberty to say. I gave my word." This surprised me not. He was known for his honesty, discretion, and piety. To those such as Vortimer, these were mere words. For Bedevere, they were a creed, an oath.

"Such currying of favor is common."

"Not this sort. When I mentioned Arthur and my pledge to him, they said that by the time of the vote, Arthur would be of little consequence."

Kay looked bewildered as I absorbed this new information. Begging Bedevere for the names of his supplicants would do no good. That reputation for honor and honesty I mentioned was well earned. And if Eleonore's death did have something to do with the election of a new Rigotamos, I doubted that those behind it would approach Arthur's chief aide themselves. They would send others to probe his loyalty.

Bedevere had returned to Castellum Arturius solely for the consilium, to see his old friend become Rigotamos. He lived at the barracks with the common soldiers, eschewing the habits of Kay and other officers of high rank. There had always been something of the hermit in him.

"That's all that was said?"

He nodded. "Made no sense to me either, but I was cautious not to probe too deeply."

This was disturbing news indeed. Logic told me that the statement meant that Arthur was to be disgraced or assassinated. Only by these methods was he to be disregarded. Assassination seemed all but impossible; here in Castellum Arturius he was well protected. Perhaps the death of Eleonore was an effort to disgrace him. I knew that there were those rivals who would have Arthur's place, but murdering servant girls seemed an odd way to lay disgrace at Arthur's feet. Who stood to gain?

That was always the question. Vortimer stood out as the one who bore the most consideration.

But the girl? Why her? I was struck by the coincidence that Lord Tristan courted Eleonore and also counseled treating with the Saxons. Could Tristan be part of such a conspiracy? Could he have told Eleonore of it in an unguarded moment? I shook my head, trying to dislodge all these insistent thoughts. Perhaps I was letting too many bedevil my mind.

Kay extended the invitation. "Will you stay with us, Bedevere?"

The burly officer paused to consider. "Aye, 'tis been too many a moon since I shared a meal with Malgwyn."

"Then join us."

The three of us continued on to Kay's timber house on the main avenue leading from the hall down to the barracks. I still had my doubts about Kay, but the closer I kept him, the more chance I'd have to observe him. That Bedevere joined us was an added pleasure. We had shared many campfires. Aye, we had both blocked battle-axes aimed for the other's head.

We spoke of inconsequential matters as we neared the house. As we reached our destination, I was surprised to see a small figure sitting on the ground to the side of the door. It was young Owain, Nyfain's son.

" 'Tis late an hour for a youngster such as you to be wandering the lanes," I said, cuffing his ear with my one hand.

"I sought you at your hut, but you were not there. A soldier in the great hall told me he saw you heading toward Lord Kay's house. I ran here."

"What brings you out so late?"

He frowned. "I was waiting at your hut earlier, during the banquet. Eleonore came to see you. She claimed it was urgent that she meet with you, but she would not tell me what secret she held. She said it was for your ears only.

"When I heard she was dead, and that Arthur had appointed you as his *iudex* to investigate, I thought I should tell you straightaway."

I tousled his hair. "You were right to tell me. But it could have waited until morning. Why aren't you abed?"

"Father Accolon and Mother have not come home. I do not like to be alone at home." He hung his head in embarrassment at this confession.

I looked to Kay, who nodded, smiling down from his great height. "What do you think? Can you find a corner in your stables for this yearling?"

"You shall bed here," Kay agreed. "I'll send a servant to find Accolon or Nyfain and let them know of your safety."

The boy's eyes brightened and he turned to me. "Do you have work for me tomorrow?"

"Perhaps, if you can get up in time after a night out carousing with screech owls."

"I'm sure Master Malgwyn can put you to good use," Kay said. "Go have Cicero find you a bed." The lad scampered inside.

"You are a strange man," Bedevere said, studying me with a wry expression.

"How so?"

"You have practically raised that boy, yet you don't wish your own child to know you are her father. Aye, you threatened to beat Cuneglas senseless when he let the truth slip."

Scowling, I turned away from my old comrade. " 'Tis not as simple as that," I murmured. No matter how much I had wronged her, my mind was not on Mariam. If Eleonore was

serious enough about some matter to seek me out, she had
something of import to tell. But I had no proof, not a kernel
of cracked corn to tie this to any alleged conspiracy. I could
not allow myself to be distracted.

Merlin was still locked away at the barracks, and I still had
no evidence to free him. While Owain slipped into a peaceful,
if lonely, slumber, Bedevere, Kay, and I sipped watered wine,
served by Kay's crotchety old servant Cicero. Arthur's trust
seemed ill-placed at best. I said as much.

Kay removed his cloak and began to make a fire in his wide
hearth. Spring was coming, but so far it had not warmed the
evenings. "Remember when we were at the river Glein?"

I nodded.

"The Saxons seemed so weak, so few. Even Arthur was
puzzled. But it was you, Malgwyn, who sensed the deception.
It was you who counseled Arthur to send riders around the
Saxons' camp and behind the hills beyond."

Vortimer and the then youthful Lauhiir, I recalled, had demanded a head-on attack against the Saxons we saw across the
river. Something in their manner, as distant as they were from
us, gave me pause. Double their force had been waiting beyond
the hills, waiting for our attack, so they could flank and surround
us. We would have been massacred. "It was nothing," I said finally, still remembering the clamor of voices around the fire.
"A feeling only."

"I willingly hazard my purse on your feelings, old friend."

I snorted. "As you wish," I answered, rising and making for
my bed. In time we too fell victim to exhaustion. The day to
come would be wearing indeed. There were many to question
and many answers to find. As I lay on my simple pallet in Kay's
house, I could hear in the distance the rock masons working

still at some task set for them by Ambrosius, some fancy of his, I supposed.

A rustling at the door revealed Kay, bending to step into the room. "Kay, I may be a drunkard and a whoremonger, but I'm not a prisoner to be guarded either."

Kay's handsome face burst into a smile. "Maybe I fear you will slip out and empty my larder."

"Old friend, as exhausted as I am, I couldn't raid the largest warehouse of wine in all of Britannia."

"Perhaps. But I will stay awake while you rest—"

"There is no need for that!" I protested.

"My life would be forfeit if you lost yours. That is the way of it, and you know this as well as I."

Kay fell to sharpening his sword, while I shook out the furs on my bed, checking for any bedbugs or other visitors, and then fell asleep with little trouble. I dreamed of my Gwyneth and a laughing, merry child whose clothes ran scarlet with blood.

CHAPTER FOUR

With the pink fingers of a new dawn came new thoughts; I had slept no more than a couple of hours, maybe three, when I rolled over and saw the sun begin its ascent. Kay, exhausted as I, sat on the stone floor, his back propped against one of the posts. The morning's dew left a dampness in the air that penetrated to my bones. With those thoughts came more thoughts, more memories.

Old comradeship, a feeling of pity, those were not the reasons that Arthur had come to me. That he had respected my talents in war, I knew. That he loved Guinevere enough to throw me a bone from his table, I doubted not. But there was a more important reason Arthur turned to me in this matter.

While I lived at Ynys-witrin, training as a scribe, a particularly horrible event occurred. In those days, the abbey was but a round wooden stockade surrounding a group of twelve huts. The village below was hardly even that, just a cottage or two and a trader.

One black night, I rolled over in my sleep and irritated my arm, still raw where it had been severed. As I tried to readjust, a screech broke the still night air, a screech not like that of an owl, but that of a human, a young man's screech.

Springing from my pallet, I found the brothers gathered around one of the wooden huts. Inside, lit by the flickering of torches, was the crumpled figure of Gnaeus, a fresh-faced newcomer to the abbey, a boy hardly old enough to know the taste of a barber's knife, more naïve than experienced, always eager to help.

Coroticus, newly appointed abbot then, wearing lots of jewelry and a heavy, gold cross, arrived as did I. With staff in hand, he motioned everyone back. I saw that two of the stouter brothers held a grubby, local thief of the name of Gareth, who struggled fearfully. "Whence came he?" I asked.

"One of the brothers caught him fleeing the abbey after the boy's scream was heard." I did not know who answered, so many were talking.

"This man," said an old brother named Aneirin, whose face held a bright red birthmark, "killed young Gnaeus with this." He held up a bloody-edged rock in his right hand.

"And this?" Coroticus indicated the thief.

"A common thief, my lord."

I watched the bandit carefully for a moment. "Let him go," I ordered, though I had no authority. Coroticus nodded and the two brothers released the smaller man. I took a pebble from the ground and tossed it to the thief. He caught it in his left hand. "He may be a thief," I said, "but he didn't kill this boy."

"How know you this?" Coroticus asked, a questioning smile on his face.

I shrugged. "For one thing, he's too short. Gnaeus would have had to have been lying down, and from the way he lies, it's obvious that he was standing and fell to the ground."

The brothers all looked at me then. "And anyone used to battle knows that a left-handed wound is usually caused by someone right-handed. This man is left-handed." At this the brothers considered me with open disbelief, but none of them had seen battle.

"Seize him and lock him up tightly," Coroticus ordered. "We will test this theory on the morrow when there is more light."

"But my lord . . ." Aneirin began to protest. "This man," and he indicated me, "is not of the Christ." I had never liked Aneirin, whose eyes wandered to places they should not. He had a nature ill-fitting a man of the Christ.

Coroticus held up a hand. "Perhaps not, but he is of the world and that is what we need. Tomorrow will be as good a time for reckoning and handing this thief over to the decurion as now. And our minds will be sharper."

With that, all was done as he commanded, but not before I saw that there were no signs of the little thief forcing his way in. Whoever had killed the boy had been let in. And besides, there was nothing in a brother's cell to steal. More likely, the thief had been after the abbot's storehouse. On my way back to my own cell, I stopped at the storehouse and saw fresh scratches in the wood where someone had tried to pry it open.

The next day brought two surprises. Gareth, the little thief, had escaped from the cell where he had been so securely placed, and Aneirin, the old brother with the bright birthmark, had hung himself.

All agreed that the thief had been the murderer of the boy, and the old brother, who had been especially fond of Gnaeus, had killed himself out of grief. Coroticus never asked me about the affair, other than to comment on the scrape on my cheek the next day or the fact that the door to Gareth's cell had been opened from the outside. No dishonor had come to the abbey, and though the decurion sent a patrol out to find the culprit, Gareth had disappeared. Yet, people wondered and stories travel.

This day, I knew, I must move swiftly in my inquiry. The longer I took, the less likely I would arrive at the truth. My mind was occupied with two necessities. One, I needed to account for the girl's movements that night. Two, I needed to find, if I could, where she was killed. Knowing those two facts would lead me further along my thorny path. And if our land held anything in abundance, it was thorns.

I remembered then that I had promised the abbot at Ynyswitrin that I would copy a manuscript for him. A stack of secondhand parchment leaves lay on a table in my hut. He needed only an extra copy and did not require better materials. As always, though, he would want the hair sides facing and the parchment sides facing, an annoying detail, but one I was bound to abide. That would be a task for later.

"Rise, Kay! The sun has beaten us from her bed. Eleonore will remain unavenged while we laze around."

Kay's eyes flickered open and he blinked quickly, hoisting himself onto his elbows. "I need some water."

"You do not drink Arthur's *posca* in the morning?"

Posca was an ancient Roman drink, vinegar with enough water in it to make it drinkable. The old Roman soldiers, one hundred years before, had drunk warmed posca in the mornings. The bitter, biting taste did much to clear the cobwebs from your head, but left your mouth tasting like soured wine. It was one of Arthur's Latin affectations, one that I gladly ignored.

"I would fain drink bear piss than that rot. Arthur is a fine man, but he leans too heavily on some of the old ways while ignoring others."

"You mean his belief in the Christ." It was not a question.

Kay nodded. "I believe in the Christ too, but I know many who wonder what it profits them. A farmer near Ynys-witrin asked of me not a fortnight ago if Jesus would make his crops grow larger, if Jesus the Christ would put food on his table. They say the gods of old watched over a man's crops, if a man made proper sacrifices for their pleasure."

"I am not a religious man. But that is not the way of the Christ. His way is not about putting food on tables or making the land more fertile. Nor does he seek sacrifices for his pleasure. He is about more than that."

"Be careful, Malgwyn. You'll be wearing a monk's robes soon," Kay chided me. "And yes, you are correct, but many of the lords have their men working as passionately as that busybody Patrick does in Ireland. But they are not converting people to Christianity; no, they are leading people back to the old gods."

A thought struck me. "Kay, what of the Druids I saw in the fort? Are they truly with Vortimer?"

"Aye. He brought them here to irritate Arthur." He paused, a crease marking his brow. "Some, but others came on their own, during the feasting."

"Cuneglas thought as much. Why does Arthur not send them away or, better still, imprison them?"

Kay hung his head. "Malgwyn, you know that I do love Arthur as a father, but of some things he is afraid."

"How so?"

"He fears that paying too much attention to efforts designed to lessen his chances to succeed Ambrosius will simply bring his opponents more converts."

"Well, Vortimer should buy them better robes. Those they wear are not suitable for holy men. I thought Druids wore white."

"He cares not for that. He is cheap; white cloth is expensive. We have few fullers to whiten them. Besides, he cares only for their effect on the people."

That suited me as well. Fullers used urine to whiten the cloth, and the smell was worse than fermenting woad or the tanner's stench. "What of these Druids? Are these bards? Or are they acolytes?" What I knew of the druids, I knew from my father and the old men of our village. Before the Romans brought schools to our towns, only the Druids could read, and they were divided into three classes: those who had priestlike duties and presided over their festivals and sacrifices, those who were bards and held the histories of their peoples in their memories, and those who knew all legal precedents and decided questions of law. At least, that much my father told me.

"I know little of them, Malgwyn," Kay answered with a shake of his head. "Arthur frowns on any of us being seen near them. He considers them ungodly and blasphemies on the Christ. But he has no control over Vortimer and Mordred. At least not yet."

"Mordred is courting the Druids?"

"Mordred courts anyone he thinks might raise his standing with the people."

"Arthur should remind the people that Druids believe in human sacrifices," I pointed out. "That would be enough to turn me in other directions."

I threw back my fur and set my feet on the ground and saw that Kay had a queer expression on his face. "What?"

"Human sacrifices! Could not the Druids have had a hand in this matter?"

I considered it. "Perhaps. But Druids only kill at certain times of the year. In another fortnight or two it will be time for Beltane, their sacrifice to the gods for good crops, but this is too early. And though Eleonore was strangled and disemboweled, she was not murdered a third time. Druid victims are killed thrice."

The sun had finally risen above the mist shrouding our land, and I stared out the door at the Via Caedes, the lane, as it ran through the fort, beginning to fill with people on their daily chores. Even now, early in the spring, the land was a vibrant green, painted only with daubs of blue and yellow from spring flowers. On a clear day, you could stand atop the walls of the fort and see all the way to Ynys-witrin, the land lying out before you like some plush, fertile blanket, coating the earth as it would a woman's curves. Large blocks of a deeper green paneled the fields, copses of trees—oak, beech, elm— tall and thick and ancient. I was not a traveled man, but I often wondered if there could be a place more beautiful.

Kay got up and started stumbling around searching for food. I roused myself and pulled a platter of old bread from a shelf and set it on the table. I fetched down a jug, a piece of rope tied around the neck, and jiggled it. Empty. I tucked it under my half an arm and snatched up the bread.

"Here." I shoved the platter at him. "I'll see about some water."

He leaped to his feet and reached for the jug. "No, Malgwyn, do not bother yourself. Cicero!"

But I spun the jug from his reach. "I've only lost one arm, Kay. I still have another and two legs to walk on. Besides, Cicero is old and does not need four mouths to see to. I'll get the water." I hated when people tried to do things for me, and I hated even more that it was sometimes necessary.

"No, let me get the water!" Owain's voice broke across the room, and I had to laugh as the little urchin rushed into the room and snatched the jug from under my arm.

"Go then! And don't break the jug, you little thief!"

"Your voice holds not half the ill will that your words do, Malgwyn," Kay observed. "Do I detect a hint of kindness in your black and hardened old heart?"

"Choke on your bread, and worry not about the condition of my heart," I cautioned him, but a smile found its way to my lips. "He's a good-hearted lad; his mother is a . . ."

"I know of his mother. She does not keep herself only for Accolon."

"Aye, and a shame it is. She was a fine woman, once. But hunger has brought her low."

Once a beautiful lass, hunger, drink, and use had coarsened her features and lined her face. Times were hard for a woman and her child with no man to provide for them. I did not judge her harshly for the path she had chosen.

Owain returned then, holding the jug by the rope tied to its neck as it banged heavily against his leg.

"Are you hungry, boy?"

He looked away and nodded. I broke half the bread off and went to a pit in the corner of the room. I lifted the wooden lid and reached into the coolness where I knew Kay kept cheese, wine, and what vegetables he might have. Pulling a chunk of cheese out, I handed it and the bread to him. "Go, share that with your mother."

Owain took it but did not move to the door. "I will try and find her in a bit."

"Oh," I said gruffly, not wanting to increase his discomfort. Besides, Nyfain was a grown woman; she could fend for herself. "Very well. You are a growing lad, and you could use some meat on your bones. We'll help you find her later. Hurry up and eat. I have work for you."

The lad nodded and began to eat energetically.

"You are in danger of becoming a good man, Malgwyn," Kay chuckled.

I snatched up the jug and threw it at his head. Laughing, he caught it deftly. "Cease your prattle," I snapped. "We too have work to do. Where is Bedevere?"

"He arose early and went to rouse the soldiers at the barracks."

While Kay ate, I instructed the boy on his duties, that of sharpening my quills and making my ink. I learned a simple process from the monks at Ynys-witrin in which the wood and bark of thorn trees, cut before they have leafed or bloomed when the sap is still high, is boiled and rendered unto a powder, then revived with good wine and vitriol. The task was easy enough for Owain to commit to memory. I required only that he keep a pot heated to boil the wood and bark. Using vitriol was too touchy a task to leave to a boy.

In moments, we were ready for the day. I cuffed the boy on the shoulder as we started out the door. "Come, bring your food. We'll get you started at my hut. You must earn that bread, lad. Don't even think of leaving until your work is done."

"Yes, Malgwyn," he said, so little-boy soberly that I wanted to laugh out loud.

"Well, I'll see if your mother is about." My ears burned, as I knew without turning that Kay was grinning at me. I moved to change the subject.

"Owain? Are you sure it was Eleonore, the serving girl at Lord Arthur's hall, who came seeking me?"

"I am positive, Master Malgwyn. I've seen her many times in the castle, and she often watched me when my mother and Father Accolon were busy."

"And she told you naught of what she wanted?"

"No, only that it was important that she see you."

I frowned. Eleonore had never come to see me before. And yet she came on the night she was killed. This was worthy of note. I was drunk, as usual, watching the procession, watching more carefully the serving women for the other lords. But if it were as Nyfain said, if it were about conspiracy and assassination, why come to me? Why not Kay, or directly to Arthur? That question would never be answered.

With a sigh, I gestured to Kay and we left.

After we took Owain to my hut, we looked about to see if anyone had been there overnight, but nothing seemed out of place. With the boy engrossed in his work, we turned back to the castle. The cobbled road made a slight turn as it headed up the hill toward Arthur's headquarters, just after it passed through the southwest gate, a sturdy wood and stone structure built into the first of three mighty palisades encircling the fort. Castellum Arturius, as Arthur liked to call it in his precious Latin, was a large fortress, the largest in the region for a day's ride in any direction. A rock wall, of dressed stone, was surmounted by a solid wooden wall. Guard chambers were cut into the stone on either side of the gate. Above the gate was a kind of towered rampart with a walkway for guards. In front of the gate, at staggered intervals, were wooden barricades, mounted on swivels to be swung into place in case of attack.

Guard posts stood every thirty yards or so, requiring thirty guards per watch, sixty when trouble threatened. Not that Arthur lacked for men. Arthur's castle held a complement of three hundred foot soldiers and seven hundred cavalry. Two long, low wooden barracks and a row of stables at the opposite end of the plateau from Arthur's hall held the common soldiers and perhaps a hundred of the cavalry. The primary cavalry encampment lay outside the fortress to the south.

The cool spring day reminded me that this path was called the Via Caedes, "the Killing Way." Old bards sang older tales of a massacre that happened along this path into the fort in Roman times. Nobody remembered why, just that men, women, and children had died in droves along this path. One of the workmen that laid the cobblestones told me once of finding bones buried in the road. The Killing Way. An appropriate path for the day's activities, I mused, pulling my fur cloak around my shoulders to block out the chill. I chanced to touch the fibula that held the cloak up. It was a big, heavy, cast-bronze piece in the shape of a crossbow. Arthur had given it to me after one of our battles with the Saxons. He said that it came from one of his ancestors, a Roman officer, and would bring me luck. The memory warmed me and steeled me to my task.

As we passed the guard chambers, a thought struck me. "Kay, do not the vigils report for duty at the southwest gate?"

"Aye. What of it?"

"Accolon told us last night that he saw Eleonore on the Via Caedes as he reported for the midnight watch."

Kay shrugged. "Then he misspoke, a harmless error. Hardly of note."

"Everything is of note, Kay. A favor?"

"Of course."

"Go and find Accolon's partner on watch last eve; bring him to me at Cuneglas's house."

"Why there?"

"I must track her movements, and starting at her home seems logical."

With a nod of understanding, Kay split away from me at the fort's well just inside the gate and took a simple footpath, one used by the guard patrols, that led more directly to the barracks.

Not as many used the Via Caedes as used the main gate which entered the town from the southwest, near unto Arthur's great hall. Sober and in the daylight, I approved of what Arthur had wrought when he refortified the town. The main streets running at either side of the hall all the way to the barracks were evenly cobbled with clean stone. Ditches, lined with flat rocks, ingeniously carried the filth and garbage of the houses out of the fort. I had seen similar construction in old Roman villages, and it surprised me not that Arthur had adopted it for his fort. It kept the foul odors low and the lanes cleaner.

An open area of hard-packed earth lay in front of the great, timbered hall. I remembered hearing that Arthur wanted to cobble it as well but had not yet done so. On the outer edges were wooden stalls for merchants to sell their wares. Brightly colored pennants—red, green, blue—flew from the roofs announcing their wares. Wine, pottery, brooches to fasten a tunic, furs, leather, linen for the wealthier class. I could hear the unmistakable rhythm of the hammers beating their singular cadence at the forge.

Arthur, I knew, had the wealth to import pottery from distant lands, fine expensive amphorae and platters. I myself had no interest in such things. Food did not change its taste based on the cost of the plate. I noted a handful of *servi*, slaves, scurrying through the lanes. For the most part, they belonged to merchants traveling through. Arthur did not believe in slavery, but it was still accepted. Many of them were Gauls, some were Picts and Scots, captured in battle and impressed into forced labor.

A breath of foul wind blew through the lane and my nose crinkled at its approach. Fermenting woad. I knew the smell well, as the dye-makers worked in a hut not far from mine in the old village. Arthur hated the odor so much that he banned woad-making within the walls of the castle.

I suddenly noted that others trudging along the lane were staring at me. Some, walking in pairs, whispered to each other as they passed. The attention disturbed me, though I could not tell if they were disapproving or merely curious. Usually people paid me no attention. A few had tried to put a coin in my hand, but I had dropped the coins as if they were diseased. I tucked my head down and walked faster into town.

Cuneglas's house, a stout, timbered affair with a thatched roof, was located on the southwestern side of the town, along one of the back lanes. Those houses on the lane leading from the square to the barracks were timbered as well, but of two stories, aye, and some with balconies too. Those were owned by merchants and some of Arthur's nobles. Gawain kept such a house here and elsewhere. When not in residence, he had a pair of servants, an old couple whose best working days were behind them, to keep the place safe and clean. Others belonged to soldiers' families and what *civites*, civil authorities, as there were. Arthur did not like to share his authority.

Though Cuneglas's home was not such a palace, it was a respectable home for a thatcher and gave proof that he had prospered at his trade. Some children played in the lane, toying with three or four kittens, just old enough to be fearless. A yellow-haired lass of six, her eyes laughing, rose from the kittens and tripped back toward my brother's house. At the sight of her my heart seemed to pound loud enough for the monks at Ynys-witrin to hear.

Mariam. My daughter.

The smile faded from her lips and the laughter fled from her eyes as she hid behind the woman with her. She hung her head and stepped warily for the door, just as it opened and a short, handsome woman came out. Ygerne, a redheaded woman of thirty winters, was a mystery to me. My family had opposed their wedding because Ygerne was of the Pictish tribes, whence sprang her red hair. But somehow she had convinced them to accept her.

She was not a beautiful woman, but strangely attractive. No chalk whitened her face, as did most women of her class, for her natural skin was pale enough. Though her lips were too full, she did not paint them with red ochre. Nor did she use antimony or ashes to darken her eyelids. Her breasts were almost too large for her size, and though she had borne three children, her waist had not thickened as most women's did. Like all the women of our land, her hair—a bright, shining mass—flowed down her shoulders and touched her hips. Although I did not know her well, she had a bluntness that I had always appreciated, and no man could have asked for a better mother to his children.

My child buried her face in Ygerne's skirt. "Mother!"

"Go inside, child."

Mariam fled through the door.

I hung my head. It hurt to see her run from me. Once she had known me as her uncle, and she would gleefully leap into my arms and tug at my beard. We had been close, as uncle and niece, close enough to play games together, to joke and tease each other. Then, just a few moons before, Cuneglas, in a drunken slip, let it be known that I was her father.

She did not understand why her own father would lie to her, why, if it were true, she did not share my hut. Since that day she would not speak to me, aye, she would not even let me touch her, try to explain our deception. No, she would have none of it. And I had come up with no way to right a serious wrong. To convince her of the truth was difficult enough; all she had known as mother and father were Ygerne and Cuneglas. To explain why I had left her with them took more words than I had at my command.

Now she was lost to me completely, and I could find no way to heal the wound.

"It would not be like this if you had let me tell her the truth some time ago," Ygerne scolded me.

I excused my neglect with my behavior, a tried-and-true answer. "Better that she have a mother and father, than half a man who spends half his life in a wine jug."

"That much is true. Look at you, Malgwyn. You look like you sleep with the pigs and cows. What have you eaten today?" Before I could speak, she pointed inside her house, silently commanding me to enter. I frowned, but somehow it seemed wrong to disobey.

My brother's home was clean and neat. The hearth, like

mine, sat in the middle of the floor. A hole in the roof drew the smoke and expelled it. I saw that Ygerne was fortunate enough to have an iron spit on which to roast meat. In one corner, a large wooden pallet covered a sizable storage hole. Against one wall were stacked the furs they used to sleep on. A fur curtain partitioned off the back of the house, and I guessed that that was where Ygerne and Cuneglas slept. In cold weather, I knew, the whole family would share one space.

Sometimes, when I campaigned with Arthur, we would find the remains of a Roman villa, fallen into disrepair. I would walk through and marvel at the ingenuity of Roman engineers, how they provided running water in the houses, their methods of heating homes in the often brutal winters of Britannia. The floors were often mosaics of colorful stone.

We had none of that any longer. In some ways, independence from Rome had taken us several steps back, and I feared it would take us many more years to recapture what we had lost. Even the furniture in our common homes was less polished, less fine.

A wooden table, newer and better built than mine, took up a space near the storage hole, but though it surpassed mine, it still was a handmade affair. Cuneglas was seated at it, frowning, shoveling some porridge from a bowl into his mouth. A second stool sat empty, and Ygerne pointed me toward it as Mariam huddled in a corner, playing with some carved wooden figures. Instead of sitting down, I went over to her.

"May I join you?" Though it sounds odd, before Cuneglas's besotted declaration, I had often found much pleasure in playing with Mariam. Together we had named some of the figurines. But now, as she had done for the fortnight past, she refused to answer me and turned her back. My heart sank, but I forced a smile onto my face and returned to the table.

"Why the unhappy look, brother?"

I would have thought him sad at the girl's death, but this was a different kind of look. One that did not fit with sadness.

He shrugged, grunted, and looked to Ygerne bending over a pot on the fire. "Must my brother sit here hungry?"

Ygerne straightened and brought me a platter of boiled cabbage and beef. Her hand lingered on my back as she served me. I smiled at her, grateful for the tenderness. Cuneglas frowned at the gesture. She looked at her husband, sadly I thought, and took Mariam by the hand and led her back outside.

"So, how are you today, Cuneglas?"

"Tired," he admitted with a half-smile, "and off my desire for food. I am not used to those same sights that you have seen, Malgwyn. To see that poor girl split open like a deer, and her heart laid out on the table . . ." He shuddered.

"When did you last see her?"

He pushed back his bowl and thought for a moment. "She came home after the evening meal at the hall and changed her wrap. Near unto the midnight, she left again. I asked her where she was going, but she was a willful child and laughed at me."

"So no mention of who she was going to see?"

Cuneglas shook his head. "No, nothing. Why?"

"Remember what Accolon told us. He saw her near the gate on the Via Caedes about midnight as he headed to report for watch. She was with someone, but the person was hooded, and he could not tell who it was."

My brother frowned. "My belly was unsettled. I did not

listen closely." His frown grew deeper. "I thought as much. But how came she to Merlin's house from the gate?"

"That is the question that must be answered."

"And you think, perhaps, that whoever she was with at the gate may have had a hand in this?"

I shrugged. "It is possible. We know of no one else that was with her. But, all things are possible."

He pushed back his platter and rose. "I must get to work. I have repairs to make on Arthur's hall before tonight's feast."

"Will you be at the gathering?"

Cuneglas smiled. "I am only the thatcher. I do not receive invitations to feasts at Arthur's table."

"And I'm only 'Mad Malgwyn,' " I pointed out.

"Enough remember you as 'Smiling Malgwyn' not to question your seat at the table. Good fortune, my brother, as you search out the culprit in this affair. She was a wonderful lass, and I shall miss her greatly."

"You take an odd interest in the girl." Could my own brother have some part in this affair? The idea seemed inconceivable, but I knew that he strayed from Ygerne often, and Eleonore was a beautiful girl of some eighteen seasons.

He laughed. "It harms me not to say that I was in love with Gwyneth as all little boys fall in love with their older brother's wives. Eleonore had just enough of Gwyneth in her to give her a special place in my esteem." At that, he stopped laughing and clutched my arm at the wrist. "Find the doer of this deed, Malgwyn."

I shook off his hold. "You must tell me, brother. Did your love for the girl go beyond simple lust?"

"Did I bed her? And what if I did," he said. "What would it be to you?"

"It might have given you reason to kill her." I did not feel a liaison between Cuneglas and Eleonore strongly, but I knew he was unfaithful to Ygerne, though why I could not fathom. We had argued about it over the years, but he was not alone in his wanderings. Other men were worse.

"I did not kill her, and I did not bed her."

"You have bedded others; why should she be any different?"

"She preferred a nobler sort, the likes of your friend Kay and King Mark's son, Tristan. Aye, and she was no stranger to David and the others." Somewhere in his words I heard other words unspoken.

"The answer will come, in time. May God watch you this day."

He looked at me quizzically. "Why say you that? You're not a religious man."

"Perhaps Arthur is converting me," I joked, but I wondered too at why I said that. It just came out.

Cuneglas laughed. "Aye, and I'll believe that when the snow birds come in the summer." And then he was gone.

Our conversation had ended on a light tone, but one tinged with strain. It was as if Cuneglas knew more than he was telling, yet no words of mine would force them from him. We had been like that in recent years. When I left to join Arthur in his campaigns against the Saxons, Cuneglas and I quarreled. I accused him of cowardice; he accused me of simply seeking revenge. I learned on the field at Tribuit that at the very least he was right.

Before I had time to turn back to my cabbage and beef, Ygerne appeared in the doorway, without Mariam. "Are you well?" I asked.

"Well enough," she answered. "Your brother is short of temper of late."

"The death of someone so close is like to shorten a man's temper. And Cuneglas was always a lad whose feelings lay upon his shoulder as lightly as a bird perches on a branch."

She nodded. "She will be buried this noon in the burying place that holds Gwyneth and their parents." We still held with the tradition of burying our dead close to their homes and family. But Coroticus at Ynys-witrin was championing the idea of creating graveyards on church property, "sanctified ground," he called it, blessed and prepared for our empty shells.

"See that the priest lays her soul to rest well."

"You will not come?"

"I have much to do," I said, dropping my head. "What say the people in the lanes about this?"

This time Ygerne had a ready answer. "That the old fool killed her in his madness or in one of his evil rituals. And that rather than charge a drunken madman with seeking the truth, Vortimer's Druids should be allowed to sacrifice Merlin to appease the gods and keep them from visiting their wrath on us all. I'm sorry, Malgwyn, but such are the whispers in the lane."

"I know what I am, Ygerne. And it may be that Merlin did this awful thing, and if so, I will be the first to demand his punishment. But Arthur is right; let us be sure of the truth. A life once taken cannot be returned.

"As to the Druids, in truth, I want no part of gods that demand death for their appeasement."

"You are an uncommon man, Malgwyn. Would that your brother were more like you." The sadness I had seen earlier returned.

"You would rather he be a drunk?"

"He lacks your constancy, your passion."

"My passion? For what? Serving girls?" I stopped even as I

shoveled some cabbage toward my mouth. I immediately re-
gretted the words. I started to apologize, but felt a hand on my
shoulder.

I looked up into her eyes, and they were bright and gentle.
They regarded me with an interest intense in its depth. "I
know, Malgwyn. But I meant your passion for the truth, and I
remember your passion for Gwyneth. Mariam comes from good
stock, though she knows it not. At first, she was too young to
understand. Then when Cuneglas told her, there was nothing I
could do or say to convince her of the truth or ease her pain."
She rubbed my back and laid a gentle kiss on my brow. "You
know why he did it, don't you?"

I shook my head.

"Jealousy. Anger. He didn't like the way that she spoke of her
'uncle,' the love that was in her voice. So, drunken, he snapped it
out at her. Oh, he got what he wished; she clung to him then and
turned away from you. But Malgwyn, he broke that little girl's
heart and caused her far more damage than you ever did by leaving her here."

A sudden pressure, painful and real, struck the back of my
eyes, and I realized that tears were pushing for release. It was a
feeling I had not experienced for many years. "It was not a lie.
You and Cuneglas are her parents. And so it should remain."

"Malgwyn!" A voice came from the door. I wiped my eyes,
and turned on the stool to see Kay standing there with a soldier
I recognized as Paderic, a cousin of Arthur's from Dumnonia.
He was not the brightest of Arthur's kin, but a goodly lad.

"Come, Paderic. How be it with you?"

He was a big, cheerful fellow with sandy hair and a quick
grin that he displayed nervously at me. "Well, my lord. Well."

I waved him off with my one hand. "I am not your lord,

Paderic, though I appreciate the thought. Tell me of last evening. What did you see and hear as you made your rounds?"

"Nothing unusual. Just people moving to and fro in the lanes. Until Accolon shouted for me when he found the maiden."

"What people?"

"A few drunks. More drunks than usual. Another group of Druids had arrived. A surly bunch, to be sure. At least Vortimer's Druids would speak to you. These only grunt. With the consilium and the procession, it was more like a festival."

"Did you see Eleonore, the maiden, before then?"

"I saw her earlier, near the great hall, but that was hours before. Not long after the evening meal."

"Accolon says he saw her talking with a hooded man on the Via Caedes as he went to report for watch. Why would Accolon be on the Via Caedes when you report in on the southwestern gate?"

Paderic grinned and shrugged. "Maybe Accolon visited a woman. He saw one ofttimes in the old village."

I looked uncomfortably toward Ygerne; such discussions were not for women's ears. "Perhaps you should see to the children."

She propped her fists on her hips and glared at me with blue eyes. "Perhaps you should hold your conferences elsewhere. I know of such women, Malgwyn. I'm not a fool."

Kay and Paderic hid smiles behind their gloved hands. I reddened, and after a too long moment of hesitation, turned back to the men. "What of Nyfain?

"I saw her go to her home with . . ."

"With whom?"

"Just another soldier." Paderic was hesitant; I could understand why. No one wanted to admit that he knew the wife of a fellow soldier was not faithful. But I did not press for an answer. I knew who she had left with.

These questions were not bearing fruit. "How did you hear of the girl's death?"

"I was patrolling on the lane behind this house. I heard a shout and then the sound of the alarm at the barracks." Arthur had erected a kind of large bell, though it made more of a clanking sound. When aught happened, when one of the watch cried for the alarm, it was sounded and roused a company of soldiers to rush to their posts. The same could be done if the lookout in the watchtower behind Arthur's hall saw a signal from Ynyswitrin.

"And?"

"And then I followed the sounds of the shouting until I reached Accolon."

"Then what saw you?"

"Accolon standing over the maiden. Lord David, Tristan, Mordred, and others, and some of their men arrived as did I. Others were there, but beyond the light of the torch."

That Arthur's family had spawned such a simple lout amazed me. But he meant no harm by his lack of inquisitiveness. I was sure that he never thought to look. "How long did it take you to get to the spot when you heard the alarum?"

Paderic shrugged. "A minute, no more certainly. I ran."

"From what direction came the men?"

He thought for a moment. "From the watchtower, behind Arthur's hall. I saw them there earlier. That's where Accolon and I meet as we make our circuit."

"What were they doing?"

"Drunk. In arms singing a song."

Typical.

"You may go, Paderic. I thank you for your help."

The oafish boy turned, hesitated, then turned back. "Malgwyn, the old man, Merlin?"

"Yes?"

"He did not do this thing. I have seen him often with the girl, and he treated her as he would a daughter. Even with a devil in him, I cannot see him killing her."

"A devil in him?"

"Aye, that is the talk. I heard it in the barracks this morning."

"Where is Accolon? I need to speak to him again. There are questions yet to be asked."

"He left just after sunrise and I have not seen him since."

"If you see him, tell him that I wish to speak to him."

Paderic left, and I sat and stared at the now cold, boiled beef and cabbage.

"Malgwyn?"

I ignored Kay for a moment, before finally I turned to him. "Let us go back to Merlin's house so I may see it in the daylight. Perhaps I will see something that darkness hid."

"You ate nothing," Ygerne said.

"As it has done to my brother, this affair has stolen my hunger. Thank you, Ygerne. Cuneglas is lucky to have you."

"Thank you. But I oft wonder if he shares your faith. Do not be long in coming the next time, Malgwyn. Our home is yours as well."

The way she said it, the urgency in her voice, left a strange feeling in me, of jealousy. Jealousy that Cuneglas could call her his own. An uncomfortable sadness that I couldn't. I tried to brush aside the thought but it would not go away, not completely.

With Kay at my heels, I left the house and trudged across the village. A noble in my wake made the townspeople more guarded in their comments, but the looks cast my way left nothing to guess about. Before, I had simply been an odd man. Now I was an odd man trying to save a madman and a murderer. That this was not quite true made no difference. I was sure that Arthur's enemies had been promoting the half-truth all evening and morn.

We crossed from the cobbled lane to the earthen square in front of the great hall and turned up the lane separating Merlin's home from Arthur's. Next to Merlin's was the kitchen for the great hall. At feasting time, a seeming river of servants crossed back and forth between the kitchen and Arthur's table. The meat was cooked in the hall, over the open hearth in the middle of the great room, but the porridges and breads and cheeses were ferried back and forth by cleanly tuniced and gowned servants from the kitchen.

As we entered I saw three servants, two girls and a boy, mashing new vegetables in bowls of a blue-black wash. I had seen such bowls before. They had raised bumps inside, the better to mash vegetables.

The girls were young and Gallic in looks. The boy, a Pict, was older, near unto being a man. He was ruddy-faced and unpleasant, tall, but not as tall as Kay. They stopped their work and stood in a line before us.

"You were serving with Eleonore last eve?" I asked.

The girls nodded, but the boy turned away with a snarl.

Kay stepped forward and slapped the boy with a gloved hand. The pop of hand against jaw was muffled but distinct, and the boy fell to the floor in a heap.

"Kay!" I held my hand out to stop him.

"This one is insolent! I told Arthur to sell him to the merchants from Brittany that passed through last month."

"And he did not?"

With a disgusted frown Kay shook his head. "Arthur does not believe in selling or buying slaves. He won these in battle."

"Then why does he not free them?"

"Because he is evil!" the boy shouted.

This time I slapped him. "Curb your tongue," I said as the boy rose from the ground. "Arthur is slow to move, to decide, but he is not evil." Typical Pict, stubborn and defiant.

The women seemed strangely unaffected by all this. I studied the lad's face and saw the reddish tinge of old blows healing.

"Lie to me," I warned them, "and you will be sorry. Now, what do you know of Eleonore's plans for after the feasting last night?"

One of the girls frowned. "She was to meet some man." Her tone and expression showed her displeasure.

"You did not approve?"

"She is a slave," Kay countered. "Who cares for her approval or disapproval?"

"Never underestimate a slave, old friend." I turned back to the girl. "Answer."

"A woman should not throw herself on men."

"And that was how you saw her?"

"Pay her no mind!" the boy shouted. "She was just jealous of Eleonore."

"Jealous? Why?"

He sneered at the girl, and I knew he enjoyed taunting her. "She hated the girl for being free. And she hated her because the nobles wanted her."

I looked carefully at the girl. She was plain, not handsome, but not unpleasant either. Probably, she was taken from a raided village when she was very young. I felt sympathy for her situation, but it was not an uncommon one.

"Does he speak the truth?" I asked.

Her head whipped around and her eyes seemed to drip with venom. "She did not know her place."

"Perhaps," I allowed. "Do you know who she was to meet?"

She pointed a finger at Kay. "I thought him. But I cannot say for certain."

The Gaul had made me curious. "Why do you think she was killed? Do you think it was Merlin?"

The girl laughed and for an instant she seemed prettier. "No. Old Merlin worshipped the girl and she doted on him. I reckoned that it was him," pointing again at Kay, "or one of his fellows."

"Why?"

"I reckoned that she had promised something she wasn't willing to give. This person, whoever it was, grew angry and paid her for her teasing."

"And you!" I said suddenly, spinning around and pointing at the second girl. "What say you of this affair?"

She was a pleasant-looking girl, of marrying age. A maturity marked her eye that touched not those of her fellow servants. "I know nothing of this. I liked Eleonore. She was that sort."

"What sort?"

"The sort that could make you laugh when you wished for nothing but to cry. They are rare people in a dangerous world, my lord. I wish that she were still among us."

"What is your name, child?"

"I am called Nimue."

"Tell me what you know of Eleonore's movements last eve."

"Little. It was a busy night with the consilium among us. As we cleared the table, she mentioned to me that she was meeting a fellow later in the eve. I asked her who, but she just smiled and would not say. I knew it was not Lord Kay she was meeting though."

"And how did you know this?"

Nimue smiled at Kay, who reddened. "Her voice took on a different tone when she spoke of Kay. She called him her 'darling giant.' Forgive me, my lord. I think she favored you above all others. But she was young and willful. Had this thing not happened and had you been patient, I think the prize would have fallen to your hands."

A hint of moisture touched Kay's eyes, and he nodded his thanks to her. I watched closely for sign of deception. I saw none.

"That is all you know, though, of last night?"

"I'm sorry, my lord, but yes. After we finished cleaning, I went to the hut that we have been assigned and went straight to sleep."

"Thank you for your help." The other two turned away from us and went back to their labors.

We started for the door, but Nimue rushed up and caught my elbow. "My lord, the boy?" she whispered. "He is prone to anger, and he wanted Eleonore for himself."

"Thank you."

With that, we slipped through the door and onto the lane. A few people passed by, giving us a wide berth. "We are not welcome today, Malgwyn," Kay said.

"That much is obvious."

"Do you think the boy had something to do with this?"

"No. Too many twists and turns lie in this road for the answer to be that simple. Although I would wish that it be. Owain and Nyfain say Eleonore wished to see me. I doubt she would have left such a message unless it was important. Unfortunately, she is unable now to deliver the message herself."

"Where now?"

"Guinevere," I said, without further explanation.

We found her in Arthur's chamber at the great hall. She had not been awake long by the looks of her, and it had not been an easy night.

"Come, Malgwyn." She held the door open for us. "I knew you would want to see me."

"How did you know that?"

She sat down before a table, took up a comb, and began stroking her long hair. "When Arthur told me he was coming to see you, I knew it would not be long before you knocked at my door.

"I saw you watching last eve, from the kitchen. You were trying to bed one of the serving girls, but you were watching us as well, all of us. Drunk as you were, I could feel you absorbing everything and everyone."

I felt naked, stripped of my clothing. No woman had ever laid me so bare, but that was Guinevere's gift. She could see into the hearts of men and know their thoughts. I had known Guinevere all of my life. She was a distant cousin on my mother's side, of a noble family whose nobility had escaped my family. We were a small land, and most of us knew each other and many of us were related in some way. Guinevere had always been special, in action and in beauty. And she sparked jealousy in women the way that freshly cooked food sparked hunger.

"I will not argue with you. Yes, I was watching from the kitchen, amusing myself by watching all those pompous lords.

I saw Eleonore serving Arthur, and I saw your scowl when he touched her on the back." Speaking straight was the only way to treat with Guinevere. She would have it no other way.

She laughed then, stopped stroking her hair. "For a man worried about keeping his cup filled with wine, you were very thorough in your watching. That is so like you."

I did not respond.

"So, you want to know if I could have done this thing?"

"I want to know if you can shed any light on it. And yes, I must ask that question as well."

"I know that Eleonore would have bedded Arthur in the blink of an eye if he had given her a sign. Stop, Kay!"

My companion had made to protest, but Guinevere's sharp rebuke quieted him.

"I know you loved her, Kay," she said gently. "And, in truth, she was not a bad girl, just willful and stubborn. She understood what power her beauty gave her over men, and that was a knowledge she would have been better off without." Her tone was marked with a wistfulness, a sadness, as if Guinevere might have been speaking about herself at a younger age.

"Yet you had no fear that she would succeed with Arthur?" Guinevere was certainly a beautiful and alluring woman, a woman of special qualities. But Eleonore had her own charms, it seemed. I had known Kay for many years; he was not given to falling in love. Like myself, he had seen too much blood wetting the grass of too many pleasant glens to harbor such romantic notions.

For his part, Kay stayed silent.

"No," Guinevere answered finally, "Arthur's nature is one of constancy; our bond is too close. He cleaved to her, but as a father would to his child. No more, no less."

"But you didn't like it?"

"I thought she used her place in his affections for her own good."

"Do not all women?"

Kay's face, so solemn and stern after Guinevere's rebuke, broke into a smile at that. Guinevere scowled at me, much as she had scowled at Eleonore last evening.

"As you say, Malgwyn. But you must know that I had no hand in this. I was here with Arthur all night after the feasting."

"You do not mourn her."

"You wrong me, cousin. I mourn the death of any so young. I did not like her, but I mourn her." She turned back to her combing. "Malgwyn, I worry that Arthur has set too much of a task on you. I hear whispers, whispers in the lanes, that there is more to Eleonore's death than an old man's fantasies about hearts."

"How could there be? She was just a girl."

"A girl who kept the wrong company. I saw her immediately after the feasting last night consorting with Vortimer's men, aye, and those of David, Lauhiir, and Mordred as well. And then, there are the new Druids."

"Say what you mean plainly."

"More Druids arrived last night. Arthur and I took note of it as we walked in the lanes after the feast."

I shrugged. "Just more of Vortimer's band."

"Do not take so much at face value. I fear you disappoint me. You, the captor of the demented monk. Where is that perception that Coroticus so hails?"

"Coroticus would be better served to worry about his abbey and not my perception." I had no interest in discussing the monk with Guinevere. A change of subject was needed.

"These Druids, they are not with Vortimer? They were not with the rest?"

"Not last night. They were in the lanes, following in the wake of Lord David and Lauhiir."

"With them?"

"I could not tell."

"What difference does it make?" Kay interrupted impatiently.

"I do not know," I said honestly. "But it seems strange. Two days past, you could not find a Druid. Now, you cannot stroll the lanes without kicking Druids from your path.

"Be at peace, cousin," I said finally. "I truly do not think that you had a hand in this. Murder is not in your heart." Plus, she had Arthur to vouchsafe her story.

Guinevere put down her comb and cupped my cheek in her hand. "You will succeed, Malgwyn. You are an uncommon man. This Arthur knows, even if you do not."

"Aye," I said, shaking my head. "It seems that I am the only one that does not know this." I stood. "Come, Kay. We have more questions to ask elsewhere."

"And now?" Kay queried.

"Up the lane to Merlin's house. Let us see what we can find inside."

At midday, not many bustled about the lanes. A sprig of early spring flowers had been laid beside Merlin's wall, near where Eleonore had been found. I studied the cobblestones where she had lain, unsure of what I was looking for.

Some of the now blackened blood stained the stones, not much to be sure. I saw no bits of clothing or weapons or anything else, for that matter, in a wide circle around the spot. "Kay, look around the sides of Merlin's house. See if you find anything unusual." He went off to do my bidding.

After staring at the stains, black on the surface but oddly transparent in the cracks between stones, for what seemed like hours, I stood. The blood told me only that she had lain here, not who or what brought her to this end. Kay reappeared at my side. "I found nothing, Malgwyn."

"My search has been fruitless as well. Let us see if anything within may help us."

We made our way into Merlin's home once again. A smell of decay filtered through the one room, and I remembered the heart that I had wrapped and had stowed at Arthur's hall. "Kay, see if there's a boy about in the lane. Send for a horseman. Her heart needs to be buried with her body."

Lighting a lamp, I looked at the contents of a long, low table running against one wall. Pots and small vials, like those I saw often at the abbey, lined the back of the table near the timbered wall. Another table along the opposing wall held stacks of parchments. I opened the top of each vial and sniffed of the contents. Kay returned while I studied the table.

"A rider is on the way." He winced as he shifted his sword. His wrist was hurting him.

I smiled and took a small vial from the table. "Here, drink this. It will remove the pain."

Kay eyed it suspiciously. "What is it?"

"An extract of willow tree bark. I learned of it at Ynys-witrin. It is safe and will help."

"What of the rest of this?" He motioned at the table.

"Simple medicines like those the monks prepare." I picked up a covered pot and sniffed. "This is carpenter's weed, made into a paste. It can be used for stanching bleeding and treating sores. Nothing of harm. Merlin is a wise old man who has seen much in his life, but I fear that his memories of yesterday are not as clear as those of a thousand yesterdays before."

Kay picked up a parchment from the other table and handed it to me. "What of this, Malgwyn? What says it?"

I unrolled the ancient parchment and read the Latin words. "It is a story, a story of a man called Joseph of Arimathea, who came here after the Christ was killed and rose again. It says that Joseph is buried at Ynys-witrin with a great treasure."

My friend's eyes widened. "Do you believe this?"

"It is only an old story, probably written to keep some lord at bay, to keep him from destroying the church. But I know that Joseph is supposed to be buried near unto a certain well and that this secret is kept well hidden by the monks."

Just then something large and solid slammed into the wall, rattling the old house and causing the parchments to roll from the table.

"Murderer!"

CHAPTER FIVE

Another stone assaulted the wooden door, jarring the walls, and the cry of "Murderer!" was taken up by a dozen other voices.

The house only had one door. Neither Kay nor I wanted to risk it, but we saw no other way. To stay in the house meant facing a mob in a small space. At least under the open sky, we could try and fight our way clear. If we made it that far.

The crowd of voices grew louder. The thud of stones grew more rapid, more fierce.

Kay drew his sword and I took the door handle in hand.

With a quick nod from Kay, I jerked the door open. A dozen stones flew through, reaching even to the pots, breaking them, spilling their contents on the table and floor.

As Kay charged forward, a stone struck his wrist, his bad wrist, and his sword clattered to the ground. Another struck him in the shoulder, and a third slapped his throat. He went down.

I saw the stone just as it hit me, against my temple, tearing the skin and sending a flood of blood rushing down my face. Staggering back, I managed to grab the door and steady myself, but the jeers and shouts of the crowd grew louder and I would not have given a silver brooch for our chances.

Then, above the shouts and screams of the crowd, I heard horses' hooves clattering on the cobblestones, and from another direction, a familiar voice rose above all others.

"You will stop!"

Arthur. Again coming to my rescue. But this time I welcomed him.

Kay was lying next to me on the lane. Blood flowed from his throat, but it was only a glancing blow and that had but torn the skin. Propping myself up on my stump of an arm, I touched my temple and felt that the cut was not deep.

The rain of stones stopped as abruptly as it began. The crowd drew back as Arthur strode in front. A rider, the one that I had sent for, reined his horse next to Arthur, blocking them from us.

"Why do you do this?" Arthur asked.

"We come to destroy the house of the evil one, my lord. He is a murderer!"

"Murderer!" the crowd murmured in agreement.

"These two men are not murderers; one is my fellow and the other my councillor."

"They protect the evil one, Lord Arthur. We know it is so."

"Who told you this?"

The spokesman, a tired, ragged-looking old fellow, pondered the question. "Why, everyone, my lord."

"Go to your homes!" Arthur commanded, his shoulder-length hair flying in the breeze.

"We seek justice, my lord."

"And so do I. Malgwyn is my councillor in this affair. And he will see that justice is done. He protects no one."

The peasant drew himself up to full height, encouraged by the shouts of his companions. "He protects the evil one, Merlin, my lord. If something is not done, the gods will avenge themselves on us. The three gods will kill us all!"

I pushed myself to my feet and helped Kay to his. Once I was standing, I could see that some of Vortimer's and Mordred's men stood silently at the back of the crowd, most with sneers on their faces. Wiping the blood from mine, I saw that the crowd could turn even more violent with ease.

"The three gods will do you no favors for destroying this house or killing me!" I shouted.

"But you protect the evil one!" someone repeated.

"Who says this? Let him stand before me now! I protect no one, not Lord Arthur, not Merlin, nor even the Rigotamos. I want only to find the truth!"

A one-eyed man who lived near me separated himself from the crowd. "Leave Malgwyn alone!" he said. "I have known him for too long. If there is any protecting of villains, it will not be him doing it." He cast a squinting, sidelong look at Arthur. "Others will do their master's bidding."

Kay started after the man, but I touched his sleeve and shook my head. Now was not the time for retribution.

With the one defection, the crowd began to melt away in twos and threes, all still muttering, leaving a black stench in the lane. Arthur ran his gloved hand through his long hair. "Malgwyn, you are hurt. As are you, Kay."

"It is nothing, my lord. Just a scrape," I assured him. Kay followed suit, but an ugly purple bruise spread across his throat, putting the lie to his assurances.

"My Lord Arthur!"

We turned to see Vortimer round the corner of the great

hall with half a dozen of his followers at his heels. Their swords were drawn and their step was light. "We heard you were in danger and came quickly."

I stifled a bitter laugh. I had no doubt that they were the very ones stirring up the crowd.

Vortimer had aged since I had seen him last. He was tall and had a chest round and thick, and his hair was beginning to turn white. If anyone had suffered from Vortigern's disgrace, it had been Vortimer. He and I remembered each other well from the battlefield. In truth, he was a brave warrior, struggling always with the ghost of his father, peering over his shoulder. Of all those who wished to see Arthur off from his perch as Ambrosius's successor, none had a stronger claim than he.

"Perhaps it is time to stop this foolishness and put Merlin to the sword, Arthur. I do not doubt Malgwyn's skills, but the people are growing more angry with each passing moment. I would not have your authority dependent on the life of one old and useless man."

But Merlin's death was exactly what Vortimer wanted. Arthur and I knew it, and Vortimer knew that we understood. Mordred too could see this struggle building. But this cousin of Arthur's was as sly and cunning as his other cousin, Paderic, was good-natured and slow. Mordred's hair was shiny and long, with braids over either ear. His eyes were set too close together, and his nose resembled a hawk's. Casting a look about, he sheathed his sword. Having started me down the path I followed, Arthur had no alternative but to see it through. Were he to give in to Vortimer now, then, in the people's eyes, Vortimer would be the winner.

"Vortimer's right, Arthur," Lauhiir chimed in.

"Malgwyn has had hardly twelve hours to sort through this

matter, Lauhiir. No one could find the truth in so short a time."

Lauhiir smoothed his hair from his face and smiled. "My lord, I'm not sure that you have much time left before the people do more than throw a few rocks."

Arthur's eyes narrowed. "Be careful, both of you. Be careful that you are not found pushing the people to such actions. You or these Druids either, for that matter. They may be banished from this city more easily than you."

The younger man bowed with great circumstance. "My lord, I would never challenge your authority in your own castle. But the Druid priests serve other masters, more demanding than I. And they hold the people's hearts more closely than you. I think it well that you not challenge their authority either." With that, Vortimer, Lauhiir, and Mordred strode away toward the barracks, their bands of followers close on their heels.

The wind shifted, and the smell of chicken dung drifted up from the tannery west of the fort. The rancid odor burned my nostrils, and I thought fleetingly that I would forever match that abominable smell with the memory of Lauhiir, whose real name was Ligessauc, though all about called him "Lauhiir," which meant "long hands" in our native tongue. He had no love for Arthur and made no secret of that.

"Arthur, why do you allow him, any of them, such liberties?" I asked.

Arthur sighed, the twinkle fading from his eyes. I could see in the wrinkles at their edges that the discharge of his duties was swiftly aging him. "I am being pressed hard by certain members of the consilium, pressed to name Mordred my Master of Horse. If I want their votes, I must agree,"

I suppressed a smile. Yet another of Arthur's Romanisms. The Master of Horse was the noble appointed to lead all the cavalry. "And you will not."

He shook his big, shaggy head. "I know him too well. Horses have become too much a key part of our defenses to put under Mordred's control, but by denying him that post, I sow the seeds of discontent among certain members."

"Like Mark?"

"Aye. And David, Vortimer, perhaps even Gawain and Melwas. To do what should be done with Mordred would cause greater dissension among the consilium. For he serves as a spy for some of them, seeking chinks in my armor."

"So you endure him to keep the peace?"

"Until the consilium decides on a successor, it is in my best interest to simply leave Mordred alone," Arthur said sadly. "What say you about this affair, Malgwyn?"

I noticed, for the first time, how much older he looked than he did in our fighting days. Dark circles rimmed his eyes, and gray streaked his thick brown beard. His fingers, weathered and beaten from a hundred battles, were not long and slender, but short and blunted. Indeed, the middle finger on his left hand was severed at the joint, gift of a Saxon spearman's good aim. But he was still Arthur, still in many ways that brash young officer who had served Ambrosius Aurelianus so well, honest and often reckless. I had trusted him then. And though I would never admit it, I trusted him still. Even with half an arm, I would follow him into battle in a second, and I would trust his judgment without question. Though he could mete out punishment as severe as any lord, he was fair and just.

And even now, despite all that had passed between us, I saw the same trust in his eyes that had held me across the campfires in our war councils. He trusted me yet, and I could not find it in my heart to disappoint him in this matter.

And if his enemies were cunning, so too was Arthur.

"Merlin did not do this thing," I said bluntly. "But I cannot prove this to you or any man. The evidence is heavy against him but for one thing. The girl was strangled to death. The knifing and the removal of her heart came afterward. Merlin is too old and too weak to choke a strong, young girl to death, and he lacks a reason. Something more is at play here."

"How so?"

"To strangle a woman speaks of passion, but to rip her body from throat to belly and to take out a heart is a calculated move. Also, she was not killed at Merlin's, nor was she gutted there. Not enough blood darkens the pavement—aye, very little indeed."

Arthur's deep brown eyes bored into mine. "I trust you in this, Malgwyn. But you see what is at risk. My position is a grave one, on all fronts. Tristan is here to treat on behalf of Mark, and they wish the consilium to enter into a treaty with the Saxons. Ah, and the Saxons are creeping into our lands, little by little. My patrols have found new Saxon villages along the southern coast and not five days' ride from here to the east. The day is coming, my old friend, when we shall have to face the Saxons again, but we must do so united! We must have Mark and the other lords with us. We cannot do it alone, and we cannot allow the Saxons even an inch of our lands."

A deep rumble of anger had entered his voice at the thought of Saxons. "I trust Vortimer not. Nor do I trust Mark or David. They would ally themselves with the Saxons in a second if they could name one of their own as the Rigotamos. Vortimer may be an honest man, but he is his father's son. Most of all, I cannot lose one measure of the people's faith at this critical hour. And though I cannot rid myself of any of them, neither can I give them more spears to use against me."

Ambrosius walked up, a pair of soldiers at the ready behind him. "Malgwyn, you must bring this affair to a close quickly. I have delayed the consilium from voting on a successor until this is over. I do not want a shadow clouding their minds at such a time."

"I will do all that I can, Rigotamos. But I promise nothing." Above all things, I desired a jug of mead or wine or anything to blot out the task Arthur had laid upon me.

"You will succeed, Malgwyn," Arthur said. "Not for the people. Not for me. Not for the memory of Eleonore. A puzzle such as this is a personal challenge to you, and you will master it or die trying."

A clattering of hooves drew my attention away from Arthur. 'Twas the rider come to speed the heart to Eleonore's burial and now grown impatient with the crowd to disperse so that he might be on his journey. I looked around and saw a slave boy holding the leather bundle at arm's length. I took it from him and handed it up to the rider.

"What is this?"

"Never mind. Just take it to Camel, to the burial of the maiden. Have it placed in the grave with her."

The soldier looked at Arthur for his approval and received a nod. "Do as he says."

Jerking hard on the reins, the rider sent the horse leaping to the side, almost stamping me with his tremendous hooves and forcing me down to the ground yet again, my cheek pressed against the cold stones.

From that odd vantage point something caught my eye. I cared not that I'd been knocked down yet again.

Arthur was shouting something at the rider, but he was gone, galloping down the lane and out of sight. I was more interested in the large black stain on the stone in front of me. A bloodstain four or five feet distant from where Eleonore's mutilated body had lain.

I rose to my knees and looked for more.

A few feet away was another.

And beyond that another.

"Malgwyn!"

"Later, my lord." I had no time for Arthur's orders. "This could be important. Kay, come with me."

With Arthur spluttering in the lane, I followed the trail of bloodstains along the cobblestones. I had not seen them the night before because of the darkness. Even now they were almost invisible on the damp and sometimes mud-covered stones. But drying blood shines, and the clear liquid that separates from man's blood shone also in the cracks of the stones.

"This way!" I shouted to Kay. Now that I knew what to look for, following the stains was as simple as tracking a deer through a dew-dampened field.

The trail led us around to the rear of Arthur's hall, and beyond that the few yards to the base of the great watchtower. The tower stood on four great legs, braced with sturdy logs crossed on each of the four sides. The guards' path ran behind the tower, and I knew that they had a small shelter there to fend off the sometimes biting wind.

The path of blood did not go to the guards' refuge, rather underneath the tower itself. There, in the perpetual shade of the great structure, I found what I had been seeking. Great masses of blackened blood covered the ground and bits of entrails as well. A dog had sniffed out the cache and was licking at its edges. Kay kicked it, and I raised my hand, willing the sight from my vision as the whimpering dog scampered away.

"So this is where it happened," Kay whispered. I remembered then that he had loved the girl. I had been alone so long that I ofttimes thought little of others' feelings. It was not a trait of which I was proud.

"Kay, why don't you fetch Accolon? I can seek out what needs to be found here. I will need to speak to him once more."

Relief was evident in his voice. "Are you certain, Malgwyn?"

I nodded. "Go. Bring him to me here."

Kay gladly left me alone with the lifeblood of Eleonore hardening on the ground. I could see now that she had been killed here. Some strands of her hair clung to one of the tower's legs, just at head level, as if she had leaned back against it. Her footprints, smaller than those surrounding her, moved about, and I could tell by the depth of the impressions that she had been moving under her own strength. I saw too the faintest impression of her body, lying back on the ground at the rear of the tower. Whoever had picked her up—and I saw at least two sets of prints—had stood her and carried her between them. Therein lay the reason for the puddle of blood and bits of entrails. They had spilled out of the mighty wound in her body.

I searched carefully up and down the tower's leg where her hair had caught. Near the snagged hair was a smear of blood—hers, I believed—telling me that someone had pushed her head forcefully against the wooden upright, just as they might if they were strangling her. The scene began to take shape in my mind with clarity.

She met someone here, either on her own or forcibly. He strangled her. For some horrible reason, he laid her lifeless body back on the ground, ripped her open and removed her heart. Then several men stood her up and, propping her body between them, walked her to Merlin's house, where they left her in the lane. At least two, if not three or more, were involved in the affair. This much the blood, the entrails, the footprints, the dab of blood and hair told me. This much I could prove to any man in a fair and dispassionate hearing.

But the people were not inclined to be dispassionate at that moment. Simply proving that Merlin had not committed this act would be of little use. I knew that I would need to hand them another culprit to satisfy their anger.

Kay returned as I was musing. "Accolon has disappeared, Malgwyn. He is nowhere to be found, and no one has seen him since the formation this morning. I searched his home and neither he nor Nyfain were there."

Accolon gone! He was a key witness in this affair. To kill and rape a serving girl, aye, such happened all too often in these times. But for Eleonore to be killed and butchered, not raped, on the night the consilium first met to choose a new Rigotamos, all to place the blame at Merlin's feet. Something more was at play here.

"Come, Kay."

"What shall we do?"

"Someone, somewhere, saw Accolon this morning. We will talk to everyone in the castle if we must. He has to be found."

Once more in the lane, Kay and I visited each house in the town. No one could remember seeing Accolon or any soldier since earlier that morning. For a big, brawling bully of a man, he was talented at disappearing.

With Arthur's blessing, we raised the alarum for Accolon. Patrols were sent forth to scour the countryside for him. Next, we attacked the barracks and talked with his fellows, but they too could tell us nothing. Finally, at the gate near the old Roman village, we found a soldier on patrol.

"Aye," he said. "I saw Accolon after formation this morning. He left the castle through this gate, on foot."

"Did you see where he went?"

"No, only that he moved quickly. And he looked about him constantly, as if he were afraid he would be followed."

"You did not speak?"

"No, I rarely speak to Accolon, and he's a strange one anyway. Keeps much to himself."

I excused the soldier, and we continued questioning the people that lived in the huts just beyond the gates. We found out nothing new and returned to the castle to report to Arthur.

"Think you that Accolon did this thing, Malgwyn?" Arthur asked. We were in his private chambers at the great hall. Before him lay the plan for his new church, the one that remained unfinished because Coroticus would not bless it. I smiled at the thought. Coroticus was demanding lower taxes for the abbey before giving his blessing. Arthur refused. Neither would budge. Each was true to his own nature.

Arthur's chambers were simple, as befitted the warrior he had been. His shield hung upon one wall, and his mighty sword, a gift from Ambrosius Aurelianus, lay across the table, holding down the plans.

"I do not know, my lord," I answered. "But I know that he has much to answer for, and if we can throw a light upon him, perhaps the people will turn their attentions away from Merlin."

Arthur sighed. His eyes were sad, and more wrinkles ravaged his face than had the night before. "Tell me what you know." No command marked his tone; he was making a simple request.

"I know more than I did; that is for certain. She met a man at the northeast gate on the Via Caedes about the midnight. Then she went to the watchtower, either with the same person or another person. I will tell you only what actions that I know occurred. I will not speculate on the causes. She was backed against one of the posts and her head bashed hard. She was strangled. Then more than one person laid her back on the ground and then is when she was butchered. These same people stood her up between them and walked her to Merlin's house where they left her lying in the street."

Arthur shook his great, shaggy head. "And the woman Nyfain?"

"I do not know what her disappearance means, if anything. She may be lying abed with some soldier. Or, Accolon could have killed her. As yet we know nothing of her, only that poor young Owain tried and failed to find her the night before. Nor have we been any more successful today. The only thing that ties her to this affair is that she claimed that Eleonore told her of a plot to assassinate someone. There may be something to it, as Owain too says that Eleonore hunted for me last night."

"Malgwyn," Arthur began in that voice I knew too well, "you must hurry. You saw for yourself today how the people are ready for revolt. I have reports today that rumors of Merlin and the murder have spread to the small villages. The lanes are becoming clogged with people heading to town, and I think they are not coming to trade for goods or to pay homage to the consilium."

"My lord, I can only move as fast as information comes to me. I think if we find Accolon that much may be made clear."

"Were my servants any help?"

"Only one, the girl Nimue. She—"

"The boy was insolent. Sell him, my lord!" Kay interrupted.

Arthur rested a hand on Kay's shoulder. "You know I will not do that. I will have him spoken to, though. He is trying." He rose before I could plead Nimue's case. "I believe strongly in you, Malgwyn. Do not fail me."

"This I can tell you for certain. Merlin did not do this. He has not the strength. Proving that to the satisfaction of the people may not be easy. Arthur, we will need to question Tristan and perhaps other members of the consilium."

"They will be offended."

"If my task is as important as you say, then let them be offended. We must have the truth and one of them may hold some of that truth."

"Then, on with your chores. You have my commission as *iudex pedaneous*. Ambrosius will concur and grant you his commission as Rigotamos. Question who you must. I must meet with the builders for my church."

And so young Tristan and the other members of the consilium were our next stop. They had taken quarters in camps surrounding the massive castle with its wooden and rock ramparts, and we found the most of them in the camp of Vortimer, casting die and playing at swords. The encampments were not large; most members had only brought a single troop of cavalry. Anything larger would have rendered their intentions questionable.

Vortimer, Lauhiir, and David were eating a midday meal around their campfire, no vegetables, I noticed, just roast pig. The servants here were all male slaves. Vortimer would allow no female slaves in his marching camp. They were a distraction and served only to slow the troops down. The success of our forces lay in their ability to move swiftly and strike hard. Vortimer saw no place for women in that strategy.

Off to one side, Tristan and Mordred were practicing their swordplay. A young blue-eyed lord whose name I could never remember was throwing spears. Mordred lived in the castle and had a house there, though he had but recently returned from a tour of our eastern border with the Saxons. But on this day, he was spending his time with the visiting lords.

Leaning back at our approach, Vortimer patted his belly. "Come, Malgwyn and Lord Kay, sit and share our simple fare."

As we had not eaten since early that morning, we sat against logs piled around the campfire. The morning still held something of a chill, though the springtime was beginning to dispel the cold, and the green grass was marked still by the silvery glint of frost. I reached out and tore some meat from the pig roasting on the fire.

"Tell me, Malgwyn, have you found anything in this affair of the girl yet?" Vortimer asked, belching and reaching for a jug of mead.

"I have found many things, my lord. But none that leads me down a straight path to the truth." I waved off the mead jug as it came my way. This was one audience where I knew that my survival depended on my wits.

"Seems obvious to me," Lauhiir said. He had just been appointed to fortify the great tor at Ynys-witrin. His ancestors had worn the purple, it was said, and Roman ancestry was highly regarded. "The crazy old man killed her. Just shows that Arthur will play favorites."

"Do not all men?" I asked.

"The proper noble will champion truth and justice, not crazy old men with insane ideas." Since I knew that Coroticus had just paid a hefty bribe to Lauhiir to keep the abbey open, this pronouncement seemed a little out of place.

"Hmm. Have any of you seen Accolon the soldier, husband of Nyfain?"

Lauhiir and Mordred looked at each other. Vortimer made a point of not looking at any of them. "I saw him last night," Lord David said. "But not afterward. Is he missing?" His question was so innocent sounding as to almost make me laugh.

"It matters not. He will appear sooner or later," I answered.

"Lord Tristan?" I said, so suddenly the young man dropped his sword.

"Aye?"

"I understand you showed a special interest in the dead maiden."

If a man's face could be said to be white, Tristan's was. "I thought she was interesting, one to bed." His false bravado trembled in his voice. From the corner of my eye, I saw Kay tighten at Tristan's words.

"Did you see her last eve?"

"Only at the feasting." That tremor in his voice quavered still. He was lying, but that alone did not mean he had killed her.

"Not afterward?"

"No. Only then."

I nodded sagely. "She was seen later with a hooded man. I thought you might have arranged a liaison with her."

"N-n-no," he stammered.

He had seen her. That much was certain from his lies. His eyes gave him away. But still, it did not prove that he was the killer. Honestly, I could not see him as such a butcher, but looks alone often were mistaken. Panic had driven many a man to butchery.

"So you retired alone after the feasting?"

"No," he stammered. "I drank with Lords Lauhiir and Mordred until very late."

"You did not go with them, Lord Vortimer?"

He laughed a deep, throaty laugh. "I am too old to keep up with these young ones, Malgwyn. I came back here until the discovery of the girl's body. When the alarm was sounded, I mustered a squad of men and went to see if I could help. When the excitement settled, I returned here and retired."

"Why all the questions, Malgwyn?" Lord David asked. "Surely you do not suspect a member of the consilium in this madness."

Before I had time to respond, help came from an unexpected quarter. "Now, now, David," Vortimer began. "Malgwyn is just fulfilling his duties as *iudex*. I, for one, welcome his questions. I would see the doer of this deed brought to justice."

"You are too kind, Lord Vortimer. I am but a common man set an uncommon task."

"Humility does not become you, Malgwyn. We have fought side by side too many times. I know something of the affair at the abbey. You have skills that other men do not possess. I would ask just one thing."

"Yes, my lord."

"Seek out the truth no matter where it leads."

His intent was obvious, but little did he know that I had

warned Arthur that I would do just that. "Of that, you can be certain. Lord Kay and I have work left to do, and we have taken up too much of your time."

The old man was my next stop. They had moved Merlin to a storage building next to the barracks where he could be imprisoned without having to be tied to a post. I paused at the door as Kay unfastened its latch, then recoiled as the smell of human filth blasted out.

"Find another place for Merlin. No man should have to live like this." I sent one of the guards off on the errand.

"Malgwyn, is that you?" A cracking voice emerged from the blackness.

"Aye, Merlin. It is. Come forward, old friend." I didn't worry too much about his safety in the confines of the barracks.

The ancient fellow stepped out gingerly and blinked his eyes at the sunlight. "That's better." He rubbed a wrinkled hand across his forehead. His scraggly white locks framed his face as he nodded his approval. "Is all this nonsense over? Can I go back to my house? I have work to do."

"No, Merlin. The people are enraged. They think that you killed Eleonore, and they want your blood as payment."

He blinked with milky-white eyes. "She was but a child, Malgwyn. I wouldn't harm her." His voice rang soft and weak, and truthful to my ears.

"I do not believe that you did, Merlin. But many others do. Vortimer and the rest have enraged the people against you." Merlin's lips firmed in the same straight line that Owain's had, and I thought for a second how much they looked like each other, the old man and the child. "Arthur cannot help me, for that would cancel out his talk of equality and justice, his Christian principles." The eyes that looked so milky and old before stared at me straight and hard. "You are his answer. He has placed my life in your hands."

"They are good hands, Master Merlin," Kay hurried to say in the pause that yawned open, but the old man waved him away with a shaky hand.

"I am content. Arthur has done the best for me that he can. Malgwyn is superior to most men. When he's sober. Are you drunk, Malgwyn? If you are, I'll take a stick of firewood and beat you sober."

From any other man, I would have taken it as a mortal insult, but from Merlin, who saw into men's hearts with a surety I thought reserved for the gods, I could only bow my head in shame. "No, Merlin. Kay is with me to keep me from the mead and the wine."

"You will have questions," he said, squatting on the ground. "Ask."

"When we spoke last night, you said that you were dragged out of bed. How long had you been abed?"

"Not long. I had been in the great hall, showing the servants my new hat. I just finished it last eve. It must have been after the midnight. They were almost finished cleaning the hall."

"Eleonore did not help with that?"

"No, she had already taken her leave by then. Arthur was in much an ill humor with her."

"Why so?"

Merlin waved a hand as if it were of no great moment. "I love Arthur as a son, but he becomes like a small child when people do not do as he wishes."

"He is to be the Rigotamos," I pointed out.

"Aye, but the kind of lord that he wants to be relies on his subjects' goodwill more than fear. You do not create goodwill by forcing people to leap whenever you command."

The old man made much sense. "But why, Merlin?" I pressed. "What was she doing that Arthur did not like?"

He shrugged. "I do not know. I did not ask her."

I felt a tug at my sleeve and turned to see Kay at my shoulder. "The argument was about Tristan, Malgwyn. Arthur did not want her to permit his suit, but she was a willful girl and would not listen. They argued about it last eve and Eleonore took her leave early."

The vision of Arthur arguing anything with a serving girl was more than my poor old mind could comprehend and I said as much.

"I've tried to explain it, Malgwyn," Kay began. "She was more like his daughter than his servant."

"It is true," Merlin agreed. "Arthur felt of her as he would his own child. And though I loved her dearly, she knew the place of honor she held in Arthur's eye, and she used it to her advantage like a harpsman plays his harp."

"She could be as sweet as a lark, Malgwyn," Kay hurried to say, but I waved him off.

"Of course she was. All women can be willful at times and sweet as honey at others. So," I said, retreating into my mind, "she left the hall after an argument with Arthur. She went home, stayed long enough to change her clothing, and then went out again. Accolon saw her at the gate on the Via Caedes about the midnight with a man. We know that she later went with someone or met someone beneath the tower. Either that man or another killed her there, took her heart, and with help carried her to Merlin's house and left her in the lane."

"Took her heart?" Merlin asked, horrified.

I remembered then that we had not told him about that. "Aye, ripped her open from neck to her legs and took her heart. We found it lying on your table."

The wrinkled old head nodded with understanding. "So, they sought to lay blame on me by using my theory on eating hearts."

"That is how I see it."

"They are not striking at me, Malgwyn. This you know well. It is Arthur at risk here. His love for fairness and justice are spreading across the lands. Should he be named the Rigo-tamos, he will hold tightly the reins of government, demand-ing that the nobles end many of their greedy ways, stealing from the people, taking bribes from the church. Even in Brit-tany, across the sea, they have heard of him. That rascal Sido-nius, the one that is friends with Vortigern's sons, is always writing Arthur and playing on his sense of equality."

I knew vaguely of Sidonius, the son-in-law of a one-time emperor in Rome. He fancied himself a poet, and he wrote let-ters to everybody, including the brothers at Ynys-witrin. They spoke of him with laughter in their voices, the laughter of ridicule.

"So, you went home after the meal, Merlin?"

"Yes, I went back and worked on some new ideas until sleep overcame me. I had not been abed long before they came and grabbed me."

"Who arrested you?"

Merlin cocked his head, thinking. "It was just last eve, but I do not remember everyone. Bedevere, Paderic, Arthur's cousin. Let me see . . . two of Mordred's men."

"You were not among them?" I asked Kay.

"No. I was . . . I was not feeling very well."

I could not blame him. My own reaction to seeing Eleonore's body was too fresh in my mind. And Kay had known and loved her.

"What sent them to Merlin, Kay? Other than the body lying outside his door."

"His knife lay beside her."

I remembered then. "You said last night, Merlin, that you had loaned the knife to someone. Do you now remember who?"

"One of the vigiles, I think," Merlin answered. "But I cannot be certain."

"Master Malgwyn." A tentative, small voice sounded below me.

I looked down and found Mariam, my daughter, staring up at me. Yet her face turned away with a mixture of fear and curiosity, so like my Gwyneth. I forgot about Merlin and Kay and knelt down. "And how may I help you, my lady?"

"Mother says that you are to come to our house right now." Her forthrightness was amusing. Her little mouth was shaped just like her mother's, and now she held it in a straight line, serious and determined. I wished to reach down and hold her, hug her. I knew, though, that such an action would not be welcome.

"And why is that?"

"You are to attend the feasting at the great hall tonight. Mother says that you dress like a pig and that she will not have you eat at the Rigotamos's table attired like one of the animals." She said it as if she had committed it to memory and was repeating it just as Ygerne said it.

"Was that all she said?" I asked, suppressing a smile, knowing that she carried her mother's trait of sensitivity. You could laugh with and to Gwyneth, but you could not laugh at her. Her daughter was the same. "Your message seems rather brief."

"No, she said that you must bathe as well. You smell like a pig in a sty."

At that, even Kay and Merlin could not suppress their laughter.

She rebuked them with a stern eye. "Laughing at other people is not nice."

"Thank you," I said as gently as I could. She could not be more like her mother. She was a tiny Gwyneth.

But she did not respond to my attempt at kindness. Her message delivered, she spun about and marched from the parade ground. I stared sadly at her departing figure, posture straight, a miniature of her mother.

"She is your child, Malgwyn. Of that there is little doubt," Merlin said. "What will you do now in this matter?"

I was not certain. "Until we can find Accolon, I can think of nothing else to be done. I know that she was killed beneath the watchtower and taken later to Merlin's house. I know that more than one man had a hand in it. Beyond that, I cannot say with certainty. Perhaps someone in one of the houses near that area heard or saw something. I should talk to Paderic again, but that can wait a while. As much as it grieves me to confess, my brother's wife is right. I can hardly go to Arthur's table dressed in this manner." Placing my hand on Merlin's shoulder, I squeezed it softly. "Be patient, old friend. I will do my best to resolve this affair quickly. You should concentrate on who you gave your knife to."

"More depends on this than my old bones," he told me with those sharp eyes.

I simply nodded. "Kay, after Merlin is settled in finer quarters, join the search for Accolon. He is the key to this whole matter. We must find him. I will meet you later at the feasting. If you find him, confine him somewhere safe, here at the barracks. Put double the normal guard around him. Let no one see him or go near him. Maybe a few hours alone will loosen his tongue."

"If he is to be found," Kay pointed out.

CHAPTER SIX

I had old Vivienne sew you a fine tunic from imported linen. I want to see if the size is right," Ygerne said, spinning me around and casting an appraising eye on me.

"Why did you do that? Such linen is very expensive," I protested. I had come straight to Cuneglas's house from the barracks to find Ygerne waiting.

"Yes, but you can afford it."

"Ygerne! You take liberties!"

"For your own good, Malgwyn. Now, turn around again." She was using needles to pin up the tunic where it bloused too freely. Mariam sat on the floor with the assessing eye of youth. I sensed a difference in her manner now. That same eye held curiosity, not reproach, and I mused for a moment at the change. She seemed to have lost her fear of me and I wasn't sure why.

Ygerne spoke the truth about my money, though. I had a pot of coins hidden in my hovel. Denarii of Honorius and even some of Valentinian. Few new coins graced our purses and those came from our far western shores where merchants from Rome still traded, but the people still valued the old coins. Otherwise, we traded services for goods. Though I was not rich, I had more than my share of coins, and they sat uselessly at home. Mead, beer, wine, and bread were cheap. Unfortunately, that was all I spent it on. And it had taken a heavy toll on my old body. Once I could work a field all day and still feel lively enough to dig a new storage pit for Gwyneth, or, in later days, ride half the night and fight all the next day. No longer. Even climbing the road into the castle left me winded.

She took the cloth and with an "I'll return," left my daughter and myself alone.

As I prepared to bathe, filling the tub with hot water, Mariam stood just inside the doorway, a great frown on her face. The air between us was frigid enough to freeze the river Cam.

Finally, I could take it no longer. "May I be of assistance, my lady?"

"Why did Father lie and say you were my father?"

The severity of her question would have made me laugh had it not been a serious question. I stripped my shirt off, though such would have shocked a grown woman. It revealed the arm that a Saxon sword had severed, leaving the elbow red and scarred, in scars and cracks and crevices like those of the northern mountains, near the wall that Emperor Hadrian built. Mariam looked closely at the stump, but she asked no questions. 'Twas the first time I had ever revealed it to her.

"He did not lie. But you were a babe; you needed a mother and a father, not half a man."

"But if that is true, you were not wounded when you left me with them," she said crossly.

"How do you know this?"

"Mother told me."

My drinking was not going to convince her of anything. She would brush aside such an excuse as she would brush away a fly. "I was filled with hate, hate for the Saxons because they raided and killed."

"Why? It is their nature."

I looked at her face, so stern and serious. "Where did you hear that?"

"Father. He says that Saxons are bound to conquer us because it is their nature. Ours is to farm and work the land."

"That is not true."

"How would you know?" she said haughtily. "If you truly are my father, why did you not return for me when the wars ended? Other fathers returned to their children. But, if I am to believe you and not my father, you abandoned me." Her face closed down, like a shadow falls over the earth, darkening it, blurring its contours. She was so confused, two fathers yet only one truth and she didn't know which to believe.

By the gods! She was a child of keen mind! I was lost for words to explain, though I loved her with all my heart.

"Never mind. I know why," she said quietly, her tone clutching my heart and breaking it in half.

"And why is that?"

A tear streamed down her face, a tear that told me she did believe Cuneglas. "You don't love me. You don't want me."

I turned away. Those same tears flooded down my face as if the forbidden words had been a dam that held them back.

"I am very busy at my work," I said lamely, not knowing how to extricate myself from this quagmire.

Ygerne entered then, took in the scene with a woman's eye. "Go play with the other children. I must take this back to Vivienne, and Malgwyn must bathe." Mariam trudged from the room and Ygerne sighed. "I am of two minds with that child. I would give anything that Cuneglas had told her the truth from the beginning. And I wish with all my heart that I had birthed her." She started toward the door and then stopped. "Have you seen Cuneglas today? He did not come to the burying."

"No, not recently."

I noted with uneasiness the way that she eyed my chest. I turned my back to her.

"Malgwyn? Have you a special woman?"

I shrugged. "No, no one special. Why?"

"It was just a thought."

Her tone of voice made me wonder if she was apt to stray from Cuneglas. Not that the lanes were not full of his straying. The town knew of Cuneglas's appetite. But I would never do that to my brother. I did not think so, at least. With a glance over her shoulder, she slipped from the room. I shook my head. Were she to truly glance my way, I was not sure how loyal I would be to my brother. He and I shared a talent for choosing exceptional women and a weakness in resisting them.

The hot water felt good against my skin. I took my time and delighted in it, bathing the wounds I had suffered that very morning. The water stung the cut on my temple. More had happened in the last few hours than had happened to me in the four years since I returned to Arthur's castle. Though the weight of my newfound obligations were heavy upon me, I felt something I had not believed possible. I felt needed. I realized that it was a sensation that I had not felt in many, many years. Not since Gwyneth died.

As I continued cleansing myself, I came finally to the stump of my arm, still strong in the shoulder, but weakening as I moved farther down to the hideous, puckered scar covering what had been my elbow. A part of me knew that I had been fortunate, but I could remember so well those first few days of consciousness when I realized my loss, and I cursed Arthur's name as loudly as I cursed the Saxons that took my family and my limb.

A quick knock sounded at the door, breaking me from my reverie, and Ygerne slid my clothes in and laid them carefully on the floor. She averted her eyes, at least partially. "I have sometimes wondered what it would be like to be with someone else." She would not know. She had been a virgin when she married Cuneglas.

"It depends on the reason," I answered honestly. I felt her hand touch the skin of my back and experienced a man's reaction. She rubbed across the skin, over the shoulder, and down to the nub that was once an arm. Her touch showed no revulsion, just an odd tenderness. I quickly covered myself, ashamed of the reaction her touch spurred in me.

"I wondered, and I thought you might give me an honest answer."

" 'Tis a difficult question," I answered, my throat tightening. "There is love and lust. Your reason for being with someone defines the experience."

"You should not be ashamed of your arm. It is an honorable wound, and all the more handsome because of it." She turned and left, and I felt longing and relief at the same time. Such a thing was more than I could bear at present. After my Gwyneth passed, Ygerne had always stirred thoughts in me; that glowing hair and those heavy breasts called to me like no other woman in the castle. But she was my brother's wife, and I would never take that step.

I dwelled on these thoughts as I donned the camisia, the undershirt of linen, and then my breeches and my tunic. Putting the arousal of moments ago from my mind, I turned to my new clothes. Strapping on my belt, with its row of iron studs, I realized that I had never, in my life, been dressed in such finery as Ygerne had laid out for me. What Gwyneth would have thought of me! She would have laughed in that deep, throaty way of hers and told me that I was a farmer no longer. For no farmer, she would have chided me, would dress so well when there were hogs to slaughter and crops to be planted.

Outside, I heard the thump of hogs banging against the wall. Most houses had a small yard in back where swine were kept. Even through the wall, I could smell the odor of the dung.

A knock came at the door. "Are you clothed?" Ygerne asked.

"Aye, and finer than I have ever been."

She slipped in and appraised me. "That is better, for certain. Now you look more like a king's councillor and less like Mad Malgwyn."

"Has Cuneglas returned?"

"No, but Kay is here and anxious to see you."

"He has news of Accolon?"

"He did not say."

As she turned to leave, I touched her sleeve. "Ygerne, why are you so kind to me?" The question had been gnawing at me. "I have been nothing but a drunkard for years now. I pushed my own child off on you. I live but fifteen minutes walk away, yet I rarely darken your door."

She looked at me straight and true. "You are my husband's brother and Mariam's father. If I knew nothing else but that, I would know enough to treat you fairly, no matter how your life is lived. But you are more than that, Malgwyn. You are a man that others turn to when danger calls. You are trusted when others are not. Cuneglas told me once that men such as you are not common, and that you should be protected, sometimes even from yourselves. And I trust you, and respect you."

"Cuneglas is my brother, my younger brother, and it is not strange for him to think more of me than others. But I know too that I am also Mad Malgwyn the Drunken Fool, and he is worth little in this world."

"For tonight, leave Mad Malgwyn and his flaws abed and live up to your brother's dream of you." And with that, she whisked out of the shed.

I finished lacing my leather shoes and followed her back to the house, where Kay was squirming impatiently in a chair, his mail shirt bunched at his hips and the tip of his sword digging a trench in the dirt floor.

"What word, Kay?"

He leaped to his feet. "None. Accolon has disappeared. None of his fellows have seen him since he left the barracks this morn. It would seem that perhaps he is more guilty than we think."

"Or," I offered, "perhaps he too has become a victim in this tragedy. And we are meant to believe that he is guilty." But Kay was right. More and more Accolon seemed to be a guilty party.

Kay frowned, a big, heavy frown that weighed down his face. "You are a frustrating man, Malgwyn. Is nothing ever clear for you? Must you always be asking your blasted questions?"

I chuckled. Kay's temper had become famous among the soldiers. But though it was easily sparked, it was just as easily dispelled. "Surely there is truth to be found, but accepting the first answer given you is not the way to the truth. Our first answer was Merlin. We both know now that that was wrong."

"True," he conceded.

"If Accolon did this thing, he did not do it by himself. That much I know for certain." I recalled to him what I had found at the watchtower.

He waved a gloved hand at me. "Aye, all that is true enough, but you would still drive a man insane."

Ygerne looked at me with questions floating in her eyes, but I could not tell her all of it. Not yet, at any rate. And the way she looked at me made me want to take her and hold her. This I could not do either.

"Come. Let us go and see what mischief Vortimer will provoke tonight."

The lanes, at least those not yet paved by Lord Arthur, were ankle deep in a thick gray mud, smelling of manure and the fetid stench of rotting straw. Vendors lined the streets, selling wine, some cheap in goatskins and some expensive, in large amphorae from the docks at Ynys-witrin and far to the west near Castle Dore. With all the merchants' stalls, jugglers, and simple folk gathered from the countryside, this was no ordinary feast, no ordinary gathering of nobles. The procession yesterday told them that if nothing else. The entire consilium, the entire group of lords, all the tribes of Britannia, had come to Arthur's castle for one purpose and one purpose only—to name a new Rigotamos, a new high king to govern over all. It was as if a great festival had been pronounced, and the people entered into it with a vengeance.

The murmur of the crowd quieted even further as Arthur emerged from the door of his hall, flanked by Kay and Bedevere. As if on cue, Ambrosius Aurelianus rode into the square, and all present, nobles and peasants alike, took a knee. Though in his last years, Ambrosius was a symbol of Roman rectitude. Arrayed as a Roman cavalry officer, he rode erect on a snorting white horse. He wore a bejeweled helmet, tufts of white hair pushing out and framing his craggy features. Were his shoulders any straighter, I would suspect he wore a wooden frame beneath his tunic and brooch-joined fur cloak. But such a one as he would never stoop to such vanity.

I laughed at all this ceremony. Ambrosius had been here since the day before, and indeed had feasted at Arthur's hall last night as I well knew. But such displays served two purposes. The people expected it, and Ambrosius's pride demanded it.

Ambrosius was followed by four attendants, and his only allowance to age was for the attendants to help him, ever so slightly, from his horse. I noticed the tremble in Ambrosius's arms and legs as he dismounted. Ambrosius never moved very quickly, as I recalled, but he moved even more slowly now as he approached Arthur, touched him on the shoulder, and signaled that he should rise. Turning a bit, he signaled that all should rise.

Too much chatter filled the square to hear Arthur's welcome. The old man had served us well, but plainly if the Saxons were to be kept at bay and unity was to be upheld in our lands, a new leader was needed. And as much as I had come to hate Arthur, I knew that only he could hold all the factions together. No matter how much I respected Arthur's abilities, the fact that I was who I was, what I was, stood between us. Before that day at Tribuit, I was a good man. Now I was useless, and Arthur had done that. We had seen friends, comrades, die on the battlefield, die a warrior's death. Why couldn't he have honored me the same way? I brushed the thoughts away to concentrate on the task at hand and made my way into the hall.

Coincidence gave me a view of the great hall and the consilium gathered around a large table. I watched with curiosity
to see who spoke with whom. If Ambrosius were to nominate
Arthur he would stand little opposition, but Cuneglas was probably right; there would be some. And some is not the same as
none. Ambrosius's support would carry enough votes to anoint
Arthur—unless I failed.

I heard a murmur from the women in the great hall. A new
arrival had joined the feasting—Guinevere. The murmurs had
a nasty lilt to them. She was dressed, rather plainly, in a deep
green peplos gown with a Roman cut. A small bronze brooch
with three-diamond-shaped pieces of quartz held the gown in
place, and her jewelry, a necklace and bracelet of gold, was
modest in design. The brooch was called a fibula then and had
come down from our grandmother and her grandmother before. Once, it seemed, our forebears had been gentle, worn the
purple perhaps. Her long brunette hair was swirled into a knot
at the back of her head, revealing her pale, delicate features,
lips slightly full and high cheekbones.

If you asked the women of the court why they disapproved
of Guinevere, they would tell you that it was because of her
past. In reality, it was jealousy. She and Arthur had been together for a long time, but Arthur would not marry her, could
not, to his way of thinking, marry her.

But at that moment, with Guinevere's entrance accomplished, I watched as the great lords and ladies in their silk and
fur took their seats and the serving girls began to bring the
food around the table.

Arthur's hall was a timbered affair, with stout wooden beams
and posts holding it in place. Woven banners, most graced by
the Cross, hung from the rafters. At the back of the hall stood

a single doorway into Arthur's own chambers. An open hearth had been built in the middle of the hall, dug into the hard-packed earthen floor and lined with rocks, and two suckling pigs were roasting over the flames. On a previous visit here, I was told, Ambrosius Aurelianus scolded Arthur for not having a proper mosaic floor. "Later, perhaps," Arthur had told the old man. "But for now, earth will do."

Though his floor was plain, Arthur kept a very Roman table. I could not say I minded though. To eat roasted pig was a pleasure I rarely enjoyed. Such an extravagance was not possible for me. To roast a pig or any meat in such a fashion required an iron spit, and that was beyond the means of most.

The two serving girls brought platters of the dark, flat, un-leavened bread that was typical for our tables. I noticed that Arthur, ever mindful of hospitality, had kindly provided imported red bowls, piled high with mashed pork and chicken for those whose teeth were too worn to eat from the bone. Hanging over a steaming kettle was a large white cloth, bundled around vegetables. One of the servers would take the softened vegetables later and mash them into a kind of paste. Other platters appeared, laden with oysters steamed in their shells.

The hall smelled deliciously of the roasting pig, garnished with honey, but beyond that tantalizing smell lay the unmistakable scent of garum, a Roman sauce made of fermented fish. Like the soldier's posca, the vinegary drink, garum was another of Arthur's Roman affectations.

I knew that we were early, but I wanted to watch the others arrive. With that in mind, I took up station at the front of the hall, near Arthur's chambers, facing the main door. Kay wanted to stay with me, but I instructed him to mingle with the group and hear what gossip he could.

Bedevere was next to arrive, elegantly dressed in a mail shirt over a knee-length tunic, with a richly woven cloak draped about his shoulders and fastened with a fancy bronze brooch. Like me, a leather belt with iron studs circled his waist, although, as befitted his station, his belt contained twice as many studs. Iron was expensive, and you could easily judge a man's position by how much iron he wore on his clothing.

Even as I thought this, Tristan entered with Mordred at his heels, and I took a moment to consider Mark's son. He was tall, though not as tall as Kay, and handsome in a pale, protected sort of way. Mark doted on the lad, it was said, and he wanted for nothing in his lands. His tunic was as fine as Arthur's, but his shield, carried by a servant, was not emblazoned with the cross as were all those who served the Rigotamos.

Tristan surveyed the hall haughtily, his mouth curved into a knowing smile. Behind Tristan and Mordred were two or three of Tristan's men, arrayed in their war dress. They wore sneers on their faces to match anything Mordred could offer. Almost in unison, the pair studied the large white banner with the red cross hanging from a sturdy rafter over Arthur's table, and they shook their heads in disdain. Two birds perched on the same branch, I thought.

The fat little Lord Lauhiir, new to the consilium, fell into deep conversation with Tristan. Gawain and Mordred also spoke quietly, apart from the others. That was not unusual. They were brothers, sons of Arthur's uncle. The others mingled about, talking to first one then another, sipping from their wine and waiting for the feasting to begin.

Following them came Coroticus, the abbot of Ynys-witrin, clothed in his drab brown robes, his hood pulled back, and the cross of his office hanging about his neck from a gold chain.

Though I thought Coroticus a good and decent man, Arthur was not fond of him, and he no friend of Arthur's. They fought over silly things. The latest argument was over Arthur's cruciform church, planned for construction near the center of the town. Coroticus said the shape was sacrilegious; Arthur said it was a tribute. Neither man would give. And, as I've said, the crux of the matter was lower taxes for the church. Despite their enmity, in a matter of this importance, Arthur had to include the church. For Ynys-witrin the election of a new Rigotamos was of as great a concern as for the rest of the land.

Gathered here were representatives of all the lands controlled by the consilium come to Arthur's table to hear the suit of Tristan for a treaty of peace with the Saxons.

"So, Malgwyn. I see you have cleaned up quite nicely." The oily voice of Mordred abused my ear, and I turned to see him standing at my shoulder. "Poor Coroticus. His day is done, you know. The people cry for the old gods."

"And you shall lead them back?" I finished for him.

"It is what the people desire."

"I am not a religious man, Mordred, as you know. I look at men's actions for their motive. Some men's motives are pure of heart. Others," and I stared him straight in the eye, "have motives spawned by the devil."

The smile he flashed chilled me to the bone. "Be careful, Malgwyn, that your investigation does not uncover affairs that you would as lief not know." Mordred was drunk, I realized. He would not normally be so bold.

"And be careful, my dear Lord Mordred, that you do not get caught under my heel. For I will grind you into the dirt."

His smile never faltered. "You are as courageous as you are

insolent. 'Tis just as well," he said with a mock bow. "We understand each other."

"Perfectly."

Arthur and Ambrosius stepped out of the chambers at the rear of the hall. Arthur was finely dressed in a crimson tunic, belted with brown leather and a shining gold buckle. He did not enjoy such trappings, but he knew that they were necessary for formal occasions. While the common folk honored him for his bravery and his fairness, others respected him only for signs of wealth and victories won.

Ambrosius approached the head of the table, and in ritual deference to his rank, all waited until he had seated himself before they joined him. Two male servants, one the recalcitrant boy from the morning, wearing plain dark tunics and Roman sandals, lifted the roast pig, still hissing and crackling from the fire, and, carrying it on the spit, placed it on a platter in the center of the table. Bowls of porridges and vegetables appeared from nowhere and platters of flat bread filled the empty spaces.

A pretty maiden circled the table filling cups with watered wine from a jug. Another worked from the opposite direction with a jug of ale, a brown, heavy drink that was replacing mead as the poor man's choice. Soon everyone was busily eating pig and drinking. The politics would come later.

"How goes it with you, Malgwyn? We miss you at Ynyswitrin." Coroticus sat next to me.

"All is not well. You have heard about the girl?"

He nodded slightly. "Great danger exists, my friend. Nothing is as it seems. Of that, be certain."

With all my might, I kept my head from whipping around. "You know something of this?"

Smiling at someone across the table, he let his chin dip in

that faint nod again. "Arthur is not my favorite person, as you know, but he is far preferable to the pagan Saxons and their murderous ways. I cannot say with certainty, but I have reason to believe that the girl's death is part of a larger scheme to weaken Arthur's position and grease the path for the Saxons."

"By whom?"

"I am not at liberty to say."

"How do you know this?"

"I was courted because of my dislike for Arthur."

"Then tell me all of it. Tell Arthur. Merlin's life hangs in the balance, and it seems the entire land's future does as well."

Coroticus smiled at me softly. "I cannot, Malgwyn. What happens to Ynys-witrin if I side with Arthur and Ambrosius and their enemies win? They have promised to leave us alone and let us continue God's work."

"They lie."

"Often. But not this time, I think. It is in their best interests to leave us to our work."

"What of right and wrong, Coroticus?"

His hand reached over and grasped my shoulder, pulling me closer as if sharing a confidence. "That is your task, Malgwyn. Arthur was hesitant to come to you for help. He feared your drinking and dissolute life had drained your considerable abilities. But I whispered a word in a certain ear, a certain female ear, and the message, that you, and only you, could weave us all clear of this maze, was delivered."

I knew, of course, who the woman was. But the timing was all wrong. "How is that possible? Arthur came to me within the hour of Eleonore's discovery."

"Arthur was coming to you before that. You were to be here tonight had Eleonore been serving us at this very moment. He simply seized upon the opportunity to enlist your aid, just as others seized upon Eleonore's death to turn it to their own advantage, I think."

I smiled at him with strong aggravation lurking beneath the surface. "You are all plagues on the face of the earth. I should have sent him away with my foot up his arse."

"You could not do that."

"And why not?"

"You are a good man, Malgwyn. And good men always do what truth and right require."

"And you are more a scheming lord than a priest."

"An abbot has to be."

On that cryptic note, our attention returned to eating. But I understood more of his comment than not. Followers of the Christ had been treated roughly by the departure of the Roman legions. Pagan worship, like that of the Druids, was returning to the land, and many people turned away from the Christ. They returned to burying their dead with grave goods for the afterlife. They returned to their feasting such as Beltain. In the east of our lands, rumor had it, they had returned to human sacrifices.

One of the serving girls, Nimue, carved some of the pig and placed the herb-laden meat on my platter. In so doing, she slid a bit of parchment into my hand. "From my lady," she whispered. I looked at Guinevere and she smiled. A bowl of the strained vegetables lay close at hand, and I alternated eating pig with my dagger and dipping a spoon into the green puree. Though I felt horribly awkward, a simple glance around at all the diners showed their faces buried in their platters and the sounds of teeth gnashing on meat filled the room. Even in a crowd, only I was witness to my own discomfiture.

Arthur's fare was certainly better than that at my own table. And better served as well. The wine was imported from Gaul— I noted with a frown that mine was thinned till it was little more than flavored water—and the porridges were served in large bronze bowls, decorated with designs from our ancient past. Around the campfires, late at night, Arthur often said that to know our future we must know our past.

To that end, while we ate and while plates and jugs and bowls clattered, a bard sang an old song about ancient kings, one who went mad, betrayed by his own family. Brightly dressed in a red, white, and green tunic, the old fellow accompanied himself on a lute. Would that his voice were as sweet as the lute.

Just as the bard finished his song, Ambrosius, wiping his dagger on his sleeve and resheathing it, stood and held out his arms. "The consilium welcomes Lord Tristan from the lands of the Dumnonii."

In his turn, Tristan rose and faced the group. "I bring you greetings, Rigotamos, from my father Mark, whose enemies flee at his approaching footsteps." He stopped with that, and I was glad. Such greetings often lasted thirty minutes or more and encompassed the prowess of all his ancestors.

Having made their opening statements, Ambrosius and Tristan sat back down around the large round table, built of the stoutest oak. Arthur did not fancy long, rectangular tables. He told me once that with a round table it was easier for him to see his guests, easier to watch all their actions and easier to read their intentions. I saw now the truth of his statement.

Brushing a few bits of pork from his long beard, Ambrosius bowed his head to Tristan. "Please, begin."

"I come before you and your great lords to discuss a matter

of the utmost importance. We have, within our grasp, a chance to bring peace to this island and stop the incessant fighting with the Saxons. Their requests are small; they wish only to be able to freely traverse our lands to the western sea and to trade in our markets." Tristan spoke with his arms extended and palms upraised, as if in supplication.

With Tristan's words came a thunder of whispers all around the table as nobles and guests expressed their feelings.

"They only wish to have the doors of our forts opened to them!" bellowed Kay, his voice echoing off the walls. "They wish only for us to lay down our swords and accept their dominion!"

"No, no, no, my Lord Kay!" Tristan remonstrated. "They come as friends, as helpers to bring peace and prosperity to our lands."

"They betrayed us before; they will betray us again. It is in their nature," Bedevere lectured in a more measured tone.

"Are you afraid that the people will not remain loyal to the Rigotamos? That they might rebel against him?" Vortimer's voice irritated me as much as ever.

"Isn't that what you've been plotting for years, Vortimer?"

The other lord hung his head and shook it, his long hair flowing about his shoulders. "You wrong me, Bedevere. I have fought at Ambrosius's side as oft as you have. Why should I want to see him overthrown?"

"Why, indeed," Arthur said, entering the fray. He regarded Tristan with a tired frown. I paid close attention now. All before had been but preamble. Negotiations were about to begin. Ambrosius, as a sign of Arthur's stature, would allow him to take the lead. "You see, Lord Tristan, how the other lords are arrayed against such a treaty. Perhaps, if there were additional restrictions. . . ." His voice trailed off.

"What type of restrictions, my lord?" Tristan asked quickly.

Arthur stroked his heavy beard. "I have not given it enough thought to be specific. Perhaps if the size of Saxon parties crossing our territories were limited in number."

"Certainly." Tristan nodded vigorously.

"And perhaps if the goods their merchants would trade with us would not compete against our own people's wares."

"I feel sure that such could be arranged."

"Perhaps," Arthur continued, with the slightest of grins, "if the Saxons would agree to go unarmed."

"Yes, yes," Tristan rushed to answer, without the barest of pauses. "I am sure they would agree to these stipulations. It would only be fair and prudent."

Coroticus cocked his head at me and smiled. I knew immediately what he intended to convey. Never would the Saxons come into our lands unarmed. Such would be death to them.

"Of course," Tristan said with a firm set to his jaw, "because the western shores are so far from Saxon lands, it might be necessary to allow them to establish permanent camps in far Dumnonia."

"Lord Mark does not feel threatened by this?" It was a logical question from Ambrosius.

"I give my word that such would be acceptable to all the Dumnonii of the west." Tristan nodded in agreement.

Once again his assurances came too hastily, and Coroticus and Arthur both looked in my direction. More was amiss with this statement than the obvious, but I could not yet grasp the shadowy element, the hint of treachery lying therein. So, rather than make an accusation, I simply raised my eyebrows, letting them know that I too found it suspicious.

Ambrosius stood, causing Tristan to almost stumble back into his seat. The Rigotamos stroked his long beard and said nothing for a long moment. "This is a grave matter," he grumbled finally. "One that bears more thought than a night's counsel can give. I will give it the consideration it deserves and set aside a time for the consilium to discuss it." He sat heavily then, as if he felt some grave burden.

Vortimer arose and faced the gathered lords. "There is yet another matter, my Lord Rigotamos. The death of the girl and the selection of your successor."

The cagey old noble fingered the golden disc about his neck. "I see no connection between one and the other."

"With all my honor to you, Rigotamos, it is no secret that you favor Arthur. But if Merlin, who is as close to a father as Arthur has now, is the mutilator of this girl, and he does not pay for this carnage, then Arthur's vaunted honor, equality, and justice, aye, his *Romanitas*, are just words on the wind. Some other, one who would hold the people's loyalty, should be chosen."

Arthur sat quietly as Bedevere stood. "You once believed in the Christ, Vortimer, as we all do now. But you have returned to the Druids. They kill. They sacrifice. Let us say Merlin did this thing. Why should it be any different? How can you make such an argument?"

Vortimer spoke not to Bedevere, an insult that sent Arthur's hand to hold Bedevere in place, and addressed Ambrosius. "The Druids sacrifice for the people's sake. They sacrifice for better crops, for better weather. They too have laws that are just. But the killing of this girl is madness. It brings no fertility to the land. It offers no homage to the gods."

"Clever words from the son of a traitor!" Bedevere could

hold back no longer. Around the room, Vortimer's bodyguard went for their swords as Arthur's went for theirs.

"Enough!" Ambrosius rose to his full height, stretching his old bones as high as they could go. "You will spill no blood at this table! I will say it now. Arthur is my choice. But the members of the consilium will vote. Should Merlin prove to be the culprit in this affair, I will withdraw my support of Arthur. Love of the Christ has no place in it for such butchery."

A bellow sounded outside the hall, shouts, screams. The main doors burst open and two guards rushed into the hall, red faced and agitated. "Murder, my lords! There has been another murder!"

CHAPTER SEVEN

Revolt! The people are revolting and besieging the barracks!"

Arthur and his men leaped to their feet in such haste that platters and jugs went flying. I kept my eyes on Vortimer and his followers. As I suspected, I saw no surprise, only the most fleeting of smiles. Tristan, on the other hand, looked decidedly ill.

"What work of the devil is this?" Arthur bellowed.

"My Lord Rigotamos," one of the guards panted. "The body of a second woman, killed as the girl, was found in the lanes. The people believe that Merlin did this thing too. They are rioting at the barracks, trying to seize Merlin to be hanged!"

Arthur's eyes darted quickly to me, and my hand rose just the slightest bit, as if to say, *Be calm, I will deal with this.*

"To the barracks, men!" Arthur ordered, and I followed behind him, out the door, and straight into the arms of an angry mob, my second of the day.

"Stand aside!" cried Kay and the others, but the motley crowd, mostly peasants from the countryside, not townsfolk, were not in a mood to obey a noble. Their clothes, patchworks of bright-colored cloth, created an odd, festive look in the torchlight.

I gasped as I surveyed the lane in the flickering light. From the great hall to the barracks, the entire length of the lane, people blocked our path.

"Malgwyn!" I recognized Arthur's call to me. He needed no words to tell me what my duties were. The mob was his; the murder was mine.

"This way, Malgwyn," I heard Kay shout above the people's din.

Kay and two soldiers stood in a side lane fifty yards from Accolon's old house. He was too poor to afford better quarters, something talk in the lane said led to violent arguments with the status-hungry Nyfain. And so he took a house on a back lane, not far from Arthur's hall.

I rushed forward and saw a clutch of people gathered around a spot in the lane next to Accolon's house. Just out of sight of the main road lay another bloody body, its legs sprawled apart, its arms flung about as if broken. I thought for a moment it might be the missing Accolon.

But I knew before I saw the face that it was not Accolon. No, this broken body belonged to Owain's mother, Nyfain. She would never more embarrass the youngster. Her life's breath had been stolen. The boy was now alone in the world.

I shoved aside my thoughts of the boy to focus on her body. The foul deed was most perplexing. For, like Eleonore, this woman too had been ripped apart. I quickly knelt beside her and examined the now familiar mutilation. "How came you to find her?" I asked a vigile standing near.

"Some of the townspeople found her. I hastened here, and once in the lane, I saw her."

"You!" I shouted at one of the soldiers. "Go to my hut and fetch a fur. Hurry!"

I remembered then Paderic telling me that Accolon had left the barracks early in the morn. Could Accolon have been the master of these events? He was the one that found Eleonore's body, and the last man known to have seen her alive. As for Nyfain, she strayed more often than she shared his bed.

I knew he had been drinking. Could he have seen Eleonore, lured her to the tower, and in trying to take her, killed her? Then concocted the tale of seeing her with another man to protect himself? Then, later, finding Nyfain and still in a murderous rage, killed her? Perhaps. It was not unlikely. His hatred for Arthur was as great as mine, and if he were drunk, he might have struck out at one close to him. Surely, he knew that the girl stood high in Arthur's esteem. She might have been a prime target for his anger.

Here, then, was my substitute for Merlin. For a moment I felt relief. I sat back on my haunches and considered the affair from all angles.

Accolon had reason and the chance to kill Eleonore. He could have killed her beneath the tower, moved her to the lane in front of Merlin's house, and then raised the alarm. He lied about seeing her with another man to divert suspicion from himself. Like a sword in a sheath, it fit snugly.

Still, other questions nagged at me like a wife. The soldier, as irritable and gruff as he was, never struck me as a man who would kill a woman. An enemy in battle? Yes. Arthur in a fit of anger over a woman? Maybe. But I could not see him committing this kind of butchery. Yet here was a second woman who had crossed his path who ended with her entrails on the ground. And this second death brought more questions than it answered. For this new theory did not account for all the footprints at the watchtower.

And, as with Eleonore, I could tell by a simple look that Nyfain was not murdered here. No great splashes of blood marked the lane. Indeed, it was as neat as if freshly swept. She had been killed elsewhere and placed here later. That bespoke more than one person, just as in Eleonore's death. If the old soldier had done this, he had had help. But who?

And why kill the woman Nyfain in the same manner? And how and why was her body dumped here, probably as we feasted, to be found? Nyfain's death seemed to accomplish nothing except excite the crowd. And what of the other footprints at the tower, the proof that more than one man had helped in this matter? Were these things meant to point at Accolon or Merlin? Were we supposed to think that Merlin had killed both women for their hearts? That did not seem sensible to my old brain. For why then was there but one heart on Merlin's table? Why not the both of them? And where was Nyfain's heart?

If Accolon was not the man I sought, then why had he returned to the castle this morn? Nyfain had been dead for hours, not quite as long as Eleonore, for her wounds were still a little fresh, but she had been killed in the early morning hours for certain, before Accolon was last seen. But Kay had come to this house searching for Accolon earlier and had seen nothing of her. Where had they kept her body? These discrepancies ate at me like a disease.

I checked her hands and fingers for signs of a struggle, but there were none. The look on her face was peaceful and her eyes were closed. I caught a strong whiff of honey mead from her open mouth. No great effort had been needed to kill poor Nyfain. She must have been senseless from the mead. And I saw no marks on her throat. Feeling around her mass of dark hair, my hand came away bloody. I pulled her head up and turned it to find that the back of her skull had been caved in.

"Here is the fur." The soldier brought it to me and laid it at my feet. He stared down at Nyfain's gaping wound and backed off a step or two.

"Cover her with that and stand your guard," I instructed. "Come, Kay. We have more work to do, and Accolon to find."

"Mother?" The small voice came from the atrium, and I turned to see Owain standing, hands dangling at his sides, staring at his mother's lifeless body. He must have followed the soldier back.

In the name of Arthur's God! Could I not be granted any fortune in this affair? I snatched the fur from the gaping soldier and flung it over Nyfain. With carefully measured steps I snatched up Owain under my one arm, tucked him safe though he fought me like a wildcat, and hustled him off to Kay's house. A pair of old women in the lane stared at me as if I were mad as I hauled the screaming, bawling child along.

Once inside, I set him on his feet, and one of his fists caught me sharply on the temple, breaking loose the stone's wound and sending blood streaming down my face yet again. "Owain! Stop it!"

"You killed my mother!"

"No! I didn't. Listen to me!" But his onslaught continued, and with just one arm, and no desire to hurt the lad, all I could do was fend off his blows. At last, Kay strode forward and pinned his young arms to his side and held the wriggling worm still.

"Owain, have I ever lied to you?"

He slowed his struggles and shook his head. Tears were streaming down his face.

"Your mother is dead. It is true. I would have given my one arm to keep you from having seen it, but I did not kill her."

"Then who did? The magician, the sorcerer, Merlin?"

"No, Owain. But I suspect that someone wants us to think that. I promise you, boy, I will find your mother's killer. Do you believe me?"

It took him a long second to reply, but finally he nodded his tear-streaked, grimy face.

"You must do as I say, Owain. It is very important. Stay here in Kay's house. Do you understand?"

Again the nod took its time in arriving, but it came. His shoulders relaxed and Kay released him.

"But Malgwyn, she must be buried."

"And we will, Owain. I promise you we will. But the only way to catch her killer is to hasten along this path that I follow. I would not lead you astray."

His lips tightened into a straight line and his eyes narrowed. "Then I will do as you say." Owain walked to a stool and lowered himself as a man of one hundred years might. His fingers fumbled with each other and he stared at them for long seconds. "She loved me. I know she did."

"I know she did too, lad." I cast about for something for him to do. "Work on the quills. Go fetch them. I will be back later. You will stay here tonight."

"Really? I may stay with Lord Kay?"

For Kay's part he smiled gently.

I knew nothing else to do, so, at the risk of disappointing him later, I nodded. "Yes, you may stay here. Cicero can watch after you. Stay here until I return or I send for you. Now, Kay, let's play the game and see how it ends."

We returned to the fray growing around the barracks. I knew some of them, from villages nearly a day's journey away, and I wondered at how they knew to come. Our enemies must be spreading their tales far afield.

"Kill the sorcerer! Kill the magician!!" The shouts rang off the walls of the town.

None of them heeded Kay's cry, nor did they cringe at the sight of the Rigotamos. A different kind of fear marked their faces, not the fear of authority, but a deeper fright. Someone had fed them a story of magic and murder, and they had inhaled it as one would the spring breeze. But they found the odor rancid and poisonous, and now they were going to strike out at the nearest target. I did not have to look far to find the source of the ill wind. Lurking in the shadows of the buildings were the Druid priests, their faces darkened by their hoods. Many of the people seemed to cling to the priests, something that affrighted me.

This was my doing. I could see that now. I had underestimated Vortimer's cunning, and how deeply involved he was in this affair. Obviously, he knew the woman was dead. He had led his followers to the stream, and they had but to wait for Kay's men to arrive before drinking from the waters of revolt.

I held my tongue. I knew that nothing I said—or that Ambrosius said for that matter—would sway them. And, as I knew would happen, the thunderous clatter of horses' hooves on the cobblestones did more than any king's command.

The crowd scattered as a troop of Arthur's cavalry stormed down the lane, opening a path as neatly as an axe splits wood.

"Hurt no one!" Arthur shouted as the mounted soldiers

drew their lances. The mob quieted as the horsemen twirled their lances, aiming the points at the sky and using the blunt ends to herd the people. I marveled at Arthur's bearing, his intuitive sense of the people. Vortigern would have had the leaders skewered on the lances already. Not Arthur.

We ran down the now-cleared lane and faced a sight even more frightening than that at the hall. One hundred peasants and townsfolk were struggling with twenty or so of Arthur's men. Only their lances were keeping the people at bay. Curses, shouts, filled the air. Rocks, dung, pounded against the wooden stockade. The horsemen formed a wedge in front of us, protecting our flanks and speeding our advance.

As the stockade grew closer, I could see the reddened face of Paderic bravely defending the gate. Fending off the thumping shower of stones with their shields, the soldiers steadfastly held their posts.

"Enough!" thundered Arthur, climbing halfway up the wall, his shoes finding purchase in the planks. The word rolled out and echoed off the houses and stalls, Arthur's jowls reverberating with each repetition.

For a wonder, they became silent. And the only sound that marred that silence was the uneven patter of stones and sticks dropping on the cobblestones.

Arthur surveyed the mob. I could see his jaws clench and unclench, his beard tightening against the skin with each movement of his muscles. This was Arthur, struggling to control his anger, searching out a solution to this thorny problem. I had seen it many times.

With palms outstretched, almost supplicating, he cocked his head to one side and smiled gently. "Who speaks here for you?"

This was not the reaction they had expected. Violence they had expected. Threats. But not an offer to parley. I watched as heads snapped back and forth like a crowd of confused chickens. Quickly, I searched the mob for Vortimer. My eye caught him lingering in the shadows of the torchlight, on the edge of the mob.

"My lord!" A voice shattered the silence.

"Make yourself known!" responded Arthur.

A single figure separated itself from the throng, a tall man in peasant's clothes. "I am Elvain of the lands near Ynys-witrin." For such one of low birth, he was very well spoken.

"Speak, Elvain."

"My lord, you hold a killer within your walls, a killer that has struck twice, most brutally. We demand justice. The justice that you so loudly proclaim. The facts are clear; the old man is unsound. He has murdered two women. You must put him to the sword before he kills again!"

"Good Elvain, he is locked safely away here in my barracks while we seek the truth of the matter. He is no harm to anyone."

"But he's a sorcerer, able to slip such bonds with magic!"

This brought the mob to life again. "We have seen him, my lord!" cried an anonymous voice. "We have seen him disappear before our very eyes. This stockade could hold him no better than a tree holds a bird in flight. He is a magician!"

I could not be certain where the voice came from, but I thought my ears pulled it from the shadows.

"He is an old man, and old men's minds often say things they do not mean." I entered the fray at last, stealing the mob's attention from Arthur.

The mumbles from the crowd were different than before.

Many of them knew me, but they knew me as "Mad Malgwyn" and not arrayed as a king's councillor. This caught them off balance, as I knew it would.

"Malgwyn is my councillor in this affair. I have appointed him my iudex pedaneus, my investigator," Ambrosius said, emerging to legitimize my role. I rolled my eyes at his use of the old Latin term. Only the older folk and Arthur would recognize the official title. I had heard that in the larger towns like Londinium, a citizen still carried the title and duties, but here in the country, such offices had fallen fallow, like a field too often planted. Aye, in some places *iudex* was used for almost any civic office.

"Merlin did not kill the women," I pronounced.

" 'Twas his knife found with the body," Elvain protested, and others shouted their agreement.

"I will condemn no man to death until all the facts are known," Arthur proclaimed.

"The facts are known!" bellowed a new voice. "If you won't punish the sorcerer, we will."

The threat brought a new surge from the mob, pushing against the stockade wall, and its boards creaked under their weight. Arthur swayed, nearly losing his foothold, and gripped the pointed end of one of the logs in the wall to recapture his balance. The crowd roared at the sight of Arthur toppling. And they surged forward hard.

Arthur clung to the fence by one hand, and that one losing its hold.

Yet another powerful wave pounded the wall.

The wall collapsed.

Ambrosius's bodyguard encircled him and hustled him to safety amid the chaos.

The mob trampled Paderic's contingent and pushed the horsemen aside. For a wonder, Arthur was able to roll to the side. But it was about to turn horribly bloody. Some of the riders had flipped their lances so the pointed edge threatened the people.

And then they charged.

Screams of pain filled Arthur's castle.

From the corner of my eye, I saw and then heard the whistle of a club swing by my ear. I rolled away from my assailant and blasted a foot into his privates as he hovered over me for the kill. He crumpled into a ball and lurched to one side. Across the parade ground, I could see a small group of unarmed men trying to separate the soldiers from the mob; soon they too were slicked in blood.

An odd screech sounded, loud and clear, and I watched as Arthur's men, with military precision, formed up twenty yards from the mob, leaving the leaderless horde with no opponent. It was the high-pitched cry of the tawny owl, Arthur's assembly call when no other means were present.

Then, much like a dog who catches the wagon wheel he chases so fervently only to be lost and confused when the wagon stops, the mélange of people simply milled about aimlessly. Once inside the walls they knew not what they were to do. Merlin was still hidden away in one of the buildings and no one quite knew what to do next.

Arthur, his retinue recovered around him, marched onto the parade ground. "You will stop!" he shouted once more, and this time he signaled for the remaining horsemen to turn the pointed lances toward the mob. The mood of the crowd turned uglier still, but they retreated at the sharpened points. Their momentum had carried them this far and then broken like a cracked pot.

In the lull, I took the chance to take an accounting of the fracas. Arthur's hopes of a bloodless confrontation were at an end. At the center of the conflict, at the shattered gate, four or five bodies lay scattered, their limbs askew, their eyes lifeless and dead. Another dozen or so moaned with wounds that would certainly take their lives. For a moment I was back at Tribuit and the river Glein. But these weren't Saxon carcasses, rotting in the sun for my pleasure. These were my countrymen; I saw nothing to smile at in this skirmish.

From around the edge of a building came Merlin, with a troop of horse soldiers at his side. He held a brightly painted staff in one hand and wore his finest robes, marked with half moons and stars, a concoction of his in celebration of his study of the stars.

"I am Merlin!"

More than my shouts, Arthur's whistles, or the horsemen's lances, that proclamation quelled the uprising. I was proud of Merlin in that moment. Faced by dozens of his countrymen who wished him dead, he maintained his dignity and strength. Spreading wide his arms, he raised them and then flung them toward the ground. His robes whooshed as they ripped the air and then a pair of explosions erupted on either side of him and flashes of grayish-yellow light encompassed him.

Though shrouded in the smoke, he never quite disappeared from view. It was a simple trick I had seen him do a thousand times before to entertain little children, using some sulfur concoction. But in the tension of the moment, he accomplished his purpose well. Clubs were dropped and combatants took a handful of steps back.

"I submit myself to the crowd's mercy."

And this neither the crowd nor Arthur expected.

An unsettled buzz rippled through the crowd. No one knew how to react.

"Ambrosius's justice fills not their empty gullets, and so I'll offer myself up to preserve the Rigotamos and the rule of his land," Merlin explained in a dry, cracked voice. *Not to mention Arthur's claim to that exalted seat*, I thought.

"So you admit to doing these things?" exclaimed a youth near Vortimer.

Merlin shook his head. "Some say it must be so. I say it isn't."

"Then the Rigotamos must judge. 'Tis he who is the chief magistrate." A bobbing of heads ruffled the assemblage.

Ambrosius took another step into the center of the crowd, moving, in the crowd's mind at least, back into control. "Malgwyn," he began, as if nothing had interrupted us a few minutes before, "have you finished your searchings?"

"No, my lord. I have not. The road is twisted."

"My Lord Rigotamos," Lord Vortimer shouted, offering himself into the fray finally, "in a lesser king's hands this could just be a ploy until sufficient time had passed to let the favored suspect go to his freedom. Malgwyn's investigations could take years. And we have yet the election of a new Rigotamos. A time limit must be set. A day of reckoning marked."

"That is fair and just," Ambrosius agreed, his head hanging as he conjured a suitable time.

"Tomorrow," Merlin shouted into the silence. "Tomorrow at the fall of the sun, if Malgwyn has not cleared my name to everyone's satisfaction, then I'll offer myself for the Rigotamos's punishment. I will offer my head for the lives of the two women."

"Merlin, what if Malgwyn fails?" Vortimer sneered.

Merlin gave me a wink. He crossed the parade ground and stood next to Ambrosius. "I have faith in Malgwyn, and should it not prove well placed, I have enough belief in your rule to subject myself to it." He leaned closer. "You must set the terms for this or your enemies will use it against you. And should it become necessary, you must cleave my head from my shoulders."

"So let it be then," Ambrosius began, stepping into the affair. "We will meet here at nightfall tomorrow evening and hear Malgwyn's report. Should he find to everyone's satisfaction that Merlin is innocent, then he will go free. Should his proof point to another, that one will be arrested and condemned. Should his proof aim the axe at Merlin's head then so be it." And Arthur would never win enough votes to wear the robes of a Rigotamos.

"What if Malgwyn doesn't return?" some sly wag threw into the silence.

Ambrosius's face grew rigid. "Then both Malgwyn and Merlin will pay for the lives of the poor women. What say you, Elvain?" He turned to the now-bloodied man, holding a rag on his head.

"I can only speak for myself, but this is just. The Rigotamos is fair."

My head reeled at the pronouncement. But then I saw that Ambrosius had no choice. Only a truly barbaric double execution would satisfy this crowd and prove his commitment to justice above all. He turned to me as people began carrying off the wounded from the fray. "Serve us all well, old friend."

"Malgwyn!" Kay was shouting from across the parade field. "Come!"

Four men were carrying one of Ambrosius's bodyguards away. I noticed a peculiar sight and rushed to him. Two arrows had pierced his back. Yet I had seen none of the mob with bows. Aye, it was not much of a fighting weapon in those days.

But arrows are aimed. A battle-axe can wound four men by accident. An archer seeks out a target. Was Ambrosius such a target, and if so, by whom? His death would certainly throw the election of a new king into chaos. Assassination was nothing new, but for whose benefit? And who had committed such an act? Could Vortimer be that bold? Suddenly, Eleonore's warnings of a conspiracy cast her murder in a different light.

"Malgwyn!" Kay's voice broke me from my reverie.

I ran to where he stood, in an alcove of the stockade wall and the barracks, near where I had seen that new brood of Druids as the fighting began. A body lay on the ground and a small bundle of a child sat beside it, rocking on its heels.

I snatched up Mariam and hugged her to my chest, checking quickly for a wound but finding none, and then shielding her from harm. My eyes were wide and I felt fear as I've never known it, spinning around, seeking danger, until a hand caught me.

"Malgwyn!" Somewhere in the cries, I recognized Kay's voice. I felt his hand on my shoulder. "Malgwyn." He took Mariam from me. "It's Cuneglas, Malgwyn." I saw then it was my brother's body laid on the ground.

My one hand flew to my hair, and I pulled a great gob of it out. A howl of rage ripped from my throat and overwhelmed the mourning cries of family and friends as they searched through the dozen or so wounded. Kay held me about my waist as Bedevere rolled the body over. Cuneglas, my brother, had a ghastly wound across his temple.

Fury flushed my cheeks, rising rapidly from my chest. "How?"

Mariam, a strangely odd look on her face, turned her face

toward me. "I slipped out of the house. To see what was happening. When people started fighting, I hid here in the shadows. Father came for me and called to me. I started toward him and some men attacked him." She spoke as if reciting a lesson at school. "He's dead, isn't he?"

His breathing was shallow but still visible. I had seen this before. He could be dying or just knocked senseless. It might take days for the truth to be known.

"No, he lives still." Kneeling, I brushed her hair lightly with my hand. I looked up to find Arthur, Bedevere, Kay, and Paderic standing over me. "It is no one's fault," I told myself and them at the same time. "The soldiers thought he was but one of the mob. They had no way of knowing."

Arthur nodded and clapped a hand on my shoulder. "The Christ will protect and keep him, Malgwyn."

"But 'twas not one of the soldiers," a tiny voice said.

We all turned to Mariam. " 'Twas a group of men who attacked him. Not soldiers. They came from the shadows just there," she said, pointing into the darkness, near where I had seen a group of the Druids standing. That struck me as strange, but when I looked about, I saw that the Druids had disappeared.

A wave of fury rose again and I shrugged off Arthur's hand. "Kay, see her safe home," I commanded, my vision clouded with the fog of anger.

"Malgwyn!" Arthur warned. "Focus. Keep your eye on the hawk, my friend. 'Tis just what they would want, you squandering your time tracking down your brother's attackers instead of putting a stop to this insurrection."

I shook his hand off. "End this game, Arthur. You are lord of this castle. Use your men to quell this rebellion. I have other work to do. Cuneglas deserves justice and he shall have it!"

Suddenly he grabbed me by the neck and drew my face to within inches of his. The sweat of the skirmish still lay heavily on his skin and his eyes bored into me like a witch's. "No, Malgwyn. I cannot do that and you know it. I believe in truth and justice; I believe in the Christ. If I forsake all that, I become no better than Vortimer, Lauhiir, and the rest, just another scheming, conniving thief with no concern for honor, just for the heft of my purse. And I condemn our people to another generation of poverty, death, and destruction. When a man believes in something strongly enough, he does what he must to keep that belief alive. Believe with me, Malgwyn. Stronger forces are at work here. Eleonore and Nyfain were simply tools used in constructing something greater and more dangerous. Discover what happened to Eleonore and you will discover who is behind this. Then Eleonore and Nyfain can be avenged."

I took a breath then, the first I had taken since he began to speak. With that swelling breath I took control of my anger. At best, Cuneglas was an innocent victim of this intrigue. At worst, his was an attack calculated to confuse and hinder me. Either way, staying my course was the only sure way of saving us all.

I watched as Mariam sat next to the motionless Cuneglas, stroking his brow.

This was my brother, a brother who had taken my job as Mariam's father. I could not just leave him. Accolon could wait until I had done all I could for Cuneglas.

I motioned to two soldiers. "Go quickly and bring Merlin to Cuneglas's house."

They turned to Arthur for his agreement. He frowned for a long second, but then nodded. He understood. With curt gestures, Arthur directed that Cuneglas be taken to his home.

Coroticus, who had walked up, sent a soldier to Ynys-witrin for his best healers and their herbs and potions.

"Malgwyn." Arthur called me to the side. "The wound is deep. He may not survive the night."

"That is why I will stay here until his crisis has passed."

"But Malgwyn, too much is at stake," he urged softly.

"You are right, Arthur." I pointed at Mariam, following stolidly behind the soldiers bearing Cuneglas. "The only father that little girl has known may be dying, and I will do all I can to keep him alive and comfort her. He has been her father, and she should not lose him like this. Not without my trying all that I can."

Arthur's shoulders sagged.

"Fear not, my lord. I have sworn to serve you and the Rigotamos. That I will do. I will tell you this—nothing is as it seems. I need time, time for reflection to work my way through this maze."

In the pause that followed, Bedevere went about the chore of clearing the parade field, setting soldiers to repairing the stockade walls. Hooking my one thumb in my belt, I felt the scrap of parchment the maiden had slipped to me during dinner. I pulled it out and unfolded it; reading the words sent my eyes flying open. *My dear, sweet cousin.* I would owe her a great debt before this affair was finished. Though Guinevere's family was wealthier, and we saw each other but seldom while growing up, our common status as embarrassments forged a strong bond between us in later years. And I had become very protective of her.

But, true to my cause, I sat with Cuneglas into the early hours of the next morning. One of the healers from Ynys-witrin, with Merlin's help, packed healing herbs in the gash across my brother's temple. They dressed the wound with linen cut into fine strips. After a few hours, once Cuneglas's breathing became steady but shallow, Merlin turned to me.

"Only time will tell now, Malgwyn. We have done all we can."

I nodded. Accolon was still missing, but I knew how to find him. The note told me that. And I was beginning to see that his guilt might be more a chimera than reality. That Guinevere was involved spoke as loudly of his innocence as anything. Though I did not doubt the message, I had to wonder at the journey it took to get to me. A sudden rush of fear swept over me. Until then, Guinevere had just been a minor part of this affair. Now, she seemed to hold information that could make her a target. Arthur appeared in the door, there to check on Cuneglas I was sure.

"My lord!" I called to Arthur. "My lord, a horse and Kay to accompany me! I beg you. We may yet meet tomorrow's deadline."

Ygerne rushed to my side. She took my good arm and squeezed it. "Malgwyn, be careful. I wish no more harm to fall on this family."

"I'm doing all I can. The soldier Accolon holds the key and if Kay and I can find him, my family will be safe." It took a second until I saw the smile on Kay's face.

"What?"

"You said 'my family.'"

Arthur strode forward and plucked up Mariam from the floor. "This family is now part of my household, and will be protected as such." His beard brushed the top of Mariam's head, tickling her eyes as she looked up at the giant holding her. "I'll see to them," he said. "Take what you need."

"You are Lord Arthur," Mariam said, her tone as curious as ever.

Even in that scene of carnage and death, with Cuneglas a few feet away, Arthur found a smile to give her. "You may call me 'Uncle,'" he answered, bringing looks of confusion and consternation to Kay and the other soldiers.

I laughed, but said nothing as a soldier arrived with my mount. For I knew that he was right, or at least nearly so, and it was something I had never thought to hear him say. Perhaps Guinevere was not without hope after all.

CHAPTER EIGHT

I held the horse's reins tight in my hand as we negotiated the twisting, turning lane from Arthur's castle toward Ynys-witrin. The trees were not in full leaf, but so big they were that no moonlight filtered through the canopy. Narrow as the trail became at times, I navigated it by memory. Occasionally, the lane broke from the trees and bordered some farmer's field, his round, thatched hut dark and lonely in the night. The breeze clothed us with the damp, rich odor of fresh-turned earth.

Behind me, I could hear the clank and rattle of Kay's mail coat and the horse's rig, the sound of leather stretching. He tried to question me about our journey and Arthur's strange pronouncement, but I waved him off, my mind too filled with thoughts. Parts of the affair were becoming clearer; other parts were still shrouded in the cloak of confusion.

Finally, we reached the ivy-entangled stone fence across the stream from the road, opposite the giant oak and blackberry vines where I had once watched Arthur in a private moment. Beyond the stream, beyond the fence, we could see the faint yellow pinpoint of a burning candle. I jerked the reins around and walked my mount across the stream, its hooves clattering against the stone-strewn bed.

Near the gate, a voice emerged, low and soft. "Malgwyn? Who is with you?"

"Only Kay. Have no fear."

"Bring your horses inside the gate. The stable is behind the house. They will be safe and well hidden there."

We dismounted and Kay led his horse even with mine. "Malgwyn, why are we here?"

I held a finger to my lips. "All will be clear in a moment." I handed him the reins of my horse and motioned toward the stable.

My eyes saw better with the light from the candle spilling into the yard. The woman before me, as tall as me with hair of the same color, but as comely as I was haggard and beaten, reached out her hand and stroked my face softly, just once, and then her hand fell to my new tunic. "You look better without a jug of wine in hand, cousin."

"And you are more beautiful than when I last saw you, Guinevere. Arthur's choice in women knows no peer."

Her home was modestly furnished, which surprised me not. She had never been one for fancy possessions. Indeed, at one time in her life she owned nothing. We went inside, where we took stock of each other as Kay made his way to join us.

Guinevere had changed into a solid maroon dress, belted at the waist, and her long hair flowed around her shoulders as she poured us a cup of watered wine. I told her of Cuneglas. Arthur had sent her away with an escort when the feasting was disturbed.

"So, Mariam stands to lose her father." Guinevere dropped her head. "And yet not her father."

I waved the comment away. "That matters little now. Tell me. What news have you of Accolon?" For that was what her note had suggested.

She lifted her head. "After we spoke this morning, I came here for a dress for the feasting. He came to me after the midday, frightened, looking for a place to hide. I told him of a place, not too far from here, where a waterfall hides a cave. Do you know it?"

"Aye," I confirmed. "I know the place. 'Twas a good choice. What has he to tell? What had him so frightened? Did he speak of Nyfain?"

Guinevere nodded. "Aye, of her and of Eleonore too." And she stopped right there.

I remembered why she drove me crazy as a child. She loved to draw a tale out and stretch my patience at the same time. It was a true gift that she had. "Are you going to tell me what he said of them?"

"Would you not rather hear it from him?"

Even Kay was shaking his head and rattling his chain mail.

I smiled as politely as I could. "Yes, but if you tell me now, then I will have time to ponder the questions I need to ask."

She rose and fetched the jug, moving to fill mine and Kay's cups. But Kay's gloved hand blocked her as she started filling mine. I gave him as black a look as I could, but withdrew my cup from her reach.

"All right, then. Accolon saw Eleonore at the gate on the Via Caedes last eve. He was returning from looking for Nyfain, he said. She was not at home."

"No, she was drinking with Ambrosius in the great hall. I suspected as much, and he had told me about seeing Eleonore before."

"Aye, but he did not tell you that he knew who she was with."

"He said the man was hooded and in the shadows."

"He would not tell me either," Guinevere admitted, "but he was afraid of what he saw. He said he knew who it was, but he would only trust you with the knowledge. They were arguing. He did tell me that. He spoke to the man and then went to report for duty. But he saw them again, and of this he told you nothing. While on his rounds, he spied this man and Eleonore headed toward the watchtower. Later still, he saw the man again, without Eleonore, running back to the watchtower with Lauhiir, Mordred, and some other men."

"But that is it, Malgwyn!" Kay exploded. "These people with Lauhiir must have been the men that killed Eleonore."

"And whoever it was," I agreed, "his mere name was enough to frighten Accolon. Vortimer?"

"I cannot see Vortimer engaging in such wanton killing."

"Not himself, perhaps, but he would have directed it be done to advance his cause. It's in his blood."

"Accolon said that he would tell only you, Malgwyn. After Eleonore was found, he became worried—he would not say why. When his duty ended, he drank for some time with the other soldiers at the barracks and then went back to his house for rest, but in rummaging around for food, he found Nyfain already murdered in a storage shed. Later, someone, he did not say who, told him of Nyfain's death, told him to keep silent or he would end his days the same way. Accolon became truly

scared then. He believes that he is being made to be the murderer of both women. And he fears that those behind it are too
powerful for him to overcome."

"Why came he to you?"

Guinevere's face narrowed with a smile filled with a woman's
intrigues. "Accolon was one of the first of Arthur's men. He rode
with him to the monastery many times to see me. When Accolon
fell in love with Arthur's sister, I counseled him against it, told
him that Morgan's mind was as changeable as the winter wind
and that Arthur could never be made to approve the match.

"But he loved her so much that he could not help but press
his suit with Arthur. He did not know that it was Morgan herself who rejected him. He blamed Arthur, and for a time he
became one of Arthur's enemies. He soon returned to Arthur's
side, but by then he was a drunkard and embittered, and the
only place Arthur could trust him was with the common sol-
diery."

I nodded. "Accolon was always too sensitive a man. He lets
too many little things bother him." It took a moment, but then
I realized that Kay and Guinevere were smiling at me.

"I can think of another with that affliction," Kay said.

A grunt was all I would give them in reply. "Come, we must
hurry. It will take us some time to get to Accolon and we have
little to spare."

"Why is that?" Guinevere asked.

"Ambrosius was forced to set Merlin for execution at sunset tomorrow if Malgwyn has not navigated this maze. The
consilium will vote immediately after and Arthur will not be its
choice.

"And if I do not appear, solution or not, I will be hunted
down and my own head taken as well."

"How could Ambrosius—"

I raised my hand to stop her. "Don't blame Ambrosius. He was maneuvered into it. Partly by Vortimer, partly by Merlin, and partly by his own blasted beliefs." I grew angry again at this lack of will to use their power and rose to my feet. "No, he bears more blame than the others. With one flick of his hand, he could have stopped this. They could have turned their cavalry on the mob, declared Arthur as Rigotamos, and freed Merlin."

"And what would he have lost in the process?" my cousin asked. "How would you feel as one of the mob to see his men turned loose on you? How would you have felt to see him free a man you believe is a murderer? After all his talk of truth and justice and the Christ? You would feel betrayed, just as they feel right now. Arthur can be no other than what he is. And that is a good man about to be lifted high in a brutal time. He is not perfect, but he is a good man."

Her hand stroked my jaw through my thick beard. "As are you, my cousin. You are a good man, and that is why Arthur came to you. You blame him for this." I winced as her gentle fingers touched the empty sleeve.

"No, I blame him for not letting me die on the battlefield! For leaving me half a man, unable to do anything of value. Who wants a one-armed man?"

"Is it that he kept you alive with one arm, or your memories of how that missing arm left your body, Smiling Malgwyn?" The voice was so soft that for a moment I thought it was Guinevere. But no, it was Kay.

I responded gruffly. "This talk does not further our task. Our answers lie with Accolon. No matter who is at fault, we have work to do. Come, Kay. Some miles yet lie before us. The forest covers near ten hides of land."

"No," Guinevere said. "You must wait until first light. The way to the waterfall is through deep forest and you will not find your way without torches. With torches you would be easily found if anyone searches for you."

"No! We must go tonight. We will travel without torches," I argued.

"And have our horses trip on tree roots and break our necks?" Kay asked. "Guinevere is right, Malgwyn. A few hours' rest will not harm us. You got little sleep last night and it has been a long day. Accolon is safe where he is, at least for a few more hours."

The flickering lights of the candles played shadows off the walls. The fire in her hearth had burned down to a few glowing embers. They were right. I knew they were right. The day had been long, too long, and I had not yet paused to mourn my brother's injury. Poor Cuneglas! His wounding was of my making as surely as I would take my next breath.

Cuneglas! What would Ygerne do now? Times were hard for women, even harder now with all the uncertainty in the land. I pushed the thoughts away. Later, there would be time for such considerations. "No," I said finally. "Whoever is behind this evil will not sleep and neither will we. They have stayed ahead of us by half a man's step, and if we pause now, they will gain a full step or maybe more. Whatever the dangers, we must go forward tonight. We cannot chance waiting until first light."

"Perhaps you are right," Guinevere conceded. "I would have no one else die in this affair. Behind my house is a path that leads near unto the waterfalls. I will draw you a map that will bring you hard upon it. Kay, look to my food. Wrap up some bread and cheese and take it with you. You will need it, or if not you, then Accolon will be hungry."

While she fetched a scrap of parchment and a quill, Kay cast about for something to wrap the cheese and bread in. I tossed him a piece of cloth from my pouch, and he filled it with food from the storage pit. I noticed that Arthur made certain she did not go hungry. In moments, she handed me the map, neatly drawn and labeled. I looked at her oddly.

"You know how to write?"

She laughed. "You are not the only educated one of our family, Malgwyn. Yes, one of the brothers from Ynys-witrin taught me, though I fear he had in mind teaching me other things. But he was fat and bald."

"You are, in your own way, cousin, worse than me. And I am bad."

Guinevere took me in her arms then and hugged me as she did when we were children. "I have little family, Malgwyn. I know you must do this thing, but I would have you be careful. I could scarce stand to lose you too."

I said nothing, but hugged her all the tighter. Finally, reluctantly, letting her go, I turned to Kay. "Are you prepared?"

"Aye."

"Then let us go."

And we slipped into the night.

"Stand for a moment, Kay. Let your eyes become familiar with the bit of moonlight. We will step slowly from the light back into the forest; our eyes will then grow accustomed."

"We will not ride?"

"No," I answered. "The distance is three or four hours by horse, but in this forest, 'twould take us twice as long. The horses' hooves will not be as sure as our own feet, and our eyes will learn to see in the dark better than if we were on horse-back."

"And the map, Guinevere's map? How shall we see it? I brought no pitch—"

"Be calm, Kay. I brought some pitch and a flint. But we shall only light it when we must." We all usually carried a fire-making tool, some pitch, a flint, some tinder. That I had remembered mine that morning was a miracle born of pure chance. Though I knew the way to Accolon's hiding place myself, my cousin had marked some twists and turns that would shorten our journey by the flight of three strong arrows.

As we stepped off into the forest behind Guinevere's house, I sucked in the heavy scent of old trees. The air was damp and heavy here, almost oppressively heavy. Common sense told me that we were unlikely to be followed, at least for a while. Even if our enemy had set their men on us when we left the castle, they would wait and see our next move. We had slipped out the back door, and if anyone were watching for us, they would listen for the horses as sign of our departure. I knew Vortimer too well, and his men had always been lazy. They had been instructed, perhaps, to merely watch us, knowing that we would be seeking Accolon and wishing to find him for the same reason. Far better for them to let Kay and I do their work for them.

After an hour or more, they would become suspicious. They knew that our journey must be completed quickly, and they would be smart enough to draw the same conclusion that I had. A chill ran down my back.

Guinevere!

Vortimer's men would storm the house. They would threaten Guinevere! Perhaps hurt her. Perhaps even kill her.

I stopped and spun around, but Kay's hand caught me. "I know what you are thinking, Malgwyn. But your cousin is a strong and brave woman. Vortimer's men know enough to realize that they would draw Arthur's wrath if they harmed her. And, though they would never admit it, they fear Arthur more than Vortimer."

He was right. Protecting Guinevere must take second place to finding Accolon. I moved forward, almost tripping on an exposed tree root and then regaining my balance.

"Be careful, Malgwyn. We have had reports of *latrunculii* in these woods."

Bandits. Though Arthur had brought much order to the land, this was still a place of few laws and the thieves held sway in many hidden places. And bandits were only one of the hazards. The forests were almost always filled with those who had escaped Saxon massacres, starving, frightened. Runaway slaves were common too, but they posed less of a danger. "They will only bother us if we bother them."

"As black as this path is, we may bother them without knowing it."

"Then pray to the Christ that our steps stay sure and true. For the bandits will not only steal our possessions, they will steal our lives as well."

After an hour, the screech owls ceased protesting our presence, and our eyes began making out the inky images of yew trees and rocks against the grayish fog of the night. Our forests were filled with old, gnarled trees, more ancient it seemed than the earth itself. Without the owls' cries, the forest was quiet, very quiet. I took this as an ominous sign. In the far distance, around some pond or marsh, I could hear the muffled sounds of croaking frogs. At least they were not disturbed.

I wished that we had Merlin with us. He knew this forest better than anyone. He gathered his herbs and mushrooms for his potions here and knew every blade of grass, every tree, and every rock.

Poor Merlin! He had been one of the wisest men I knew and the best judge of men's true minds. Aye, that was one reason they called him a sorcerer. We knew of him as far away as the little village I called home. He seemed able to divine a man's heart and know his intentions from a single look. Some called it magic, but I knew that it was experience. Merlin had seen much in his life.

Once, around the campfire, Merlin had told me some of his history. He was born at Carmarthen, but he never knew his father. He believed, as his mother told him, that he was sired by a Roman soldier, an officer of high rank, in the days just before the legions retired from our island. But the officer returned to his family in Rome and left his woman and the son they had begotten behind. We had such families among us; I had played with such youths when I was young.

Merlin's mother had died when he was but a child, and he had lived by his wits until, one day, he met a man named Lailoken, a bard and prophet of the lands of the Picts. Some said that Lailoken was a madman, but no one yet living knew anything but tales. Even in our village his name was spoken in whispers. When Merlin came to this part of the story, he would only smile faintly and say that it was from this man that he learned much of what he knew. Of his youth, that was all he told, though I suspected there was much left unsaid. There would always be a nagging concern for me, bred around those old campfires where older men told tales of this Lailoken.

A nightingale sang somewhere nearby, breaking me from my reverie. It was getting a late start to its night's rest, I mused. Before us lay the forest, Accolon, and, I prayed, answers.

On we pushed, stopping twice to check Guinevere's map, a few moments only each time and then well hidden behind one of the giant trees that filled this ancient wood. Kay used his cloak to further block the flame, a small flame that seemed in that murky darkness as a giant and brilliantly lit torch.

The map was accurate, and I wondered at my cousin's ability to draw such a thing. Her marks showed a stream crossing our path just to the south. If we followed the stream east, it would take us to a larger stream and following that would then take us to the waterfall. But the distance was still far and I was more tired than I would admit.

Almost no breeze stirred beneath the trees. I turned to caution Kay to step carefully and stay away from the small limbs littering the forest floor. As I did so, I stepped on one, cracking it in half, the sound shattering the quiet.

"Malgwyn!" Kay hissed. "Be silent! If anyone else is abroad in these woods, they will surely hear you."

I wanted to laugh, but our quest was too serious and I could not summon up the humor.

Just then I felt the point of a knife pushing my tunic.

And I smelled sour, honey-mead breath.

CHAPTER NINE

"What have we here, Llynfann?" the voice in my ear said aloud.

I started to twist my head to look, but the knife point dug deeper.

"Ahh, ahh, ah. Just you be telling us what you are doing, skulking about in these woods at night."

Latrunculii. Bandits. They had found us, almost before we had begun.

"Mine is a pretty one, Padern. How about yours?"

"He has a pretty tunic. I think it should fit me very well. Should we kill them here?"

"No. Let us take them back to the others. They will enjoy the sport."

Any other time, Kay and I would have made short work of the rogues, but they had so taken us by surprise that we were helpless. To resist now meant the death of one or both of us. Alive, we still had a chance. The pair relieved us of our weapons and bound Kay's hands with strips of dirty wool. As for me, they took a long leather strap and bound my arm to my side, pulling it so tight, the leather bit into my skin.

"Come," one barked.

We stumbled and staggered off the trail and headed north into the densest part of the forest. I became convinced that our captors could see in the dark, and behind me I could hear Kay curse as he tripped on a rock.

"Malgwyn," Kay whispered. "We have no time to spare."

"We had better take time, my old friend. Or else we will surely have no time."

On we went, through the dark forest, tripping on tree roots and banging our shins on rocks as we fell. Our captors would laugh and yank us back to our feet, and on we would go. After an eternity, we rounded a mass of fallen trees and walked into the daylight, or so it seemed.

Their camp was cleverly fashioned. What appeared in the dark to be a mass of fallen, tangled trees was in reality a log enclosure, camouflaged on three sides and built against a rock wall. I saw immediately that it could hold thirty or forty men and their belongings.

The heat of their fire, banked against and reflected off the rocks, kept the hideaway warm against the cool April breeze. An ingenious layer of branches and leaves high above the fire dispersed the smoke to keep it from being seen afar. A wanderer might smell the smoke and never suspect its origin.

A crowd of about fifteen men sat in a half-circle around the fire. Some gnawed on chicken legs, tossing them to the side as they finished stripping the meat. A pig roasted on a spit. They were dressed in an assortment of dirty woad-dyed tunics, but all had daggers at their belt, and their beards reached down to their waists. One man was better dressed than the others. His tunic looked to be linen, dyed red.

I laughed at the sight.

The bandits looked up to see who had disturbed their feast. Kay looked at me as if I were mad.

The man of the red tunic, apparently the leader, squinted into the night, away from the glare of the fire. A grin broke across his face. "What have we here?"

"We found them in the forest, Gareth. I know we should have killed them, but you said always to be on the lookout for a one-armed man."

The one called Gareth rose and sauntered over to us. "Well, he does sport but one arm. Aye, but the man I knew would never dress so fine as this," he said, tugging at my tunic. "Yet I do think I have smelled him before."

"That is your own rotten breath, you rogue," I answered without a hint of fear in my voice.

"Malgwyn!" Kay hissed.

Our captors laughed heartily. "You spent too much time with the brothers at Ynys-witrin, Malgwyn. There was a time when you did not talk so pretty." The pressure of the knife point subsided.

"And you once did not smell as bold."

Gareth was older than the rest, with gray streaking his hair and a long, thick beard.

"You know these men?" Kay asked.

"Aye. This one," and I nodded toward Gareth, "stands before you only because of me. And," I said to the now grinning bandit, "that is something you should hasten to remember."

"How come you dressed as a noble, Malgwyn? The last I heard of you, you were drinking and whoring yourself to death."

" 'Twas true. But now I am in the service of Lord Arthur." I bowed as nobly as my bindings allowed.

At Gareth's signal his men untied us. He motioned for us to sit on logs situated around the fire. "You would be Caius, he that is known as Kay."

Kay nodded. "You know much of us."

"We make it our business to know all that we can," Gareth grumped. "We survive by our wits, not by our station in life." The old bandit eyed me with a grin. "And you, Malgwyn, you serve Arthur? If my memory has not abandoned me, you once hated him with a passion."

"Time changes many things, Gareth."

"Malgwyn! Who is this?" Kay was confused and rightly so.

"At Ynys-witrin, as I recovered from my wound, a young initiate, a boy, was found foully abused and murdered. Gareth here picked the same night to raid the abbot's stores. He was taken, and he was blamed for the boy's death."

"But Malgwyn," Gareth continued for me, "was not satisfied with that. He poked and prodded about the edges until he proved that one of the brothers of the monastery had done the foul deed. In the confusion that followed, the door to the chamber where I was held was opened and I gained my freedom." He stopped and smiled at me. "I have often wondered who unlocked that door."

I shrugged. "'Twas an old door. I am sure that the wood was rotten."

"I had heard of this from Arthur," Kay said, "but I knew not the names of those involved."

"Coroticus put about that Gareth had, in truth, done the deed. Since he was but a thief anyway, and had escaped, he could hardly argue. That allowed Coroticus to shield the monastery from the scandal."

"And what of the brother?"

"He hung himself in his cell, I am told."

"You sound as though you do not believe it," Kay said.

"I believe only what I can prove to be so," I responded, which was not quite the truth. I had no need to prove what happened to Brother Aneirin. He did not hang himself. I strangled him to death myself in a fight after I confronted him with his guilt. Aneirin was a vile and despicable creature, and it took no great effort to string him up from one of the hut's support beams. Coroticus believed that claiming he took his own life was a better lesson for the other brothers. And he wished no blame attached to me.

Gareth did not believe me, and neither did Kay, but none of that mattered. Only our mission mattered. "Are you here because of the killings at Castellum Arturius?"

"Aye. Arthur has charged me with sorting them out."

"You seek Accolon then, at the cave?"

"You know of this?"

Gareth grinned. "Nothing happens in this forest that I do not know of. We saw him sneaking through. He was drunk and made much noise. Since he had nothing we wanted, we let him pass. The only puzzle is why he hides in the cave. And why the others seek him."

"Others?" Kay queried.

"A band of men has been scouring the countryside for him, but quietly, as if they want no one to know of their presence."

Vortimer, I thought. It must be Vortimer, but why would he be quiet? He stood to gain the most if Arthur were discredited. Gareth's men would have more to fear from a troop of Vortimer's allies than they from him. I myself had set patrols out looking for the wayward soldier.

"Who are they?"

"Men who are careful not to be seen, but even the most careful of men leave signs behind. They have not yet found Accolon, and because we did not understand what was going on, we made certain that they did not."

"You act with a decency I would not expect from a thief," Kay said.

"He was not always a thief," I countered. "Just as I was not always a one-armed scribe. But that is a tale for another day. Can you provide us with a guide, Gareth?"

"Stay with us and eat from our table, Malgwyn. No need for hurry. Accolon is going nowhere."

"Not so. I must find Accolon and take him back to Arthur's castle by the setting sun on tomorrow's eve; the matter must be resolved or lives will be lost." I quickly explained about Merlin.

"As you will." Plucking bits of greasy yellow chicken dangling from his gray-flecked beard, he motioned to the one called Llynfann. "This one will take you. He knows the forest better than anyone."

"My thanks, Gareth. Your help will not go unnoticed." Kay was so sincere.

The old rogue winked at me and reached to tear another chicken leg from a roasting bird. "Tell Arthur that if he is a good fellow, I might let him pretend to be king for a while."

With Kay rendered speechless, I grabbed his arm and shoved him away from the fire and after Llynfann into the darkness.

"Be silent, lads," the bandit said. "There are but two hours until the dawning. Our danger heightens in daylight. Gareth spoke truly about the band. They move more as warriors than latrunculii."

"And how is that?" I asked, hearing a bullfrog in the distance and knowing a small pool of water was nearby. These woods were full of little streams and pools and the frogs were plentiful around them. Sometimes, the pools resided in little glens with thick grass, almost little gardens tucked away in the great forest. Other times they were dark and dank, a part of the black forest, often fed by underground springs running underfoot.

"They lack the stealth that a bandit must have. This bunch is crafty; they are woodsmen, but they make too much noise when they move. For many days they made their camp just over there." He pointed into the blackness of the forest.

"Keep going," I commanded, mystified by this latest revelation. For many days? "Time is wasting."

Tiny slivers of light were filtering through the trees by the time we reached the glen of the waterfall. They cast a strange, greenish glow in the awakening forest. The chirp of birds brightened the half-light of dawn as we crept through the underbrush, small branches poking me in the face.

The rush of the falling water could be heard loudly, drowning out the birds. The falls, majestic and tall, pointed slightly to our left, and the continuing stream lay at the foot of a sheer gray rock wall. To our far right, I could see a faint path winding through some large rocks, broken by patches of grass and weeds, the hill rising slowly toward the top of the falls. A fog lay across the glen in between, but even through that silky, silver haze, I could see that it was a beautiful place indeed.

"To get to the cave, you must go up the path to the top of the hill and then look for a break in the rocks, no wider than a man's waist," Llynfann told us. "That is the start of the path down to the cave. It is steep and narrow. The gods make your journey a safe one." He turned to disappear into the woods, but Kay caught him by the arm.

"You are not coming with us?"

The little thief grinned. " 'Tis daylight. I have to lighten the loads of travelers." With that, he was gone, on the run now, and the forest swallowed him up.

Kay started forward, across the glen to the little knoll, but I caught him by the shoulder and held him. My chest burned from breathing the heavy, damp air. My days of drinking and wenching were costing me dearly.

"If this wandering band is looking for Accolon too, we must be careful not to lead them there. Let us follow the line of the trees and scout the area before we dash headlong for the path."

We crept just inside the forest, in the still shadows of breaking morn. All was quiet across the glade. I studied the glen, glistening with the silver of morning dew. That's when I saw it, or rather saw them—eight trails wriggling like snakes through the sheen of dew.

I shivered but not from the chill of the air. My friend the bandit had been wrong. The wandering band of which Gareth spoke had found Accolon and encircled him. By this time they might have even killed him. I needed to know.

I touched Kay on the arm and held a finger to my lips as he turned. I nodded my head toward the trails, then pointed upward.

Quickly and quietly, Kay slipped his sword from his belt, handed it to me, and mounted a nearby tree. The only sounds he made were those of his leather belt and boots scraping against tree bark.

I waited nervously while Kay surveyed the glen from his perch. A slight breeze slipped out of the southwest and stirred the treetops. Too much mist and water clouded the entrance to the cave, and I could not see if Accolon was still there. If he was smart and watchful, he would secrete himself in some way where he could see but not be seen.

As the minutes passed, I grew impatient. An idea was growing in my head, but I needed to know how the land lay and if Kay could see Accolon. If Accolon knew what I believed he did, then he had the key to the entire matter locked inside his memories. For if those chasing him weren't of the castle, then he might truly be innocent, or at least he had knowledge they feared he would divulge.

"There are indeed eight."

I nearly jumped. Kay had descended and caught me lost in my thoughts. I knew then that I was tired from the night before, too tired to be traipsing about the forest and hunting murderers.

"They lie in a line and carry bows."

"Bows? They are not soldiers. No one uses bows but for hunting." An image flashed in my head, and I remembered the arrow in the soldier's back.

Kay shrugged. "They say in Gaul that the Saxons use bows in battle."

"Perhaps. I have an idea, if you are willing."

"Whatever you counsel."

I explained my plan and Kay agreed to it readily. It required more effort on his part, but he knew my strength was limited. With only a bit of sleep since Arthur threw me into this intrigue, I was finding it difficult to move. A fog, as thick as that which often blanketed our land, clouded my mind.

We separated, with Kay splitting off to our left, toward the stream, and I to the right, toward the path up to the cave. I rested while Kay moved into position. I could only pray to Arthur's God that my plan would work. Looking up toward the cave, I could just barely make out its dark, sinister presence behind the gray mist of the falls.

The seconds passed like hours, and then I heard a horrendous bellow from the far side of the glen, near unto the stream. "Accolon! Quickly, this way! My troop is just through these woods."

Almost immediately, as I waited, I saw heads pop up from the deep grass of the glen, and I heard the babble of conversation, but I was too far away to understand.

"Here, Accolon! Here!"

Kay was playing his part well, drawing Accolon's pursuers away from the cave.

With all the heads of the pursuers facing Kay, I started at a quick trot up the path to the cave.

"Now! Accolon! Come with me! My troop is through here!"

I kept an eye on the band and they moved off toward Kay's voice. I picked up my pace. In the gray/black of the cave, I could see a darker image moving about. Accolon. Trying to find out what was happening.

I was now high enough to see the mysterious band plainly, pulling away from the glen and disappearing into the forest. I strained to discern their identities, but their clothing was rough peasant gear, and I was too far away to see their faces.

As the forest swallowed them, I made it to the top of the falls and easily found the path down to the cave.

"Accolon!" I hissed, trying with all my might to make

myself heard above the roar of the water, yet praying that our foes below did not hear me as well. Squeezed between two massive rocks, I craned my head to see better into the cave.

"Malgwyn? Is that you?" His head popped around from behind the boulder.

"Aye."

"How many did you bring with you?"

"Only Kay. He is drawing off the others. Please let me come down and speak to you."

"Hurry! Quickly, before they see you."

I slipped and slid down the mist-slick rocks and nearly fell in the mud but for the arms of a very frantic Accolon. Dark circles rimmed his eyes, and they were the eyes not of a man but of a trapped animal.

"Malgwyn, the lady got my message to you?"

"Aye. You have certainly attracted a great crowd in this hideaway."

He stumbled backward and fell against the wall of the cave. "Malgwyn. I prayed that you would come. I know that we are not close, but I think we have both traveled a difficult road."

I chuckled. "That we have. What have you to tell me? Kay will lead them on a merry chase, but sooner or later, they will detect the deception. We must take you by then to the safety of the castle."

Accolon shook his head. "No, the castle is not safe for me. Indeed, there are more enemies there than here."

"How am I to protect you, Accolon? You cannot stay here. You cannot go to the castle. Where then?"

The old soldier was bleary-eyed and worn. He frowned and scratched his unruly beard. "Can you promise Arthur's protection?"

"Aye. I have Arthur's and Ambrosius's authority in this matter. You shall be safeguarded at the risk of my own life."

Furtively glancing about from side to side, he seemed torn for an answer. Finally, his shoulders slumped. "Then we will go."

"First, tell me your story that I may search for some answer."

"If we are to leave we must do it now. I trust you, Malgwyn, but I think that my knowledge of this matter is all that keeps me breathing. I will tell my story to Arthur."

My first impulse was to strike him down with a single blow. To lure me here with promises of revelation, and then deny me that which I was promised, was almost more than I could take. But he was both right and wrong. What he knew was certainly all that he owned of value, but while it might keep him breathing in some ways, that information could bring his death by others.

"Quickly, then," I decided. "Let us leave this place behind." Accolon needed no further encouragement.

Our shoes found poor purchase on the muddy path and going up took twice as long as coming down. "Kay led them away to the northwest," I said, panting, as we reached the top of the falls. "We will move south by southeast to Arthur's castle, staying away from the roads. With good fortune, we will be with Arthur before they realize they are chasing but one man."

"And if they catch Kay?"

I shrugged. "Kay knows how to deal with trouble."

"You throw your friend's life around casually, Malgwyn."

In the cool of the early morn, I turned to lecture him on the dangers that men such as we face in this life, but the gray hairs painting his beard were legion. A pair of scars, remnants of old battle wounds, marked the left side of his face, lying like wagon tracks upon his cheekbone. He needed no lessons from me.

"Much is at stake here, Accolon. This affair is about more than the killing of two women."

"I know that better than you, Malgwyn. I have followed Arthur's banner all of my life."

"If we are to preserve him, then we must do what is necessary. Kay knows this."

Despite the burning in my lungs and the weariness in my step, we started off once again.

The path we chose took us between the old Roman road and the lane from Arthur's castle to Ynys-witrin, that road known as Via Arthur. We had ten miles to cover through forests and fields, with no lanes, just mere forest and animal paths. Yet I foresaw no problems. We had the entire day, and it was but a four-hour journey even in our exhausted state. To make certain, I chose a straight path. We would allow ourselves no margin by taking a more circuitous route.

Two miles from the glen, we stopped beneath an oak tree long enough to eat some of Guinevere's food. I was ever alert to sounds of our pursuers, but it seemed that Kay was doing his job well, and safely, I hoped. The cheese was hard and cracked at the edges and the bread was stale as well, but the water was welcome and we tore at the food with our teeth.

"Tell me something of that night, Accolon."

"You would worry a sore until it bleeds," the old soldier grumbled. "We would be better served continuing our journey."

"Why did I come for you then?"

He grinned crookedly. "'Twas the only way I could be guaranteed safe passage back." The spark of humor in his eyes faded quickly. "Malgwyn, I am but an old and tired man whose life has been one of rejection and failure. But that life, no matter how miserable, is all that I have left. This knowledge is my only road back to respect, to earning the trust that Arthur placed in me by allowing me back into his service."

"But how does telling me harm your plan?"

"You are much like me, Malgwyn. We are both but shadows of what we once were. What assurance do I have that you would not kill me as soon as you have heard my tale and take Arthur's reward all for yourself?"

I clambered to my feet angrily. "What I do I do for the girl and for the truth, not for Arthur or any reward."

"I am counting on that, but in these days when treachery calls at every door, I must protect myself, even from you. Be at peace, Malgwyn. You shall know my story soon enough. And though I know not everything, I think you will, once you have my piece of the puzzle."

In truth, I could understand his suspicions. Ours was a time when a man's word was good only as far as it didn't endanger his own position. Trusting anyone was not a wise policy. Vortigern had trusted his Saxon mercenaries and watched in frustration as they turned on him. Kings of the many tribes were often assassinated by brothers and others. Such events were what made Arthur special. His love of the Christ tempered the practicality of his Roman heritage. That, as much as anything else, accounted for his appeal. But even that was not enough to bring all the Briton tribes together.

Still, too much was at stake here to accept his refusal. "What if you are killed along the journey to the castle? What then?"

The old soldier reached across and patted me on the arm. "I have weathered too many battles to die upon this road. Be at ease, Malgwyn. All will be well."

I wished with all my heart that I could taste but a bit of his confidence. "Then tell me of Nyfain. How came she to die?"

Accolon's cheeks turned red. "Those who killed Eleonore killed Nyfain too, killed her for what Eleonore might have told her.

"After duty and after you questioned me, I went to the barracks to drink and ponder over it all. After a while, I sought Nyfain at home to seek her counsel. I wanted to tell her of what happened and see what she made of it. When I arrived, she was not in our house. I searched and found her in a storage shed. She had been butchered like Eleonore. I was in a panic."

"And you ran because you were afraid that someone would blame you with both murders? But you knew that Merlin was being blamed."

"Aye. But I also knew that the old man had nothing to do with it and you would discover that truth. Nyfain was killed after Merlin was arrested. I had already spoken to you, so you knew I was one of the last people to see Eleonore alive. I was approached in the lane when I left my house. This man told me that I should keep silent or the same punishment would be visited on me as Nyfain."

"Who, Accolon? Who? A name, man! Give me a name!"

The grim soldier looked grimmer still. "I can't, Malgwyn. 'Tis the only thing of value I have left. If I give it to you, I have nothing to bargain with."

I leaped forward, my face framed in red. The quick move found my good arm pinning against Accolon's throat.

"Kill me, Malgwyn," Accolon choked out, "and you'll never get that name. Death holds no fear for a man such as me."

Breathing heavily, I released Accolon, the foul odor from his clothes filling the air. He was right. For Accolon, there was little left. I knew well how he felt.

The big warrior rubbed his throat. "You may have lost half an arm, but you are not a man I would choose to fight." A sincerity in his voice made me a little more friendly toward him. In many ways, we were much alike.

Wiping a crumb of bread from my lips, I considered his words and then wrapped our food back in its cloth. "We have miles to go. Come, let us finish this journey." I felt I had learned all he would tell me, though I yearned for more.

Accolon reached down and offered me his hand. I took it in my own, and he helped me to my feet. "You are a good man, Malgwyn. I have heard it said many times over."

I looked him straight in the eye. "Arthur did not reject you. Morgan did. It was her choice, not his."

The old warrior's head drooped in a tired nod. "I finally understood this. She was too young for me, and I would never have been happy with her."

"Then let us go see Arthur and end this current matter. I think you will rise substantially in his esteem."

The day grew warmer and warmer, hot for our land. We were both exhausted and our journey was taking far longer than I expected. Without a path, our scramble across rough ground and through dense copses of woods was slow indeed. The sun was well past its noontime perch and we had covered but four, maybe five miles, with another *schoenus*, another four miles to go, at least.

Sweat stung my eyes and dripped from my beard. My shoes were not those of a warrior and the leather was tearing. My fine new tunic was torn in a half-dozen places from thorns and low-hanging limbs. I collapsed in a copse of trees sprouting up in the middle of a rocky field.

"I must rest, Accolon. I have not a soldier's strength any longer."

"You are just fat and lazy from your wanton life."

I could not argue with him. Although I was less fat than he, I tired more easily than the old soldier. I lay and gathered my strength as he studied the land behind us. We still had some time. The ground from here to Arthur's castle was more level, less broken than that which we had covered.

"Off your lazy arse, Malgwyn!" Accolon suddenly hissed. "Your ruse has collapsed."

I pulled myself to my feet and grabbed his shoulder with my one hand. At first I saw nothing save the rock-strewn land, stretching back to the last stand of trees. Then, watching the curve of the field, I saw movement, a head bobbing. I strained to see, but only one man moved slowly, popping up and gauging the land to his front.

He did not know we were there, so close, and he was being cautious, probably so that he could return to the others quickly and alert them to our presence. But here we were, not two hundred paces away. And we had seen him before he saw us.

I scouted around swiftly. Undoubtedly the others of his band were not far behind, perhaps even in the dark line of trees behind us, just waiting for their scout to wave them forward. I cast about for a solution, thinking. "Quickly, Accolon! Help me."

Pulling a young sapling, about an inch thick, forward, I motioned for Accolon to cut it and he did. I whispered my plan to him and he quickly set to work, while I held my stick under my half-arm and sharpened one point. "Here." I nodded, pointing at my tattered tunic. "Strip some of these threads and twist them." With a jerk, he tore away a length of my linen tunic. I thought of Ygerne and how pleased she had been with it. With any luck, it would save our lives.

While Accolon worked, I found a good place to execute my plan near the opening of the copse. A deer path was worn between a pair of trees, standing some ten feet apart. The trees and bushes of the copse were thicker on either side, and I had no doubt that our pursuer would choose the deer path. And that would be his misfortune.

Soon, Accolon joined me and we prepared our surprise. "Now," I told him, "you go on across to the far woods."

"And what of you?"

"I want to have a little talk with your pursuer. It will be a few moments before his companions realize that something has happened. Fear not. I will join you."

"I do not like this, Malgwyn."

"Neither do I, but I need to know something of these men."

"Then I shall stay. Tell me what you must know."

I grabbed his shoulder. "You worry too much. Go. Wait for me in the edge of the trees."

He frowned but then set off at a swift gait across the field. I secreted myself in the mass of brush and thorns to one side of the path and waited.

And waited.

A thorn found its way to my earlobe, but I knew by then that there was nothing I could do. Nothing. Even then, I could hear the rogue's shoes scraping on the ground.

I chanced a look. I succeeded in driving the thorn deeper into my earlobe, but I caught enough of a glimpse to see him rise to a half-crouch. As I suspected, he was heading straight to the deer path, eager to ferret out any sign of our passage.

Tears flowed from my eyes, but I had to watch and see if our trap worked. I gripped my dagger in anticipation.

White spots appeared before my eyes, but I could not tell if they were from fatigue or dread.

My breathing, already ragged, grew shallower.

It happened quickly, too quickly. The sound resembled a bird flapping its wings angrily, trying to free itself from the leaves of a tree. At least until the point of our little spear slammed into our pursuer's abdomen with a sickening, wet thud.

I leaped out of my hiding place and pounced on the intruder, my one hand snaring his throat. "Make not a sound," I whispered, looking swiftly at the piece of wood protruding from his belly. "You are a dead man already." The blood, looking almost black against his rough tunic, began a small stream down his side, and he looked at me with questioning eyes.

"Who are you?" I asked.

The question had no need for an answer. I knew by looking, but when he spoke all doubt vanished. Accolon's pursuers were Saxons. He was a grizzled warrior, not unlike Accolon in his own way. But where we wore beards down to our chests, Saxons went clean shaven except for long, drooping mustaches. This one had the mustache plus an oily topknot. I had heard of such things in Gaul but had seen no Saxons here in our lands arrayed thus.

"How many?" I asked in the Saxon language. I knew little of it, but enough, I thought, to handle this.

Wild-eyed, he shook his head. Did that mean he understood me not?

"How many?" I repeated.

He shook his head again and this time he spat in my face. A rage took my soul and wrapped it in a fog. I grabbed the end of the stick, aimed it upward, and thrust it into his heart. With a gurgle and a scarlet froth from his mouth, his eyes grew blank.

No surprise marked his death face, only hatred. I had given what he expected, and rather than satisfaction at yet another Saxon death, I felt embarrassment.

Searching his clothing, I found nothing of use to us but a dagger. I shoved that into my belt, pushed myself to my feet, and ran through the small copse of trees and out the other side. His companions would not wait long for his signal before sending another to check on him. I had seen all I needed to see. My thoughts darted to Kay, and I prayed to Arthur's God for his safety. He had followed me blindly, but willingly, and such was the mark of a friend.

As I bolted across the opening, I could see Accolon waiting at the edge of the trees. I stumbled, breathless, past him and would have fallen, but he snagged my tunic.

"Malgwyn! Who are they?"

"Saxons."

Accolon's face screwed up in obvious confusion. "Saxons? Why would Saxons seek me?"

"I do not know, but there is one less to deal with."

"You killed him." It was a statement, not a question.

"He served his purpose," I said sharply, courting no further discussion on that matter.

He seemed to understand and nodded. "I thought 'twould be some of Tristan's men."

"Why thought you that?"

" 'Twas one of them that warned me. This surprises you?"

I thought for a moment. Vortimer had practically confessed by threatening me at the feasting. Tristan was always eager to follow after Vortimer. And his vote would be cast for Vortimer. In truth, only a few of the lords were committed, the majority for Arthur, but some, like David and Lauhiir, were liable to shift with the wind. If Arthur's credibility suffered, Vortimer could count yet more votes. Vortimer would always be hampered by his father's memory. That he would use someone else for his dirty work made sense. But, I said simply, "Nothing in this matter surprises me any longer.

"Come, we have more miles to cover and little time. The Saxon's friends will be coming swiftly, and they will not be as easy to kill now. Whatever you know is of importance to them, enough to risk their lives."

Accolon frowned. "I cannot put the two together. I cannot see how one is tied with the same knot as the other."

I opened my mouth to speak, but thought better of it. His caution in this matter was sound. Too many others had seen their lives ended by not keeping an eye to the horizon for treachery.

"We must go. Talk only delays our journey."

"You still think I should trust you with my knowledge."

"What I think is not important, Accolon. We have no time for this. The castle lies too far away."

Accolon nodded. "You place great faith in me. It has been many seasons since anyone has done that. I shall not forget it."

"You are wrong, Accolon. Arthur placed great faith in you by taking you back after you allied yourself with his enemies."

"Aye, you are right. I—" His eyes narrowed at some distant object. I turned to look just as the buzz of an angry bee swept past my ear.

A slicing, like that of a knife in raw meat, sounded, followed by a grunt. I turned back to Accolon as surprise registered in his widening eyes.

A spray of blood splattered me as I watched skin flap open from Accolon's skull.

CHAPTER TEN

Two more bees buzzed, followed by the dull thuds of arrow in flesh.

Accolon, his mouth still open, fell with an arrow protruding from his right arm and another from his chest.

I dropped to the ground as more arrows split the air above. With my one arm, I wrapped it around Accolon's chest, beneath the arrow, and kicking hard with my feet, dragged his heavy body behind the tree.

"Malgwyn . . ." In his throat I heard that rattle that accompanies death.

"Be still. Your head is bleeding and your arm is pierced. But 'tis the arrow in your chest that worries me."

"Do not pull it out," he croaked.

"I know." Arrows in the chest, if removed without hot iron to cauterize the wound (and sometimes even when that was available), could cause the victim to strangle on their own blood. I knew not why, but I knew that I had seen men die quickly from chest wounds that bubbled blood. Leaving the arrow in would give us some time.

"I . . ." and then Accolon passed out, his eyes closing. I knew not if it were the loss of blood or the blow to his head.

They were still approaching. I knew that. And I knew that staying there would condemn us both to death. Without thinking about the consequences, I crouched, pulled Accolon's body over my shoulder, steadied him with my stump of an arm and ran as fast as my old legs would carry us.

The arrows flicked past us, and I braced for the one that would hit me, yet never broke my stride. Ahead, across open ground, I could see a patch of dark woods. I needed no advisers to tell me that our pursuers would be right behind me, but if I could get us into the forest, I could find sanctuary where I could watch for them crossing the open ground. At least I could use the chance to evaluate our situation.

"Malgwyn! You cannot carry me. I am too much a burden," Accolon croaked.

Gulping in air, I plunged into the open and prayed for the gods to watch over us.

The ground was rough, uneven, and I stumbled under Accolon's weight, my one arm pinning him to my shoulder. My knees ached with each stride.

Arrows sped past me.

Fifty yards.

Twenty yards.

My knees began to buckle under my burden.

Ten yards.

Arrows buzzed in swarms, it seemed. One nicked my shoulder, stinging, but I knew instinctively that it was not serious.

Five yards.

I could feel the coolness of the shaded trees in front of me.

The sickening thwack of arrow in flesh sent a shudder through me, and the force of the blow sent me falling forward and Accolon tumbling from his perch on my shoulder. We rolled into the protection of the trees and a depression, a little hollow.

I quickly scrambled forward, pulling myself with my one arm and peering into the clearing behind us. In the distance, shadows dashed among the trees. I counted five. Two seemed to hold bows. The use of bows continued to bother me. They simply were not used for war in our lands, only for hunting. In all my battles I had never fought against Saxon archers, though I had heard of their use in Gaul. Another small clue that I knew must mean something, but I could not tell exactly what.

"Malgwyn—" Accolon was stirring from his faint.

Our pursuers were moving slowly, cautiously, toward us. I had a little time and so I turned back to Accolon. The last arrow had hit his shoulder at an angle from the rear. To lay him on his back, I had to remove it. "Accolon—"

"No, Malgwyn." He waved a weak hand at me. "You must leave me. I am already dying."

"Be quiet." I took the arrow and pulled it quickly. Accolon seemed not to notice. The point bothered me. It was of an odd shape, made of iron, without barbs intended to take hold of the flesh. I broke the arrow and stored the point in my pouch.

"I cannot leave you."

"You . . . must." The words came hard for him. The rattle in his throat and the pink on his lips told the tale better than any bard.

"No. We must make this journey together."

He grabbed the stump of my arm with a strength I could not believe he possessed. "Go, Malgwyn. I will tell you what you need to know, but I am done." And then as quickly as he grasped me, he released me, the effort almost visibly draining his strength.

I stared at the wrinkled face, his long, brown hair lying wet and matted across his cheek and lips. He was indeed done. Other lives now took precedence.

"Who, Accolon? Who did you see with the maid?"

His eyes opened slowly. I knew he was almost gone, and I willed him to live a little longer.

"Tell . . . Arthur I tried . . ."

"I will. I will. Now, who?"

"As I passed . . . the alcove, I saw the maid . . . arguing with a man. I did not see his face; he wore . . . a hood. But I knew . . . the voice." A fit of bloody coughing racked his body. I feared he would die before he finished.

"Accolon! Please, stay with me!"

" 'Twas . . . Tristan . . . son of Mark. Go, now, Malgwyn!"

"But later, Accolon, later, did you see him with anyone about the watchtower?"

His eyes began to glaze, but he managed a nod. "Yes, he and others."

"What others?"

". . . and Dru . . . and . . ." The effort became too much, and he closed his eyes.

I gave him the Saxon's dagger, and though I knew not if he could hear me, I whispered, "If you live, take one more with you. God grant you mercy. You have earned my respect and thanks."

I left him there, bleeding from three wounds and from his mouth. Accolon was not a bad man. He had walked down a dangerous path, but he had returned to an honorable lane at the end. Without looking back, I threaded my way through the trees, heading south by southeast toward Arthur's castle. The sun was past the meridian, and the time I had left was slipping like water through my fingers.

The forest swallowed poor Accolon up behind me. I thought I heard the anguished sounds of the Saxons as they found their fellow, but it was probably just the wind singing through the trees. Forcing my feet forward, I tried to focus on my next steps. If I did not move quickly, both Merlin and I would die.

As branches whipped into my face, I considered what Accolon had told me. Tristan was the man who was last seen with Eleonore, most probably the man she had left Cuneglas's house to see.

Tristan! I knew that he desired the girl. His suit was well known among the people of the castle. I understood Accolon's hesitation. For a common soldier to accuse a lord, the son of an ally, of murder was a serious matter. That Tristan was affrighted had been obvious at the feasting the night before. I had believed that he was treating with the Saxons, but perhaps it was the guilt of his actions that made him nervous. Perhaps it was both. Still, I did not see Tristan as the architect of this maze. Perhaps he killed the girl in a fit of passion, but he did not compound his error by cold-bloodedly murdering Nyfain. No, Accolon had been right. That act showed the hand of a shrewder, more evil mind than the boy had.

The murder was one affair. The attempt to hide it and cast a shadow of guilt on first Merlin and then Accolon was another, pointing to a cool and calculating nature, which I did not believe that Lord Tristan possessed.

Yet Vortimer came from a bloodline that would do these

things. Now it all made sense. Eleonore, Nyfain, talk of conspiracy and assassination. More was at stake than the death of two
women and old Merlin's head. Somehow, Eleonore had stumbled
on a conspiracy to kill Ambrosius. She had been killed to keep
her mouth shut, and Nyfain had been killed for what Eleonore
might have told her. But who were the conspirators?

I tried to think back to that first night, the last time I had
seen Nyfain. She had been with Ambrosius, but then he drifted
off to sleep and she fell in with some other soldiers. I remembered seeing Mordred for he had left with her, but I could not
recall who else had been there. One thing was certain. Arthur's
hope of becoming Rigotamos, indeed the hopes of all Britannia, rested on my sorting out this affair.

While I thought, I ran, faster than I believed possible. My
knees ached. My head pounded from lack of sleep and little
food. But I knew that as soon as the other Saxons found their
countryman and then found Accolon, they would come after
me in earnest. Beyond the young leaves of the trees, I saw that
the afternoon continued to wane. We had wasted much time. I
hoped upon hope that Kay was alive, and that he had realized
that our ploy had not worked. If so, he would soon be upon us
and instead of four against one, it would be four against two. I
tried to put the matter from my mind and concentrated on
reaching my destination without breaking my neck.

The woods before me extended nearly to the edge of the
settlements around the castle, but they were thick woods with
few paths. I thought more than once of heading south and
striking out for the Via Arthur, but if Vortimer was at the head
of the conspiracy, as I was certain he was, then he would have
soldiers loyal to him watching the lanes. So I stayed to the trees
and kept watch over my shoulder.

After some time, I stopped near a group of stones lying carelessly on top of each other on a steep slope. Their facings showed that someone long ago had dressed them. I studied the green slope, covered with trees save where the stones had tumbled down the hill many years before. Grass and ivy had covered the hollow created by the old landslide. I did not think they could find me in this forest, but I had been wrong many times in the last three days. From Merlin to Accolon to Tristan, the trail of guilt had led me on a crooked path. I had even suspected Kay for a time.

Glancing at the sky, I judged that I had about two hours until sunset and but another hour to travel. Even so, I had the river Cam to cross. Cam was an old and sacred river, a reason, the bards sang, that Arthur's castle was first settled back many, many generations before.

My plan was to strike the river north of the town, where the land sloped gently down to the water. The river could be forded there, but not farther upstream, where the bank rose more than fifty feet above the water. From the crossing to the castle was a ten-minute run only.

Climbing up into the fallen rocks, I hid behind one of the larger ones, with the ivy-covered hollow at my back. My stomach growled, and I took a moment to pull the crusty bread and hard cheese out of my pouch. Fortunately, my teeth were not as worn as those of many of my fellows; I drank too much of my food to bother my teeth much. And oh, how I wished for a drink of mead, or watered wine, or anything that would cut through this exhaustion.

I could offer Arthur a new murderer, but it was not one he would welcome. The crowd would demand Vortimer's death, and Arthur could not afford to execute Vortimer. He was too powerful. My evidence would have to be secure, and Vortimer was smart enough to keep himself at arm's length. He had others to do his bidding. To alienate one of the most powerful members of the consilium was not a wise move at any time. So, if I were to save Merlin—and Arthur, for that matter—young Tristan would have to be sacrificed. Yet that would alienate Mark. Every time I seemed to have an answer, another difficulty emerged from the gloom.

And then there were the Saxons. That Tristan seemed uncommonly close to our mortal enemies surprised me not. Vortimer would do anything to put Ambrosius's crown on his own brow, including directing his minions to treat with the Saxons. Tristan was young and might fall under Vortimer's spell. At the very least, Tristan could be manipulated, and Vortimer was a master at manipulation, evidenced by his way with the common folk.

But Saxons chasing Accolon, far away from their lands among the Cantii? Had Arthur not told me of Saxons encroaching on our lands again, I would have thought it impossible. Arthur's forces defeated the Saxons at the City of the Legion, driving them back to the eastern shores of our island. The victory had sealed Arthur's right to the crown, among the lesser lords such as Mark, and the sounds of battle had temporarily ceased. We had signed no peace treaty, and we knew the Saxon vermin had withdrawn from the war only to lick their wounds and plan more treachery. All who knew them understood that the warfare was not over; we were just enjoying a lull in the fighting.

Much was at stake here. For a small band of Saxons to run through our lands openly showed how precarious Arthur's position was. It also indicated the laxity of our borders. I resolved to tell Arthur to investigate the conduct of his patrols. Only someone manipulating them could allow Saxons such free rein, especially in the region between Arthur's castle and Ynys-witrin.

My hate for them did not fill my soul as it once did. I was surprised at my reaction to killing the Saxon in the copse of trees. That he deserved to die, I knew. But I felt no pleasure at his death. Rather, almost a regret at the taking of a life. I shook my head to clear it and took another bite of the hard cheese.

Tristan had argued with Eleonore, but, if Accolon were to be believed, they returned to the town together, went to the watchtower. Then Accolon saw Tristan, and others, coming from the watchtower. Paderic, I recalled, had also seen men drunk, coming down the lane from the tower. An idea was forming, a guess at what may have happened. I struggled to my feet and went to store away the cheese, but so lost was I in my thoughts that I dropped the chunk.

Sighing, I bent over to retrieve it—just as a Saxon spear split the air where my head had been.

I stared at the spear, quivering in the earth, and then I snatched it up and ran. With only a dagger tucked in my belt and the spear in hand, I had no choice. I could do little with either one, but taking one of their weapons was better than doing nothing at all. Glancing back over my shoulder, I saw six of them scrambling down the massive stones. One of them carried a bow; the others but one brandished spears. They wore their hair greased back and braided.

Seeing their numbers, I could only conclude that Kay had failed. The question remained: Did Kay know that he had failed, or was he still trying to lead them on a merry chase? The answer was of little use to me at that moment.

I headed for the banks of the river Cam and the shallow

water I knew I could ford. Swimming was not easy for a one-armed man. Though the slowness in crossing the river would give my pursuers a chance to catch up to me, I knew I would do neither Merlin nor Arthur nor anyone any good if I drowned in the sacred river.

Drained as I was, I found new energy when I emerged from the forest and saw the river across a small field, holding not much more than three hides of land, red and yellow with little flowers in first bloom. Once across the river, I was but a mile or less from the castle, and even less than that from Arthur's cavalry encampment.

The sun was setting off to my right, beyond the western lands, and shadows were lengthening. If I could make it across the river, I could reach the castle in time.

Then I heard a Saxon war cry.

But not behind me. Not in the forest. To the west. To my right.

I very nearly stopped in my tracks, but instinct urged me on as I looked across the western reach of the field and saw them. Ten Saxon warriors, bellowing their familiar cry and rushing across the field in a line.

Laughing wearily, I did the only thing I could and turned east, where I did not want to go. As I shifted direction, I glanced back at the trees and saw that those Saxons were angling down into a line as well. They were pinching me in, herding me like a goat into the one place I wished to avoid—a fifty-foot cliff over a deep part of the river.

My heart sank at that prospect, but I could not give up, not to a pack of Saxon dogs. They had taken too much of my life from me. They would not win this race.

I was dizzy from the run and from exhaustion, stumbling

now, falling. But each time I pulled myself up and forced my legs to cover yet more ground.

Sweat stung my eyes and made it difficult to see. I could smell the beginning of spring and wondered at the fates that put me in this place and time.

My half-arm ached.

My stomach was beginning to heave.

Checking over both shoulders, I saw that I would reach the height before they caught me. But that was as good as being caught. I could never swim across the river with only one good arm.

I was approaching the top of the bluff, the river flowing gently many feet below. I turned and took aim at one of the approaching Saxons, heaving the spear with all my might.

It struck him in mid-chest, lifting him off the ground and flinging him backward in a splash of blood. But the others kept coming.

And then I did something very strange, and even as I write this, I cannot explain it.

I jumped.

Any chance, no matter how slim, is better than no chance at all. If I had stood and faced off the Saxons, they would have surely killed me and more than merely my own life would have been forfeit.

As the air roared in my ears and the water rushed up to greet me, I heard an odd sound from above. The sound of horses neighing and hooves on packed earth. But I had no time to wonder at its meaning before I slapped against the water, broke its surface, and was swallowed by its depths.

The world became one of cold green water and silvery bubbles. My descent slowed the deeper I went, but then I felt a firmness, ground, beneath my feet. I bent my knees and let my weight carry me another foot farther, and then I sprang up with all my might, thrusting toward the surface. I might lack for an arm, but I had two strong legs.

When I broke surface, I found myself in the chilly shadow of the great stone bluff, and as far away from the far shore as I could get. In my confusion beneath the water, I had headed back toward the northern shore.

My legs ached and my arm ached, but I did the only thing I could. I struck out for the southern bank and prayed that I would make it before the Saxons could ford the river to block me.

Kicking with my legs and stroking with my one good arm, I began to feel hope again. I was moving swiftly. Tucking my head in, I stroked harder and felt the surge of my extra effort.

Just a little farther, I thought.

Suddenly I realized that I was moving more sideways than straight ahead.

I had forgotten the waterfall to the west.

And then I found myself flying over the edge.

CHAPTER ELEVEN

Two thoughts passed through my mind as I hurtled down the falls. First, I knew that Merlin was as good as dead. Second, I knew that by the time I had gathered my wits about me, the Saxons would be upon me. That is, if I survived the fall. As if to remind me of my danger, my shoulder slammed into some rocks and threw me out a bit from the churning waters, but I landed belly first just where the current was strongest, thereby pulling me down into a whirlpool.

Once again, I was surrounded by the murky jade water, brightened only by the churning bubbles. But this time I did not search for a quick trip to the surface. I considered not fighting the pull of the undertow, carrying me deeper into the bottomless pool beneath the falls. Within minutes, the pain that ate at my heart, the belief that I had failed in life, would all be washed away in sweet oblivion. It was an enticing prospect.

But then I thought of Mariam. If I surrendered to the lure of death, I would never have the chance to set affairs straight with her. I would never see my child's smile again.

I kicked my legs and climbed with all my might through

the suddenly cruel water, knowing that the Saxons waited
above, but knowing too that I could not just give up.

The undertow was strong, almost too strong, but I fought
it with a strength that surprised me.

Then the surface, painted by the light of a dying sun, appeared before me and I fought harder.

A dark, curling snake hit the surface, and it drifted down
toward me.

A rope.

Grabbing it with my one hand, I pulled hard, not knowing
who was at the other end and not really caring. Life brought op-
portunities. Death brought nothing. The rope tightened and
pulled me up and up.

I broke the surface sputtering and choking, but I was glad
to see the sun.

"We have caught an exceedingly large fish, Lord Kay," a familiar voice said as the rope continued to pull me to the river-
bank, the south bank.

Gareth and his band of latrunculii appeared. Kay was astride
his horse, the other end of my rope looped over the horse's neck.
Beside him stood my horse, pawing and scratching at the earth.

As I climbed up the muddy bank, I noticed that Kay's cheek
held a long, bloody cut. Gareth's men likewise were bloodied,
and their tunics showed the rips and tears of battle.

"The Saxons?" I managed to choke out.

"Feeding the dogs upon the bluff," Gareth said with a
harsh smile.

"How?" I struggled to a sitting position and fingered my
pouch in amazement that it had stayed around my neck through
all.

"When they learned our deception," Kay answered, "they disappeared. I knew that you and Accolon were in danger, so I ran like the wind back to Gareth's camp. He volunteered to help. We continued on foot to catch up with you, and Gareth sent one of his men to go for our horses. We arrived just as you leaped from the bluff. Those you left for us gave a good accounting of themselves."

I nodded, absently reaching inside the pouch and feeling for the cheese. I pulled the soaked hunk out, wrapped in a bit of torn cloth like that from Eleonore's hand. As I looked at it, clutched between my fingers, the truth dawned on me. The whole affair became clear. Quickly I rummaged through the pouch and retrieved the bit of cloth I found with Eleonore. I knew then what Accolon had tried to tell me.

"To the castle!" I shouted. "We have no time to spare." Two of the bandits helped me to my feet, and I staggered to the side of my horse.

"What is the matter, Malgwyn? We have yet minutes of daylight," Kay argued.

"Assassination! Druids!"

"Go quickly, Kay," Gareth urged. "He may be a madman, but he is a madman I trust."

I reached deep within myself and found enough strength to mount the horse, but my reserves were fast dwindling. The red ball of the sun was nearing the western edge of the sky. "No more time for talk. They will be preparing Merlin for beheading even now. And the Rigotamos is in danger as well."

"From whom?" Kay queried.

"From the consilium," I answered, bringing a frown to my friend's face.

"Go, Malgwyn!" Gareth counseled.

"Your debt to me is discharged, Gareth. You owe me nothing now."

Gareth's eyes twinkled in that devilish way of his. "My debt to you will never be discharged. You believed in a bandit when no one else would. Now, finish your task."

I nodded, jerked the reins, and aimed my horse for Arthur's castle, just a mile or so in the distance. As I kicked his flanks, the old horse laid his ears back and lunged forward.

Our route took us across an open field and intersected with the Via Arthur. Once there, we raced our sweating horses down the muddy trail.

As we approached the cavalry encampment, three soldiers moved to block the lane, until they recognized Kay and we flew past them, their mouths hanging agape. Before us, the Via Caedes near my hut began its ascent to the northeastern gate. One lane split off and skirted the base of the fort, headed around to the main gate near Arthur's hall. I ignored it and headed straight for the smaller gate. I did not believe we had the time for the extra distance. The last journey along the Via Caedes had begun.

In seconds, the horses' hooves were clattering on the cobblestone lane, and while most horsemen would dismount to lead their mounts through the double gate, we rode straight through, nearly scraping our heads on the rampart above.

The streets were ominously quiet. No one walked in the smaller lanes. Arthur's castle seemed deserted. Until we neared the square in front of Arthur's hall.

Two hundred people were crowded around the edges of the square. The merchants' booths were closed, and some children had found perches on their thatched roofs. Others were astraddle their father's shoulders. It seemed like a festival day. We had seen precious few of those in recent years.

A late afternoon cloud, dark and thick, had brought a sprinkle of rain to the castle as the cobbles were slick and the air clean, empty of even the tanners' stench. Since Arthur's hall rose on the high point of the plateau, I could look over the heads of the onlookers from atop my horse. "Kay!" I shouted.

Arthur, his long brown hair blowing in the breeze, stood in front of his hall, wearing his finest tunic, with a slave boy holding his shield and sword behind him. Off to the side stood Vortimer and his men, Tristan, who looked ill, Mordred, and a group of country folk. Ambrosius and his guard stood slightly apart. He looked old, much older than I had ever seen him. This affair had weighed heavily on him. Kneeling before Arthur was Merlin, dressed normally now, no patterned robe in sight. The last sliver of the sun was settling in the western sky. Arthur's face was as grim as I had ever seen it, his teeth clenched and lips stretched into a thin line. It took no prophet to see what Arthur intended. If Merlin was to be executed, he would be the one to do it. He would burden no other man with this chore.

As I watched, transfixed by the sight, Arthur held his hand out and the young slave placed the sword in his hand. He gripped it tightly and took a step closer to Merlin's bowed head, even as the crowd's heads turned to see us arrive.

"My lord! Not so quickly with the sword!"

Two slaves rushed up to take our horses, one slipping and falling on the wet cobblestones as he met us, and we dismounted in unison. Arthur took a step back from Merlin. That spurred Vortimer, Mordred, and Lauhiir to step forward.

"My lord, I demand—" shouted an enraged Vortimer, fighting to turn a tide only he could see roiling against him.

"Hold your tongue, Lord Vortimer!" Arthur ordered, holding up a gloved hand and releasing a giant sigh. "Malgwyn has arrived and deserves his say." He closed the distance between us and laid his hand on my shoulder. "You look worse than the day I delivered you to Ynys-witrin," he said softly. "I hope you bring good news."

"The path was filled with enemies of all shapes, Arthur, but I think I have divined a solution that will settle the affair and keep Merlin's head on his shoulders." I hoped to do more than that, but I did not want to throw my dice askew.

"But did you find the truth?"

"What is the truth, Arthur, but the story most favored by those in power?"

"Malgwyn!" he hissed.

"Be calm, my lord. Yes, I found the truth."

"Why do you wait, Lord Arthur?" Mordred was on the attack, stalking across the cobbles, his sword clanging at his belt. "Does Malgwyn wish to talk himself out of his own death?"

As for Vortimer, he stood apart from his lieutenant. He had a confused look on his face, a look that confused me also. I thought to see a cool, calculating expression. But this was definitely not one of those.

"Kill them both!" came the cry.

"My lord!" I shouted, my voice echoing off the buildings. I stepped away from Kay and moved to the center of the square. In a corner I glimpsed Ygerne and her children, including Mariam. I looked down at my torn, mud-streaked tunic, new just the day before, and I was certain my wet hair was knotted and tangled. I thought of how embarrassed I had been before at my appearance, but I felt no embarrassment at that moment. Before, it had been my own laziness that caused my filth. On this day, I wore my ragged clothes with pride at how they were earned. This was my one chance. "Is this what you came for?" I shouted with a strength I did not feel. "To see a killing? I thought it was to see justice done. More is in these deeds than can be seen by normal eyes."

They stopped their screams at that, and the taunting voices turned to low rumbles.

"What more can there be?" Lauhiir asked, his eyes narrowing. "Two women are dead by the old man's hand."

" 'Tis simple, my lord. The tale is one of treachery and treason."

This last sent the crowd rumbling even louder, and I listened as the word *treason* circulated through the mob.

"If an old man's deviltry is treason, then I suppose you are right." Vortimer was speaking slowly, cautiously. He did not know what I had discovered. He did not know how to respond.

I walked in a wide circle, and Vortimer followed me. The smell of the wet cobblestones stung my nostrils as I rounded the opening. My eyes searched the crowd until they found their quarry. Of course they would be here. They had much at stake. And they were easy to pick out from the crowd, but there were too few.

"My Lord Arthur," I began. "Master Merlin is innocent of these crimes."

"Such is easy to say, Malgwyn," Mordred challenged.

"And just as easy to prove."

The people were listening to me now. No rumbles crowded the air.

"The woman Nyfain had not been dead but a few hours when I found her body. Merlin was already securely locked away at the barracks. He could not have killed her."

"But he is a sorcerer!" a voice insisted. I recognized it as El-vain, from the night before.

"It would take more than sorcery for him to kill her from the barracks, bound to a post."

"And what of Eleonore?" Vortimer prodded. " 'Twas his knife by her body. 'Twas in front of his hut that she was found."

I nodded agreeably, keeping my eyes focused on my quarry, continuing my circle around the crowd. "All of that is true. But all is not as it seems. She was not killed in front of the hut, but elsewhere and moved there."

One of Lauhiir's men snorted.

"Her body was ripped nearly in half, yet there was little blood on the cobblestones in the lane where she lay. I found where the blood had dripped from her body as she was moved from beneath the watchtower. That is where she was murdered, my lord," I reported to Arthur.

"How come you to know this, Malgwyn?"

I noticed that Vortimer and his men had grown quiet. "There were great gouts of blood on the ground beneath the tower. And I found where her head had been bashed against one of the posts. Her hair and blood were on the post.

"They laid her on the ground and then cut her open and took her heart. The sole intent of their actions was to lay blame at Merlin's feet and turn the people against Arthur and the Rig-otamos."

"They? They? Who is this 'they'?" Mordred would not surrender easily.

I turned and smiled at him. "It was a mystery to me until I found the soldier Accolon."

For the first time in our acquaintance, I saw fear in Mordred's beady eyes. He swiped a drop of sweat from his forehead. "And where is Accolon? If he has information important to this affair, he should present it himself."

Murmurs of agreement floated through the crowd.

"I agree. But unfortunately, Accolon was killed as we tried to reach Arthur's castle."

"Very convenient," Lauhiir replied, a hint of confidence returning to his voice. "So, you will attempt to pin the blame of this matter on some poor soul with a broken brooch of a witness?"

I had reached the place where I wanted to be. Spinning around swiftly, I surprised Lauhiir, and he backed into the open square a step or two.

"No, my Lord Lauhiir, not on some poor soul. When I first searched dear Eleonore's body, I found something clutched in her hand." I paused and looked straight at Kay, half winking my eyes in a gesture I hoped he would recognize, and then I looked at Arthur and smiled. "That something was this," and I pulled the piece of torn cloth from my pouch. Taking three quick steps, I snatched up the hand of one of the hooded Druids. "And I believe it fits in this hole."

A gasp circled the crowd. The robe I displayed had a snatch of cloth torn from it, exactly the size and shape of the piece I found with Eleonore. My quarry was so surprised that he did not react at first.

"The Druids!" a voice wailed.

"But Druids only kill for sacrifice!" argued Elvain.

As quickly as my one arm would allow, I yanked the hood

back from the man's head, exposing an oily topknot. "But these are not Druid priests! These are Saxon spies!" As he spun away from me, his robes flew open and the point of a sword slipped into view.

"He has a sword!" the chant went round the square. Druids did not touch weapons, except for sacrifice. Such a weapon meant only one thing. They were not Druids. I had spoken the truth.

"Arrest them!" Arthur cried, sending half a dozen soldiers rushing forward.

Even as Arthur shouted, I searched for the others. I looked swiftly about the square, not at the crowd but at the roofs. It took but a second.

"Assassins, my lord! The Rigotamos! Look!"

I spoke just as a hooded figure launched an arrow at Ambrosius. What happened next, I could never have predicted.

Two men lunged in front of Ambrosius to protect him. For his part, the Rigotamos did not shrink from my warning, but held his back straight and stood his ground.

One man was a half-step farther away and a half-step slower to react. But in this footrace, second place did not mean just losing; it meant losing the place of honor—the right to take an arrow aimed at the Rigotamos.

No sooner had the first arrow sunk into that barrel chest than a second whistled through the air. Vortimer sacrificed himself to save the Rigotamos. The world seemed to tilt, and I felt dizzy. Everything I had reckoned about Eleonore's and Nyfain's deaths hinged on Vortimer being behind it. Once I knew Saxons were involved, Vortimer, through his stepmother, had the perfect link.

But even as my world spun, I acted. I grabbed an old Roman

short sword, a *gladius* dangling from my horse, and hurled it with all the strength my left arm could muster.

It caught the false Druid in the stomach, slightly off center. He tumbled from his perch and slammed into the ground with a thud.

I saw movement in the crowd. "My lord! Look to your flanks!"

Two more Druids rushed Ambrosius across the square, daggers drawn. Arthur bounded to meet them. He took the first one with a slash that split him nearly in half, sending huge gouts of blood spraying across the square. Arthur spun and thrust his blade into the second up to its hilt as Bedevere and Kay reached him. They formed a semicircle around Ambrosius, a barrier to further assaults.

Almost as a second thought, it seemed, Lauhiir and Mordred joined them.

All notions of executing Merlin had fled and the crowd bubbled excitedly.

A fourth Druid, on the edge of the crowd, had his arms pinned by some helpful citizens. Soon, every Druid in the crowd had been grabbed and held. I dismounted and strode across the square. When I reached the first Druid held, I studied his robes and jerked back his hood. He wore the same greasy topknot as that of the Saxon in the grove.

"It is well known that Druids do not touch weapons," I shouted to the crowd. "These too are Saxons!"

He spat in my face. Kay and Arthur moved toward me, but with my one good arm I waved them off and wiped my face. "Your days of spitting in our faces is fast coming to an end." As I spoke, men were carrying Vortimer, his chest holding the two arrows of the false Druids, out of the action. Ambrosius shrugged off his bodyguard.

"Malgwyn!

Across the crowd Druids were subdued by citizens, all Druids. "Stop! 'Tis only the ones in the dark robes that bear us ill will!" I noted with interest that Mordred's and Lauhiir's men were also spreading through the crowd.

But Mordred beat them to the target, drawing his sword and lunging at the one I held. "Kill the Saxon vermin!" he cried.

I swear by the ancient gods that he meant to thrust his sword through us both, but I released the Saxon and stepped back quickly. Mordred would have impaled only him, but our false Druid spun away faster than Mordred could lunge, dashing to a corner of the square.

My eyes grew as large as boulders as the Saxon snatched Mariam away from Ygerne and pressed a dagger to her throat. Kay and I strode forward to attack him.

"Not another step," the man shouted in our tongue, heavily accented as his words were.

Two other Saxons, swords drawn, quickly closed on him, and silence reigned across the square.

Ygerne seemed frozen with her arms outstretched, reaching for dear Mariam.

"If any harm comes to us, the child dies."

Still no one spoke.

"What is it you want?" Arthur asked.

"Horses and safe passage to the nearest Saxon settlement."

They were brazen, I gave them that. Dressed as Druids they had stalked our lanes for days, murdered two women, subverted

Ambrosius's authority, and now they demanded free passage or my daughter's life.

I had cast her away; now I was deathly afraid of losing her forever.

But she was unusually calm in the Saxon's arms. She looked at him with that penetrating gaze of hers. She was her mother arisen from the grave. As if sensing her disfavor, the Saxon pressed the dagger point harder at her throat and stepped back away from me.

"You may as well surrender," Mariam told him as we all looked on in amazement. "Father will not let you harm me."

My face grew pale and clammy. My hand shook. "Why do you call me that?" I croaked.

"Mother told me this morning that it was time. She said it was time that I accepted you as my father and time that I knew that you did love me, but I think I knew it all along. She said you were just afraid."

I stood before her, my one hand reaching out to her, the fingers trembling. To save her, I had to let the murderers go. To capture the murderers, I must sacrifice my daughter. I looked to Arthur, and he smiled oddly, as if to say the decision was mine.

"Take me. Leave the child." It was a sad response to so dreadful a situation, but I knew nothing else to do without endangering Mariam.

The Saxon who held her knew his advantage, and he was not going to relinquish it. Mariam was his guarantee of safe passage. An old one-armed man was worth but little for his purposes.

"Never!" He spat on the ground.

"Horses!" Arthur snapped.

I could not allow them to leave the square with Mariam. I glanced around, but all the people had drawn back. Arthur still stood in front of his hall. Merlin was now standing next to him. Kay was at my side; Bedevere stood between Arthur and the Saxons. Mordred clung to the edge of the crowd, but of his men I saw naught. Vortimer's blood spread brightly across the square. That worried me, but I could not concern myself with it now.

Arthur and Merlin moved closer to the Saxons as two soldiers brought three horses clomping into the square.

Ygerne was frantic. Tears ran down her cheeks as she watched the Saxon's dagger point push against Mariam's neck.

I looked quickly about, trying to see some way to prevent them from leaving. Mariam's life was forfeit if they made good their escape. They would kill her without hesitation once they were clear of the fort. This much I knew.

The soldiers brought the horses up as two of the Saxons watched them, their swords at the ready. I had developed a very deep hatred for the Saxon holding Mariam, his topknot gleaming in the early evening. One eye was dark and menacing; the other was the color of milk. His lips were thin beneath a trimmed mustache—trimmed, I knew, to further his hoax as a Druid. He took a queer pleasure in testing the strength of Mariam's skin with the point of the dagger.

I made ready. My dagger in hand, I measured the distance and considered the best time to strike. Mariam might be killed, but not because her father abandoned her to the devil Saxons. I had to try.

My Saxon turned to hand Mariam off to another as he prepared to mount the horse. That was it. I would strike as Mariam was handed back up to her captor. If I could dash between them, perhaps I could snatch her away. With any luck, the worst she would suffer would be some bruises.

The time was ripe. The milky-eyed Saxon easily leaped upon the horse. Once the reins were in his hand, he turned back and bent slightly forward to take Mariam.

His fellow lifted her slightly and took his eyes off us, leaving only one watching.

I flipped my dagger over and threw it with all my might at the third Saxon as I dove for Mariam.

My aim was off and caught the Saxon in the shoulder instead of the chest. Time slowed down then, and with all my senses concentrated on Mariam, I heard nothing of the crowd, though I could see mouths open.

I felt my tunic pulled at the back, and I guessed that Kay was trying to keep me from suicide, but nothing could hold me back.

The Saxon holding Mariam turned, and his eyes grew large as I barreled toward them.

The milky-eyed Saxon raised his sword, and my heart almost burst as I saw he had time to strike Mariam before I could reach them.

The sword started down.

Then something very strange happened.

A brilliant white light encompassed us all, blinding me just as I wrapped my arm around Mariam and fell to the ground, rolling.

I heard horses neighing, people shouting, curses, moans. I smelled the strong odor of sulfur in the air.

Then the blindness faded, and as I held Mariam tight against me, I saw Arthur's sword clash with the third Saxon, my dagger still protruding from his shoulder. Kay had joined combat with the other, backing him farther and farther toward the edge of the square.

Looking above me, I saw Ygerne, her face a study in fear. Swiftly, I handed Mariam to her and leaped to my feet.

Arthur parried a Saxon blow. The man was game, but Arthur was a mighty swordsman. Another moment, another clash of iron, and Arthur lopped off his opponent's head with a mighty swing. The head thunked against the ground and rolled a few feet toward the barracks. The Saxon's body stayed upright for a long second before collapsing, blood gushing from the great hole at his neck.

The milky-eyed Saxon was matching swords with two of Arthur's men from horsetop. He scored a lucky blow, leaving a mighty wound across the chest of one of the soldiers, and he broke free, dashing on horseback for the gate. I started after him on foot, unarmed, but with murder in my eyes.

"Stop, Malgwyn!"

It was Arthur's voice.

I slowed and turned. Arthur, his sword dripping red, dangling from his hand, breathed heavily and sweat dripped from his beard. "They will catch him at the gate, Malgwyn."

He was right. I would only waste what strength I had left. Turning, I sought out the last Saxon. Kay had forced him to surrender. Still partially blinded, he was being held by Lauhiir from behind and the tip of Kay's sword against his chest.

Lauhiir was nervous. Even as he tightly held the Saxon by his topknot, his dagger pushing against the man's tunic, I could see fear in Lauhiir's eyes. But I had questions for the Saxon.

"Whence came the light?" I asked Arthur as we walked toward the false Druid. "Merlin? Some of his special powder?"

"Aye." Arthur laughed. "I think he planned to use it to escape in case you did not arrive."

"The old fraud!"

"What now?"

"Our prisoner has things to tell us."

Walking up behind Kay, I touched his shoulder and he stepped away with a grunt. "Watch him, Malgwyn. He is still dangerous."

I wondered if he meant the Saxon or Lauhiir.

The captive had a bloody cut across his forehead, and blood trickled from temple to jowl.

"How came you to this place?"

He looked at me with hatred burning in his eyes. "We walked."

The crowd, pressed against his back, laughed nervously.

"Who helped you? Who gave you access to the castle?" I knew the answers, but I wanted him to say it in front of everyone. I wanted no mistakes about it.

The Saxon swallowed deeply, looked to Lauhiir and back to me. His mouth opened, but only a cry came out as his head was jerked back and a dagger slipped from behind and sliced his throat as neatly as it would a pig's. Great gouts of crimson answered my question, spurting from him and soaking me with the hot, thick liquid. I wiped my mouth and watched as pandemonium erupted in Arthur's castle. I knew they would never find the killer; the Saxon was pressed against the crowd. In the confusion, anyone could have done the deed and fled without a witness. Without a witness in a crowd of people, I thought.

Mordred suddenly appeared at my elbow, solicitously offering me a cloth, which I waved away.

"Lord Mordred!" Arthur thundered. "How did this happen? Find the murderer!"

But I could tell by the set of Arthur's jaw that he too knew that his command would never be fulfilled.

Lauhiir's and Mordred's men appeared, prancing and snorting like young horses, as if they had resolved this affair themselves, and dispersed the crowd. Grumbling, the people returned to their homes. A few of the merchants began to clean up from the affray.

"Father."

I looked down and saw Mariam standing there with a cloth.

"Mother said to give you this," she said, handing the cloth up to me. "She said to tell you to come to our house for food and rest. You have had a hard day and need to rest."

I knelt down and took my daughter in my one arm and held her close. Before I could speak, I felt her tiny lips on my cheek. "Thank you for saving me, Father."

I buried my face in her hair and cried.

Would that this was the end of it, but it was not. I tucked the cloth in my belt and cuddled Mariam's chin in my hand. Her cheek was warm and soft, and her eyes were just like her mother's. Yes, more was left to be done.

I let Mariam go reluctantly and sent her home as I swabbed my face, cleaning the blood and sweat away. I knew my eyes must still be rimmed in it. I could feel it drying and cracking as I opened my eyes wide.

"Come, my lord. We have another prisoner to question."

Bedevere came racing up, his face wrinkled in frustration. "Lord Arthur! The guards did not stop the Saxon. He rode through unmolested."

"Bring them here. Now!"

I touched Arthur's sleeve. "A word, my lord."

We stepped away from the crowd. "Leave them be, Arthur," I counseled. "We know they are the creatures of your enemies now. We can watch them. Having them beheaded will serve no purpose."

"But they ignored my orders; they allowed that Saxon to flee!"

"I know. But they may be more profitable to us alive. They can make up a thousand excuses for their lapse."

His shoulders slumped. "Aye, I take your meaning. Very well."

"My lord, the matter of Eleonore is not finished. Let us roll the die once more." Straightening what was left of my tunic, I marched off at Arthur's side for his hall.

CHAPTER TWELVE

All of the other members of the consilium were gathered in Arthur's hall once more. The time had come to settle affairs, though events in the market square had changed my mind about many things. As we entered, I saw that Lord Vortimer had been laid upon the great round table. Two arrows protruded from his thick chest. They had struck home despite the coat of mail garbing his body. Merlin went to him immediately, but after examining the wounds, the old man looked toward Arthur and Ambrosius and shook his head.

I walked to where Vortimer lay, blood bubbles painting his lips. He was yet conscious. As I approached, his men closed about him, but with uncommon strength, he raised his head, saw me, and waved the soldiers off.

"You thought I was the architect of the murders," he said weakly.

"Aye, but you proved me wrong when you took the arrows for the Rigotamos. No traitor would give up his life so valiantly."

A faint shake of his head. "I am not disloyal, no matter how much I disagreed with the Rigotamos or coveted his crown."

"But you knew that something was awry."

He shook his head again. "I suspected it. No more than that, but I thought to turn it to my advantage. Of that much, I am guilty."

"Be at rest, Vortimer. The shadow of guilt has passed from you. Your sacrifice will be sung in halls throughout the land."

At that, he breathed his last. His eyes remained open, staring fixedly at nothing. I sighed, remembering how much time I had wasted thinking him guilty.

"Malgwyn, the Druids were part of his company."

"The real Druids," I noted. Arthur and Ambrosius looked confused. "The false Druids, dressed in dark robes, were not in Vortimer's company. I did not realize it until I looked again at the scrap of cloth I took from Eleonore's hand.

"There were two groups of Druids—one group that arrived with Vortimer and another that arrived several hours later, wearing much darker robes. Cuneglas remarked upon it, as did Kay and Bedevere."

"Then who was behind the second group of Druids, the false Druids, if not Vortimer?" asked Ambrosius.

"I, like all of you, was too willing to believe Vortimer guilty. But you must needs go back to the murder of Eleonore to penetrate the truth."

"Accolon must have been guilty," Tristan said nervously. "Why else would he have run?"

I turned to the young lord and smiled shrewdly. "If you thought two murders and a conspiracy against the Rigotamos were to be wound around your neck, you would find any number of places to be other than here. Accolon believed himself labeled a murderer. He was a simple man, though, who had no lust for the Rigotamos's crown."

Tristan looked relieved, and very young, all at once. He bowed to Arthur and Ambrosius. "I shall take my leave. I too regret the complications that have harmed your city. I will carry your words to my father, but I cannot tell you that he will not treat with the Saxons himself."

"You will not stay for the election?" Ambrosius asked, somewhat perplexed.

The young man shook his head nervously. "I must consult with my father."

Arthur's countenance darkened, and his eyes flashed with anger. "That would be a grave mistake, Tristan."

"Perhaps, my lord, but time will tell. I feel that it is important to take this matter up with my father quickly. I will leave tonight."

"No," I said, "you will not."

Arthur drew back in puzzlement. "Malgwyn! You forget yourself."

"I think not, my lord. You asked me to investigate not only the affair with the maid but the matter of Lord Tristan's entreaty as well."

Both Arthur and the Rigotamos nodded cautiously. I gestured to Kay and Bedevere with my head, and they moved to bar the main door. A sheen of sweat on Tristan's lip glittered in the torchlight.

"When the Saxons were revealed, I had only begun my explanation of events. But it is just as well that we do this in your hall, my lord. I have tales that we will all wish to keep quiet, I think."

Merlin, frail and wrinkled, narrowed his eyes at me. He knew me too well, the old scoundrel, and he suspected that I had fashioned this entire scenario, except for Mariam.

"The Saxon spies were not the only ones involved in Eleonore's death. It is that which I wish to discuss now. We can concern ourselves later, Rigotamos, with how these spies were able to infiltrate our town."

"I would like to hear that now," Ambrosius insisted.

"Malgwyn is right, Rigotamos," Arthur said with a smile forming on his face. "That can wait until later. Continue, Malgwyn."

I turned back to the young nobleman. "Lord Tristan, what did you and Eleonore argue about at the gate?"

The question caught the young man by surprise. His head jerked up. "I . . . we . . . what do you mean? I saw her not that night. Not after the feasting."

"Accolon saw you, Tristan. He saw the two of you arguing just inside the gate on the Via Caedes near unto the midnight."

"You said nothing of that before the people," Mordred argued.

"I did not need to. This was a matter to be settled in Arthur's hall, not in front of all the people." I beckoned for Tristan to answer. "Now, my lord, what were you arguing about?"

Fear radiated from the young lord's eyes. "I begged her to leave with me and go back to Castellum Mark. There I could convince my father to allow me to marry her."

"And she would not go."

He shook his head. "No, she would not hear of it. She said this was her home and . . ."

"And what?"

Tristan averted his eyes from us. "She did not care for me. She said that she enjoyed my company, but that did not mean she wanted to marry me."

"How came you to the watchtower?"

"I asked her to go for one last walk with me. When we reached the watchtower, I drew her underneath."

All he was saying fit with what I had thought. "When you pressed your suit, she became angry. And you pressed too hard; you bashed her head against the post." I did not raise my voice. I said it softly, hoping that it would soothe him and make him tell the truth.

Tears fell from Tristan's eyes as his face tensed. "I did not mean to hurt her. Her face went pale; she collapsed in my arms. I saw the blood on the post." The lord dropped into a chair, his face falling into his hands. Across the hall, I could see Kay stretch himself to full height and his gloved fists clench and release, clench and release.

"And then?"

At last, he raised his head. "And then I went in search of Vortimer, anyone, to help me. I was frightened. I knew that the girl was Arthur's favorite. I found the Druids. I knew that Vortimer had brought them here. They hurried to help me."

"Which Druids? Those of the light or dark robes."

"I sought only the first ones I could find. They were eager to help."

"Of course they were!" Arthur broke his silence. "They were Saxon spies. They saw a way to undercut my strength and force one of our lords to their side."

"But you did not know that then," I offered.

"No!" Tristan shouted. "No, I did not learn that until they set about their work."

"How?"

He looked beseechingly around the great hall, but all of the consilium turned away from him. Tying one of them to this crime did nothing to help Tristan, and he knew it. "Why, when they took up the dagger to take out her heart. Everyone knows that Druids will not touch weapons."

"Yes." I laughed wearily. "We all know about that."

"I confronted them, and they threatened me with death if I did not keep quiet. They knew my secret and told me that if I did not push hard for a treaty, they would get word to you, my lord, and my life would be forfeit for killing the girl." He spun around quickly toward Ambrosius. "My Lord Rigotamos, I beg you to take mercy on me!"

"Lord Tristan, tell me why I should not march you into the square beyond those doors and behead you before all the people of Arthur's castle?" Ambrosius thundered, his beard shaking with every word.

The young nobleman fell to his knees and clasped the Rigotamos's legs. "I meant her no harm, my lord. I swear it! Whatever you command, I will do, if you will just spare me."

Bedevere slipped in next to Arthur and whispered something in his ear. In turn Arthur counseled with Ambrosius. Nodding in approval, the Rigotamos turned to Tristan to deliver his verdict.

"This is what you shall do, Lord Tristan. You shall compose a message to your father, demanding that he not treat with the Saxons under any circumstances. You will tell him that the Saxons have proven themselves unworthy of our trust and that the Rigotamos demands obedience from the entire consilium. Malgwyn will write your letter so there is no mistake in what you say.

"Then," Ambrosius strode over to Tristan and placed a heavy hand on his shoulder, "you shall stay here at Arthur's castle as surety against your father's obeisance. You will serve as one of his nobles, and you will honor his shield, until such time that I think it meet that you be returned to your father."

Tristan dropped his head. "I am at your command, my lord. It will be as you have ordered." The boy's face was wet from fright, and the dampness had soaked the neck of his tunic down to the middle of his chest.

With that matter settled, I addressed the assembly again. "There is more, my lord. This was a complex maze, and I am only now navigating my way clear. Lord Tristan is at fault, but Eleonore would be dead anyway. She was marked for death by other than Tristan."

"How? By whom?" Arthur demanded.

I held up my hand. "Eleonore learned of a conspiracy to kill Ambrosius and, in the election of a new Rigotamos, to secure the crown for Vortimer."

"But Malgwyn! You said Vortimer was innocent."

"And he was. Vortimer was easy to manipulate, but volatile, and as we saw in the market square, loyal as well. The conspirators could not take the chance of including him in their plans. They had to count on being able to sway his opinions. With Vortimer, not much was left to chance.

"Eleonore sought me that night to tell me what she had learned, to seek counsel, I suspect. I was gone, but the boy Owain saw her. And she told Nyfain as well. Remember, my lord?" This last I directed to Ambrosius.

"Yes, I recall."

That surprised me a little. I did not think he would remember anything. "The architect of this affair discovered that Eleonore knew. Tristan's rendezvous was convenient, and the passion of his ardor a stroke of good fortune. They were likely waiting for Tristan to leave her alone long enough so that they might kill her."

"And Nyfain?" Arthur queried.

"They did not know what or how much Eleonore had told her. Leaving her alive was a risk they dared not take."

"But Malgwyn, why did they attempt to blame Merlin?" Ambrosius asked.

"I confess that when I realized that Saxons were involved, that confused me as well. But Eleonore's death offered a way to discredit Arthur without the mess and uncertainty an assassination brings. That's when I understood that the man behind this scheme was as skilled a manipulator as I know and a man with a talent for subtlety. Saxons are not subtle."

"Do you have a name for this man?" Lauhiir asked derisively.

"Yes, I do." I had the consilium's full attention. The hall fell silent but for my voice.

"It was you, Lord Mordred." I spoke the words without looking at him. The room exploded into shouts and excited murmurs.

Only then did I face Mordred. His narrow face and hawkish eyes were relaxed, almost too relaxed.

"I trust this is not just drunken raving of yours, Malgwyn," he said, reclining in his seat, yet his hand had slid onto the hilt of his sword.

"Treason is a serious charge," Lauhiir responded in measured tones.

"Aye," I agreed, "it is." I chose my next words carefully. The realization of Mordred's guilt had struck me only moments before in the great square. It sounded too fiendish even for Mordred, but I could reach no other conclusion. I knew, however, that I was about to create several mortal enemies.

"You have proof?" Ambrosius asked.

"Of a sort. Conspirators of any kind, my lord, prefer to keep themselves a league removed."

"Just as I thought." Mordred sneered. "The ramblings of a drunk."

I sucked in a deep breath of air. This was single combat, between Mordred and me. Again, I spoke without looking at him, a gesture of dismissal. "Think as you wish, but consider what we know. Despite the urging of many members of the consilium, Arthur had let it be known that he would not appoint Mordred as Master of Horse when, and if, he became Rigotamos. It was a job Mordred lusted after because it would put him in command of all cavalry, our most potent weapon.

"Why should Tristan turn to Vortimer for help? It is easier to blame a dead man than a living one. Who was Tristan's constant companion? Mordred. 'Tis more likely that he would go to his friend Mordred in such a crisis.

"And who was the last person seen with Nyfain? Mordred. I watched myself as they left the great hall together after Eleonore was found dead. The next time Nyfain was seen, she had been cut and butchered.

"As for the Saxons, those so newly arrived that they spoke not our language, who among you had recently returned from the eastern frontier? Who among you could have arranged so easily for them to cross our borders and arrive safely here at this castle?"

All the consilium looked at Mordred with a growing belief in my words. Even Lord David looked aghast at Mordred. All, that is, but Lauhiir. He was part of the conspiracy too, but I had no evidence against him.

Mordred's expression had not changed. He smiled stiffly, but my indictment of him could not now be dismissed as drunken ramblings. Still, he was not going to confess. "It strikes me, Malgwyn, that you have no witnesses to corroborate your accusations," he said. "You are strangely out of Saxons, and I daresay that Tristan will not help you."

"Not so strangely, Lord Mordred. I have not forgotten that you disappeared into the crowd just before the last Saxon's throat was slit, and then reappeared by magic immediately after."

"Still, I am a free man and a noble of this land. You have no witnesses. You have no evidence beyond your own musings."

"Don't be so certain, my lord. One who would investigate such things never reveals all he knows."

A sheen of sweat emerged on Mordred's lip, his eyes quickly flashing as he tried to remember what he might have missed. "Then reveal it and be done!" he dared.

I shook my head. "Now is not the right time, but it will come. Fear not."

"I fear nothing."

"Then you are a fool." I meant to provoke him, wanted to provoke him. I wanted his blood.

"Lord Mordred!" Ambrosius's voice rang again, and I watched Mordred nearly jump from his sandals.

"Yes, my lord?"

"I think that you should take your company of men and patrol our western borders. There are reports of Picts coming from Ireland. You will leave now."

"My lord?" Mordred wanted to argue, but he knew that all that stood between himself and a formal charge of treason was myself and Tristan. And Tristan knew that it was wiser not to involve Mordred. Plus, he was not so sure of his success in single combat with me. And Ambrosius was right. All Mordred's death would accomplish now would be civil war.

"But the election of a new Rigotamos!"

"You will unfortunately miss it. Be gone before I change my mind." Ambrosius turned to the other members of the consilium. "We will reconvene in an hour to hold the election. Lord Bedevere, find suitable quarters at the barracks for young Tristan. He will need time to learn the routine before he establishes his own household."

"My lord," Bedevere acknowledged. Tristan left, a nauseated look on his face, but Bedevere lingered.

While grumbling came from some of the lords, they obeyed, leaving only Ambrosius, Bedevere, Kay, Arthur, Merlin, and myself.

"You performed your work well, Malgwyn," Ambrosius began. "I do not doubt your conclusions at all, but Mordred still has many friends, and he was right, your evidence was not solid."

"I know, my lord. But I still prayed for his blood on my hands."

"I find it discomforting that the Saxons were able to penetrate my fortress so easily," Arthur said, changing subjects.

"More than that, my lord," I replied. "A band of them was moving at will in the countryside between here and Ynys-witrin. No one but Gareth knew of this."

"Kay!"

"Yes, my lord."

"You will go to the eastern borders and secure them from further incursions."

"For how long, my lord?"

"Until I call for your return. Make ready for your departure."

"And Kay?"

"My lord."

"Take the heads of the dead Saxons and impale them on stakes near unto our border with their fellows as an example to them or anyone who challenges my authority."

"As you wish."

"Bedevere!"

"My lord," he answered.

"Fetch Accolon's body and return it here for a warrior's burial. He shall be honored in death as he was not in life. Then scout through the countryside for any other Saxons still there."

"Be vigilant," I warned, pulling the arrowhead from my pouch that I had scavenged from Accolon's body. "The Saxons were using archers, shooting these."

Bedevere took the odd arrow and raised his eyebrows. "These are what penetrated Vortimer's mail," he said.

"Aye," I agreed. "That I faced men skilled in their use means that new bands of Saxons are being brought to our lands."

"Go," Arthur commanded. "Report everything, no matter how small. These tidings do not bode well for our future, and we must be prepared."

Kay had lingered, and now he told us the reason why.

"My Lord Arthur! Tristan killed Eleonore. You are just going to let him walk away with such little punishment?"

"Kay, old friend, I could not behead Mark's son no matter who he killed." Arthur, looking bedraggled and weary, rubbed a gloved hand over his tunic, hooking a thumb in his studded belt. "That would bring war among the consilium and civil war is what we've been fighting so desperately to avoid. I am sorry that it seems unfair, but—"

"But," I interrupted, waving a hand at them both, "it was

unnecessary. Tristan did not kill Eleonore. Her murderers have already paid."

They all bellowed questions then, since that was not the conclusion from before. Finally, Merlin's voice rose above the others. "But you yourself blamed him for the death."

"No, Merlin. I let him believe that he killed her. All I blamed him with was bashing her head against the post."

Now Arthur was troubled. His tongue flicked out and wetted down his drooping mustache, pulling the hairs into his mouth and chewing on them. He only did that in the most frustrating of times. "Did that not kill her?"

"Perhaps it would have, my lord, but she was still alive when the Saxons took Merlin's knife to her. Remember that I found the bit of cloth clutched tightly in her hand. Were she dead already, she could not have clutched the robe with such fierceness as to tear it. It was their hands that strangled her before they began to carve her up like an animal. Ergo, they are truly responsible for taking her life's breath. Plus," I continued, "what Tristan did was accidental. What the Saxons did was intentional."

Bedevere regarded me with bemused comprehension. "You manipulated the truth to help Arthur put down this infant rebellion."

I shrugged again. "I manipulated nothing. I told the truth, just not all of it. I put to use the tools that I was given. A part of me has hated Arthur for years, but in just the three days I have returned to his world, I see that we are in better hands with him than Mordred or Tristan or the Saxons. Mordred should have been beheaded for bringing Saxon spies into this fort, and I believe he knew all along who they were, as well as knowing of the band of Saxons in the woods, but I knew too that Arthur could not do that. First, I could not prove Mordred's guilt without doubt. He stayed just far enough in the shadows to shield himself. And we know not who else from the consilium might have been involved. No, we foiled their plot and kept Arthur a contender for the crown; Mordred is too popular to be executed. Tell me, Arthur, that you did not see what I was handing you."

"No, I saw immediately what your scheme was," he replied, those dark eyes of his flashing. Arthur was as cunning as any man I knew when he chose to be.

"Since he could not be killed, sending him away was an excellent way of keeping him out of trouble."

"For a while," Ambrosius agreed.

Arthur walked up to me and wrapped his big hand around my neck. "I trusted you, Malgwyn. You did not fail me. I ask you now to come serve with me as my scribe and councillor." He held up the other hand as I started to protest. "This is no gift. You have earned it."

The offer did not seem a bad one. "Give me a night to consider it. And, if you do not mind, my lord, I will take that bed you offered a few nights ago. I am falling asleep as I stand here." I turned to Kay. "Old friend, will you tell Ygerne and Mariam that I will take a meal with them tomorrow? And please have Cicero take Owain to Ygerne. She will understand. Tonight, I must rest."

"Stay!" Ambrosius abruptly commanded. "You will dine here during the election and serve as my aide during the vote."

I wanted a bed, not a job. "I am no member of the consilium. I have no standing. For the sake of the gods, Rigotamos, have I not earned a night's sleep yet?"

"Though you have done an admirable job sorting through

this affair, Arthur's election is not a certainty. We don't know what last trick they may try to play."

And then the old warrior, the good king, did something I never dreamed possible. Ambrosius laid his hand on my shoulder. "A man is what he proves himself to be, Malgwyn. In this affair, you have proved yourself a far greater lord than any with lands and retainers. Accept Arthur's offer and I will make you official clerk of the consilium. Then, perhaps, you'll earn your night's sleep." He stopped and sniffed. "But now, go get cleaned."

As befitted his station, Ambrosius took the chair of the Rigotamos. Vortimer's blood yet marked the great table, though large splinters bore witness to the attempts of slaves to rub out the stain.

The other lords soon drifted into the room, each taking a Roman-style goblet in hand from scurrying servants and gathering into cliques. No politics at this gathering. The lots had been drawn and Arthur held the most. Most all were casting worried glances at the man soon to be the new Rigotamos.

Only a fool believed that Arthur wouldn't be chosen, yet the treachery shown in this affair had been such that Ambrosius himself had demanded my presence at the election and Arthur joined his plea. The crown had not passed to him yet, and he needed his most trusted allies to make certain there was no mischief. And such a jest it was. Myself, a trusted ally? Why, a fortnight before, I would gladly have slit his throat. But much of that love I once felt for Arthur's leadership had returned, much of the surety in his judgment renewed.

"Why comes he here?" I turned to hear Lord David demand a reason for my presence. Bathed and redressed, I resembled little the blood-dripping, battle-weary man of two hours before. "He is no lord of the consilium and holds no lands."

Ambrosius settled his ungainly figure in his chair and considered David through narrowed eyes. "He nearly held your bleeding head in his hand. He may yet." Ambrosius chuckled half seriously. "Malgwyn will serve as my official scribe and as counter of lots. And it would be my advice that the next Rigotamos confer on him the titles and lands of a lord of the consilium."

"That will certainly make the count come out as you please," a fat lord named Melwas grumbled, but I paid him no mind and neither did Ambrosius. As a lord, Melwas counted for little at any rate. Arthur, rightly, paid no heed to any of it and stood to the side, drinking wine with Kay and Bedevere. David and Lauhiir were in conference with the blue-eyed lord Celyn ap Caw, one of a group of noble brothers from Gwynned who were outspoken against Arthur and Ambrosius. One brother, Huaill, was little better than an outlaw and had openly challenged Ambrosius.

After a few moments, Ambrosius moved into place and the others followed suit. "There is no formal procedure," Ambrosius intoned. "We will take nominations and different colored stones prepared for each candidate. Malgwyn has readied stones for three candidates."

I nodded. An air of mischief floated about the room. Arthur's opponents knew they had no chance of success, and I wondered at how they would behave. I left stones of each color before each lord as two slaves heaved a giant rock onto the table. Ambrosius rose and pulled his jeweled sword, one symbol of his office, from his sheath. " 'Twas this stone upon which Caesar first stepped onto our isle. It has been our custom since the consilium began, that the Rigotamos take up the sword from the stone to defend our people."

With a wave and a flourish, he laid the sword upon the stone. The Caesar Stone was an enigma. It might have been where Gaius Julius Caesar made his first step on Britannia, and it could have been a rock from out of one of the rivers. But symbolically it stood for the first step made by an invader, and the British leader who took the sword from the stone must be victorious, as that first was against Caesar. Forgotten was that the Romans did succeed against us later and we embraced them, but some things are best left in the past. As for the stone, my old dad thought that it was probably some rock that Cunobeline pissed on.

This I did not know, but I knew that it had grown into a sacred symbol, held at the Rigotamos's castle under constant guard. And such symbols were important to a people with barely a sense of themselves.

"Who would take up this sword?" Ambrosius queried in a rumble.

Bedevere stood. "I put forward Arthur ap Uther as the new Rigotamos."

Lauhiir, in turn, stood and placed Lord David's name in nomination. It was expected. After Vortimer's death, David was the senior lord of the faction that opposed Arthur.

No one else spoke.

"Those choosing Arthur will use the red stones. Those voting for David will cast the blue," I instructed the lords, sweeping aside the third set of stones. It was only prudent to prepare more "ballots" than necessary in case of a surprise candidate. As

I gazed round the table, I felt a foreboding, a sense of dread. Celyn, the blue-eyed youngster from one of the northern tribes, flashed those blue eyes and snorted. I remembered seeing him at the spears when I went down into Vortimer's camp. He seemed eager, too eager, the kind of eagerness that is not welcomed among lords and warriors. I noted that eagerness as I held the box for him to cast his stone.

In seconds, the lots had been cast. I took each out of the box so that all could see. The reds outnumbered the blues by two to one. Arthur was to be the Rigotamos. With a nod from Ambrosius, he reached for the sword lying upon Caesar's Stone.

And then something unexpected happened.

Celyn stretched forward to grab the sword himself. "Damned if I'll let the crown go to such as he!" he cried. But before he could lift the sword and thrust it into Arthur, his eyes flashed suddenly in shock and then glazed over. The young lord fell forward onto the table, unconscious from the sturdy backhand I had given him with my gloved hand. A little blood seeped out from the corner of his mouth, and his tongue lapped from his mouth, swelling.

I wiped my hand on the young lord's tunic. "Only Arthur has earned the right to take up the sword."

Amid the clamor in the hall, Arthur took the sword from the stone and held it up.

Quickly, one voice rose above all others—David.

"Malgwyn assaulted a lord of the consilium! Arrest him!" cried David.

"Malgwyn assaulted a petulant child, a would-be usurper. He bears no guilt," Ambrosius proclaimed.

And with a smile at Arthur and a wink from Ambrosius,

Arthur became Rigotamos, high king of all Britannia. The ordeal was over.

Arthur looked then at me, and something passed between us, something warm and welcome. The past was finally buried.

CHAPTER THIRTEEN

"You have earned your rest, Malgwyn," Arthur said as the other lords, some happy, some disgruntled, left the hall. Kay nodded as Arthur took me by my one good arm and led me toward a servant's door at the back of the hall. "First, you need a bath again. You will rest easier." He shouted for a slave boy, who appeared as if by magic.

"I just need to sleep, Arthur!"

"Malgwyn, you are covered in sweat once more. Your clothes are soiled. You need to be cleaned." Arthur stopped then. "You know you made an enemy this day."

"I know I made many enemies. But if you refer to the boy lord, Celyn, I am just happy that I did not have to kill him as well. Too much killing in this affair."

"Well, beware. You embarrassed him in front of his elders. He will not forget it. Now, off to be bathed!"

The prospect of returning to Arthur's world was not as attractive as I had thought. These people had an absolute adoration of cleanliness. I sniffed my clothes and sensed nothing unusual. But the slave led on, and I went with a curse and a frown.

And that brought the affair to an end, for a while. Arthur and Ambrosius knew that Mordred, David, and the others would not go away. They would continue to be a thorn in their side. But the next morning, after a good night's sleep born of the exhaustion of my toils, I stood with Ygerne and Mariam in the great market square and watched as Ambrosius and his company marched out of the castle, on their way to Dinas Emrys and a quiet retirement. As the last of the horsemen departed the square, Ygerne and I, with Mariam in between, turned toward the house in the back lanes of Castellum Arturius, where my brother, Cuneglas, lay abed.

And I returned to the place where I had stood post on the night he was wounded.

And the vigil began.

He lay as if asleep for days on end. I spent most of my days and nights sitting by his bed, watching and waiting for any kind of movement, any sign of life beyond the rhythmic rise and fall of his chest. I prayed to the one God and the many gods, anyone, anything, that might open his eyes and set him on the path to recovery. Ygerne pleaded with me to get rest, but I could not. I had been a bad brother, leaving my own child to his care, seldom aiding in her support, rarely visiting at all, wallowing in drink, women, and self-pity, and now all I could do to remedy that was to be there and hope and pray. I lost so much weight that my clothes began to hang off me. Ygerne feared for my sanity; I feared for my soul.

Merlin came to see him every day, placing smelly poultices on the wound, which never seemed to heal. He cautioned me to have patience, and on occasion he forced some tonic or other on me. Usually I found myself asleep after taking one of his concoctions, and though I would berate him afterward, I felt the better for the rest.

Arthur came every few days, taking me aside and telling me of affairs across our land. His intent, I know, was to take my mind off Cuneglas, but his retelling of the various deeds and misdeeds of the other lords and the Saxons served only to distract me momentarily from the horror that was my brother. Still, I appreciated his concern. And some part of me knew that I must take up my duties for Arthur soon.

Mariam would often come to sit in my lap and lay her head on my shoulder. She still bore confusion in her feelings toward Cuneglas and me. Oh, she knew truly that I was her real father, but after so many years of thinking of Cuneglas as her father, the emotions she felt were complex and entangled. I hoped to help clear the fog that clouded her mind.

But the monks of Ynys-witrin and Merlin told me that even if Cuneglas did recover, he would never be the same. So I assumed the responsibility of providing for his family. It was a kind of responsibility I had once wanted more than life itself, but life regards us lightly at times. I realized that I had much to learn and the challenges were great. Arthur had helped by naming my brother's wife and children part of his household. That would allow them to be fed from his kitchens.

And the gods chose to intervene once more.

One early morn, just before the sun's rise, at that teasing of first light, I stirred from my stupor, stiff from sitting in a chair. I looked over at Cuneglas, but this time, he was looking back.

"Ygerne! Mariam! He's awake!"

He blinked a couple of times, in a confused sort of way, as if trying to understand where he was. Ygerne and the children rushed in. I sent the oldest boy for Merlin and turned back to him.

He had not spoken, just looked from face to face. He looked so much like our father in his last years that the resemblance was frightening. His face was thin and drawn, and suffering was etched into every wrinkle. He noticed Ygerne and managed a weak smile. And he forced that smile to each person present.

But when he came to my face, his look grew bolder, younger somehow. He reached out a hand slowly and sought mine. I held his hand, the grip weak and weakening.

"Malgwyn, my brother." The words came out in a sort of dry-throated croak. "Come closer."

I scooted my chair next to his bed and leaned down.

"It is not easy to talk to you," he said.

"Nonsense," I said to comfort him. "We are brothers."

"Aye," he croaked. "We are that, but you are something that I have never been. You are a man of principle. You believe in the right and wrong of things, though your actions might say otherwise." He coughed hoarsely and Ygerne hurried with a beaker of water. He smiled at her again and nodded. And when he began this time, his voice was clearer. "When they found Eleonore dead, you hesitated not. And when the crowd hungered for Merlin's life, you stood your ground. As for me, I have always been about my needs, with no concern for others. I have not been a good father or husband."

I started to protest, but he held up a weak hand to stop me. "This is an argument you cannot win, my brother. I am dying.

I feel it in every part of me. I cannot undo what has been done, but I must beg this promise of you."

"Anything."

"Be a part of this family now. Do not return to that life you lived. God has given you a second chance. Use it to protect my family"—he coughed again—"your family."

"I will do all I can, Cuneglas, but you will heal now and be well."

"Ygerne." He called for his wife weakly. She hurried over, wiping her hands on her dress and taking his in hers. Despite the scene before me, despite the death rattle in my brother's throat, I still felt that hint of jealousy at her grasping his hand.

"I . . . am sorry, Ygerne. You deserved . . . a better . . . man than me."

"Hush, Cuneglas. You are a good man. Even if you do not see it. Besides, there will be plenty of time for this later, when you have healed."

He shook his head impatiently. "No. It is finished."

At that, his body trembled and his chest fell and did not rise again. His eyes remained open, staring vacantly at the ceiling.

Merlin rushed in and assessed the situation. He moved swiftly to Cuneglas, moving his hands quickly around his body, squeezing his hand, listening at his chest, as Ygerne stood with his hand in hers, her moist eyes shining with the hurt.

Finally Merlin turned to all of us. "His soul has gone to its maker. There is nothing more to do." He took two old and used copper ases, shut my brother's eyes, and placed each coin on Cuneglas's eyelids. It was an old Roman custom. The coins were meant to pay the ferryman who carried his soul to the afterlife.

I remember little after that except hugging and comforting Ygerne, Mariam, and the other children.

We buried Cuneglas the next day on a windswept hill where our parents had been laid. The day was cool and damp as were our moods. When the last stone had been laid on the burial cairn, I paused for a moment and considered the green land that was Britannia. It was a good land. It must be. For good people had spilt their blood to make the land fertile and worthy of such sacrifice. I turned, and, with Mariam's hand in mine and Ygerne's on my shoulder, we started down the hill to Castellum Arturius.

The days passed and soon Merlin was back at his inventions. Kay and Bedevere were out fulfilling the tasks Arthur had set for them. Arthur made his appointments, but not without some complaining. Kay was named his Cup Bearer or Seneschal. Bedevere became Master of Horse. Rumors reached us that Mordred was growing fat and lazy on the western coast, drinking away his miseries. Each day I had the pleasure of seeing a miserable Tristan, crazed to be released from his "imprisonment," moping around the castle, but Arthur seemed uninterested in sending the boy home. I returned to my place at Arthur's side, as his scribe and senior councillor. Owain had gone to live with Ygerne. I moved in with Merlin, and though I sensed that she would welcome it, I could not bring myself to move closer to Ygerne, yet I could not ignore her either. Something had grown between us, but Cuneglas was still too fresh in his grave. Perhaps, someday, it would not feel so much like a betrayal of my brother.

I walked through the door of Cuneglas's house one eve, just before the sun set, and I sat down at the rickety table where Cuneglas and I had sat but weeks before. Mariam crawled into my lap and laid her head on my chest. A feeling came upon me at that moment, unlike any I had felt since Gwyneth's death. Ygerne began preparing the evening meal. With my one hand, I stroked Mariam's blond hair. I felt a hand on my back, and I looked up at the smiling face of Ygerne. The world no longer seemed so dark and cruel, and I too smiled once more, not the chilling smile of "Mad Malgwyn," but a smile that warmed my heart and made life seem worth living.

GLOSSARY AND GAZETTEER

Braccae—Breeches worn by both Saxons and the Brythonic tribes. The only extant examples come from peat bogs in Europe.

Brittany—That area of Gaul known as Brittany. Settlements by some of the Brythonic tribes were located there during the fifth and sixth centuries.

Castellum—Castle, but not in the High Middle Ages sense with thick stone walls, towers, and damsels in distress. Usually a defensive position with stacked rock and timber defensive rings.

Arthur's Castle—For the purposes of this novel, Cadbury Castle at South Cadbury, Somerset, is the location for Arthur's castle. Excavations during the 1960s identified it as having been significantly rebuilt and reinforced during the late fifth century by a warlord of Arthurian stature, although no explicit evidence linking the site to Arthur himself was discovered.

Castellum Mark—Castle Dore in Cornwall is believed to

have been the site of King Mark's headquarters. Nearby was found the famous Tristan stone, a gravestone believed to commemorate the historical Tristan, making it the one contemporary piece of evidence for the historicity of a character in the Arthurian canon.

Cervesa—The Latin name for the beer made by the local tribes during the Roman occupation. According to tablets unearthed at Vindolanda near Hadrian's Wall, Roman soldiers were not shy about drinking cervesa.

Consilium—A council. Gildas refers to a consilium ruling pre-Saxon Britannia that ended with Vortigern hiring Saxon mercenaries to help put down the raids of the Picts and Scots. It is safe to assume that any warlord that exerted influence over large areas in central and western England would have done so at the behest and the agreement of such a council of lesser kings.

Dumnonia (Dumnonii)—A tribe residing in the area of Cornwall and throughout the west lands. Mark is thought to have been a king of the Dumnonii during the general period of Arthur's life. Snyder suggests in *The Britons* that people in the post-Roman period referred to themselves by tribal designations

Durotrigia (Durotrigii)—A tribe residing in the area surrounding Glastonbury down through the South Cadbury area to the southern coast.

Fibula—A brooch or early "safety pin" used to keep togas, cloaks, and women's dresses held properly together. Some were round, others in the shape of crossbows.

Iudex Pedaneus—A Roman official assigned to investigate crimes and offenses. It is known that such titles were still used in post-Roman Britannia.

Latrunculii—A term applied to groups of bandits that ran rampant during the fifth century.

Londinium—As would be expected, this is the Roman name for what is now London.

Peplos—A type of gown worn by women, having a Roman cut.

Tigernos—The Celtic word for *lord*, sometimes used to designate local lords, but believed by some scholars to have been combined with the word *vor* to produce the name "Vortigern," or *overlord*.

Via Arthur—"Arthur's Way." A roadway or lane actually ran from Cadbury Castle to Glastonbury. It has become known as Arthur's Way. Two major Roman roads near Cadbury Castle were the Via Fosse and the Via Harrow.

Via Caedes—"The Killing Way." Obviously, this is a creation for the novel, but skeletons were found along the main roadway entering Cadbury Castle. They were victims of an ancient massacre, probably at the hands of Romans and probably in reaction to the rebellions of Caractacus or Boudicca.

Vigile—The Roman equivalent, in a sense, of both a policeman and a fireman. In Rome, they watched for fires as much as any crime.

Votadini (Votadinii)—A tribe residing in what is now northern England and into the lands of the Scots border as far as the Firth of Forth. One story of a chieftain named Cunneda (Kenneth) suggests that part of the Votadini migrated to northern Wales, but, according to Snyder, that possibility has been discounted.

Ynys-witrin—According to some sources, this was the early name for what is now Glastonbury. It is believed that a Christian community resided there during the Arthurian age.

AUTHOR'S NOTE

First of all, this is a novel, a work of fiction intended primarily for entertainment. It is not an attempt to establish history. Granted, the book offers my view of the time and place in which I think the historical Arthur lived, but this is not a scholarly attempt to prove he lived or not.

Those readers who have spent any time studying the Arthurian canon will recognize elements from a variety of scholars in my version of the Arthurian legend. I use Geoffrey Ashe's scholarship frequently, but I've also heavily relied upon Christopher Snyder, Norris Lacy, Leslie Alcock, P. F. J. Turner, and a veritable library of archaeological studies of various sites in and near South Cadbury, Somerset, England, as well as all the extant early source material.

I am a great believer in oral tradition, and I believe in two traditions: the peoples of what was then Britannia (as named by the Romans) did not conjure up a mythical hero called Arthur, who was some kind of amalgam of pagan gods or ancient legends. Nor did they start naming their children after this fantastical concoction in the years immediately following this conjuring. I believe there was an Arthur, a man around whom other men's deeds may have been wrapped, but who was extraordinary in his own right. It is our misfortune that Arthur lived in what, from a documentary sense, was indeed "a dark age."

I admit readily that I have adopted Geoffrey Ashe's identification of Arthur as the Briton leader Rigotamos mentioned in Sidonius's letter. And if he were not *the* Rigotamos, he certainly could have held the title in the wake of Ambrosius Aurelianus or preceding him. From both the historian's and novelist's perspective, it fits as well as anything does. My Arthur is a Christian, more than nominally. He is also a man of passion with an innate sense of wrong and right. He rules by right of a precarious coalition among the Brythonic tribes, and intrigues and treachery are part of his everyday life. A compassionate man, to a point, his compassion is seen by his enemies and rivals as his fatal weakness. The times would have dictated a certain brutality in any leader, and I've tried to add something of that trait to his personality as well.

As to the cultural and societal structure of the time, Snyder, in his *Age of Tyrants*, points out that it is almost impossible to reach any consensus on what life was like during the period 410 to 600 CE, but, Snyder asserts, there is much to be learned by attempting to reach such a synthesis. His own assessment, in his volume *The Britons*, tends toward a continuation of Roman cultural influence deep into the fifth century. I have chosen, after much reading, to view it as still partially Romanized. Most cultures undergoing major changes tend to think wistfully of the "good old days." I cannot imagine that the peoples of Britannia were any different.

The withdrawal of Roman troops did not mean the immediate collapse of Roman institutions and civil structure. Ample evidence indicates the continuation of Roman titles and offices well into the following period. Also, evidence suggests that there was at least a minor resurgence of Roman influences in the middle of the fifth century. Some scholars have theorized that it was out of this resurgence that the historical Arthur emerged. The question is whether that theory rests on a desire to make the historical Arthur fit with the Arthur of romance or whether it is truly an attempt to analyze the history. I tend to support the latter. Sidonius's letter to the Rigotamos, while certainly showing a fair amount of bootlicking, implies that his correspondent has a reputation as a compassionate man.

But the Britons themselves, and perhaps Arthur among them, eschewed some Roman practices. Building methods differed. Clothing styles differed. A new culture emerged, Christian and stubbornly defiant in the face of the Saxon invasion.

You will not find Galahad or Lancelot in these pages. Their appearance in the Arthurian romances came far too late historically to accord them any role in the present work. While that may disappoint some readers, a writer has to make decisions. As to Guinevere and arguments that she too is a figment of the romancers? Her reality seems, according to early stories, to hold a bit more substance. I, along with Ashe and others, tend to lend more credence to the stories of Arthur's and perhaps Guinevere's exhumation by the monks at Glastonbury in the 1100s. In fact, some authors, such as P. J. F. Turner, claim that Arthur was married to two different women named Guinevere.

The invention of "Caesar's Stone" as the origin of the "sword in the stone" legend might not be as farfetched as would first appear. That the Britons venerated places is well known. That they believed that mystic power from sacred places flowed into them and strengthened them is equally obvious. I refer specifically to the so-called Brutus Stone, said to be the spot where the founder of Britannia, Brutus, first landed, and the London Stone, an altar set up in Cannon Street to honor the goddess Diana. One legend holds that Vortimer wanted to be buried near the spot (rock) where the Saxons first made landfall in Kent (Adventus Saxonum). Is it then such a great leap to think they might assign great tradition to the stone that Caesar first stepped on? I think not.

For the inevitable errors, I apologize and take complete responsibility. They are mine and mine alone.

CPSIA information can be obtained at www.ICGtesting.com
Printed in the USA
LVOW082144260313

326210LV00003B/104/P